Thomas —

your

LATE BITE

A JOHN MATSUI THRILLER

§

EDITED BY DAVID DAUPHINEE

BOOK 1 OF 3 IN

THE TORONTO CHRONICLES

Late Bite is a work of fiction. Names, characters, businesses, places, events and incidents are either the products of the author's imagination or used in a fictitious manner. Any resemblance to actual persons, living or dead, or actual events is purely coincidental.

ISBN 978-0-9937548-2-1

To Judy, for all the reasons she knows too well.

CONTENTS

"Reason is intelligence taking exercise.
Imagination is intelligence with an erection."

-Victor Hugo

"Logic will get you from A to Z;
imagination will get you everywhere."

-Albert Einstein

PROLOGUE

Eight grim-faced cops, in full tactical gear, chase the white bars of light that slash channels of visibility through the gloom above the steaming, inch-deep swamp that forms the floor of a large storm sewer outlet. Straining to lead, but keeping no more than a pace or two ahead of their heavily armed colleagues, two canine handlers labour on the leashes as their dogs, now ruled only by instinct, pitch into full paw-scrabbling frenzy as their scent meters fly off scale.

The cacophony of barking, grunts of men barely restraining the dogs, and heavy boots splashing double-time, tells Detective Buddy Ferino, the 11th cop in the group, that they are very near their quarry, known to a terrified city as the Toronto Stalker.

Ferino, dubbed by the deputy police chief as 'the mastermind' when he got the nod for the manpower required to execute the plan, gives his head a shake. Some mastermind, Ferino thinks. He's the only one in their number in street clothes and street shoes, something he's reminded of with every soggy step as he step/slides along the slimy, subterranean runway.

The plan called for a massive deployment of officers to cover the maze of more than 40 miles of storm sewers with check points at every channel and every exit from the underground network blocked. Between the positions where police entered the sewers, more than 3,000 Neighbourhood Watch block captains linked via text messages and social media directed their neighbours to park cars on the more than 42,000 storm-sewer grates within a five-mile radius.

With five more Emergency Task Force (ETF) units closing in on this same position in the storm sewer system, the Toronto Stalker has nowhere to go. It's taken months for Ferino's plan to come together after the elusive Stalker twice escaped less comprehensive stratagems.

Nine victims were assaulted in their homes over the past 16 months but for what purpose? Nothing of value was stolen and none of the previous eight victims was sexually assaulted. Was tonight's victim sexually assaulted? Ferino doesn't know but doubts it. The Toronto Stalker is clearly a weirdo of a different colour.

The singular act that defines the Stalker's signature is the ghoulish, vampire wanna-be, twin wounds on each victim's neck accompanied by the loss of about two pints of blood. Strangely, the blood isn't left in a pool like most other crime scenes. The Stalker takes the blood with him, for purposes unknown. Possibly he draws it out with a needle, or pumps it from the neck wounds. Other than some weeping from the wounds and the odd smudge, there isn't any other blood to be found. Truly a freak, but a neat one, Ferino thinks.

The detective's attention fixes on the moment when he feels the grip of the stinky, sticky ooze that's applied a love hug on his right shoe. His flashlight reveals his foot immersed, ankle-deep, in a foul puddle that the other officers, all wearing waterproof SWAT footgear, quick step through without concern. He gives his Florsheim a futile shake, which unravels a rolled-up cuff, now a partner to his shoe in this murky ballroom. With a sigh, he grounds his foot and feels the swill squirt through his toes and up his pant leg as he resumes, a fast step/squish, step/squish to keep time with his team.

Ahead, a frenetic waltz of torch beams track a sharp turn to the left that opens into a large chamber engineered to capture and slow the flow of water during heavy storms before its white water rhumba into the Don River. The spots of light, at first as random as a disco ball's castings, one by one converge on a solitary figure near the back of the chamber.

Despite his soggy Oxford and the warmth and humidity of the sewer, Det. Ferino feels an icy jolt run the course of his spine. The flashlights reveal an incredibly tall, thin, pale, and hissing man-thing who bares gleaming, three-inch fangs, rakes razor claws through the air in challenge, and bores yellow Jack O'Lantern eyes, right into Ferino's soul. Even the dogs go silent.

Fighting to maintain his composure, Det. Ferino stammers an order for the suspect to surrender. "This is the Police. Down on your knees. We have you surrounded."

The response is not what he expects.

The creature is upon them at once, covering the 50 feet before Det. Ferino has any notion of fight or flight.

Hundreds of hours of training under stress make the tactical officers' reaction time a hair faster. Two fire tasers just as the snarling demon bowls into the pack, parting the formation as easily as a comb through hair. The tasers have little effect other than creating the briefest of pauses as the beast contemplates fleeing or charging again. In that moment, all eight ETF team members fire X3 tasers and lash out with the butts of their automatic weapons and metal batons when the man-thing falls.

"Cuff him," Det. Ferino barks once the pale creature lies still on the ground.

Two team members move in, plastic handcuffs at the ready. As each officer grips a pale, bony hand with its elongated fingers and deadly claw/nails, each horrid hand moves at rattlesnake speed, biting into a flak jacket and, incredibly, pitches the men 20 feet against the sewer's concrete wall.

The remaining ETF officers fire their X3 tasers twice more at the fallen suspect, reload and fire three more times before encircling the creature and pounding him with combat-boot kicks and a rain of metal truncheons.

"If he moves again, use live rounds," Ferino commands.

CHAPTER ONE

THE LAWYER

"Do you know what I'd really like to do with you?" sexy, red-haired starlet Chloe Castor purrs provocatively.

"I'll bite," responds the late-show, TV host and, despite the hundreds of times he's said it in the past, the audience howls with laughter.

"What did I say? What did I say?" Dragul Mangorian laughs in a practised wide-mouthed way, the better to display his fully extended, three-inch canines, as he adds a theatrical shrug that flips up his flowing black, silk cape like a parachute.

Neither the audience nor I, standing on the side stage, ever hear the answer from the buxom redhead, nor is anyone particularly interested.

But what do I care. Life is beautiful. Life is perfect. I am the agent for the world's No. 1 Late Night TV Star, who just happens to be a vampire.

Today marks the fifth anniversary of his brutal arrest, the day that I first met him. That meeting had an inauspicious start, but it changed everything in my life. Who would have guessed that at age 57, despite a threadbare pate and an extra 40 pounds in all the wrong places, women now line up to meet me or, at least, want to meet me to meet him. And for somebody who's walked in my sad sack shoes for nearly six decades, I'm good with that.

So here I find myself, Al Hamblyn, the guy voted least likely to do anything noteworthy, enjoying the rewards I'd never even dreamed of, especially during the days growing up rough in a single-parent home in Toronto's Regent Park.

In high school, my grades were average. I participated as little as possible in sports and other activities until I came across a Tobey Robinson infomercial on late night TV. Tobey told me that I could make my own breaks. So I worked my ass off and took on two and, sometimes, three part-time jobs to put myself through university. Halfway through, mom died. That just spurred me to push harder. My marks were respectable enough to get into law school and land a partial scholarship, but I still had to work at two jobs to finish my law degree.

I even put up with daily abuse from Tim Gracey who, on the surface, looks and dresses like he walked off the pages of GQ magazine. Scratch the surface, you'll find he's pure Neanderthal. Gracey, of the perfect teeth, wavy, blond coiffe and six foot, two of perfect posture, left no stone unturned in an effort to pitch them at me.

The son and sole heir of multi-multi-millionaire developer, Robert Gracey, took it upon himself to create a private hell around any aspirations I had for a career in law. What my sins were, I never knew. From day one, both directly and indirectly, the insults from the Gracey Gang came at me every day and each day more inventively cutting. I remember each of them like it was yesterday. Tim Gracey, Philip, Samuel, Franklin and George – the Gracey Gang. Each of the five, the scion of a family occupying Toronto's elite social circles. and each one of them a thug.

Gracey thought himself immensely clever by dubbing me "Shabbylyn" because of my Value Village wardrobe. As graduation approached, one of his buddies came up with "Hambulance Chaser" as their prognostication of where my career was headed.

One of their regular, so-called pranks was to Crazy Glue my lock and locker. I got used to carrying an extra lock and a small pry bar in my book bag. Once I became proficient at reopening my locker, they upped the ante by gluing all the pages of my textbooks together three days before a big exam.

Gracey actually bragged that his buddies got rewards for making my life a misery in return for invitations to his infamous parties and extra consideration from professors who Gracey Developments hired as legal consultants.

The glued textbooks finally gave me the courage to complain but, of course, it got me nowhere. There were no eyewitnesses so no one was punished. However, it did gain me an ally, my law theory prof, Dr. Jerome Hennesey – Jerry – who took up my cause with the dean. After that, Gracey's gang had to be very careful in the prank department and soon stopped the nastiest stuff. Of course, they continued with the insults, but I ignored them because I knew that when I graduated as a lawyer, I would be their equal.

Despite long-hours cleaning washrooms at the 'Y', bussing tables at André's Steakhouse and weathering Gracey's diurnal gauntlet, I graduated in the top quarter of my class by studying every other waking moment.

Gracey finished dead last and wouldn't have graduated at all without some generous help from certain profs. Two weeks after graduation, I heard he was articling with the Law Firm of Verdon-Glassmere, the 600-lawyer powerhouse with offices across Canada and a Fortune 500 clientele. A year later, a newspaper advertisement announced his appointment as an associate. The following week a business publication reported Gracey Developments hired V-G as its law firm. Six years after that, they promoted Tim Gracey to partner.

As for me, six months of applying to article with every firm within 100 miles of Toronto got me nowhere. I faced the very real prospect of not being able to practise law at all. My one law school ally and professor, Jerry Hennesey, had gone the academic route and didn't have much pull with law firms. He had, however, stayed in touch with one former student.

That was Sally Wiseman, director of the Parkdale Community Law Clinic, another alumnus of Regent Park. She saved me by taking me under her wing for the required 10-month internship in a tiny storefront on Queen Street West in the midst of a beaten-down-by-life neigbourhood.

Salvo Sally, a nickname I gave her but kept to myself, was indefatigable. She had to be. Everything was a battle: Indifferent and, occasionally, spiteful decision-makers in corporations and government versus our deeply depressed, poverty-stricken clients.

"I've never seen a person living in poverty who had good health," Sally told me when I first joined her team. For the next 10 months, I learned how true that statement was.

Day after day, we saw our clients, a sorry sea of humanity, who had bartered away their bodies for bread – broken backs from industrial accidents, repetitive strain so bad they couldn't sign documents, cancer from long-term chemical exposure.

Sally's desk was always covered in stacks of paper. Somehow she managed to move the stacks with purpose, single-handedly filing more motions, appeals and interventions than any dozen Bay Street lawyers.

Like Little Orphan Annie, suddenly turned 33, after sticking her finger in an electric socket, Sally's rusty mop of hair looked like it had never been introduced to a comb.

I never met anyone who worked as hard as she did. Sally was there in the morning no matter how early I arrived, and she was there when I left, no matter how late, a change of clothes the only sign that she had ever left the office.

Sally's sole focus was to get justice for our clients. Her personal appearance and a life outside of work never entered into it.

"Do you have someone special?" I ask her over coffee one day.

"What are you talking about?" she says, looking at me with a suspicious squint.

I recognize that squint and should have known to back off. Instead, I jump in with both feet, which then land in my mouth. "You need a life outside of work. It's not healthy," I say, pointing to the amalgam of paperwork, clothing and small household appliances that bespeak a life spent almost entirely in her office.

"The only thing that's going to be not healthy is you if you keep up this line of questioning," she says, leaning over her desk with a 'you-want-some-of-this smile.'

"I mean don't you have anything else in your life?" I mutter, unnerved by her aggressiveness.

"What else do I need or want," she says with finality, turning her attention to one of the thick files on her desk.

"Don't you want a boyfriend or anything?" I say in exasperation.

"Are you hitting on me?" she says, a wicked smile breaking across her face.

"Uhh, forget I asked," I say, scurrying out the door as fast as possible while still maintaining my dignity.

Although I enjoyed the work and Sally and I made a good team, it was that conversation that convinced me that I needed more from life than working in a community legal clinic.

When I completed articling, I slapped up my own shingle, Al Hamblyn, Attorney at Law. As a lawyer, the world was now supposed to be a feast set before me. The truth is, I still wasn't invited to the table. I remained a server for people like Gracey. It didn't matter how hard I worked, how much I had toadied up to some of those sanctimonious professors, and how hard I begged for an opportunity with the big law firms. My public housing pedigree and my magna come-short diploma, meant a lifetime of wills, small time real estate deals and, yes, ambulance chasing.

That, and an all-too-short, sad marriage to Rosalie and the birth of my son Johnny as the only highlights, occupied the next two and a half decades. Then, five years ago, Mangorian fell into my life.

As Mangorian's agent with a no-cut clause, executive producer of Late Bite With Dragul, and 50 per cent owner and CEO of Dragul Enterprises

Inc., which owns the show and markets a vast array of Dragul paraphernalia, I banked my first million in 2015, just three years ago. In the past 18 months, my net worth blew by $5 million. By late 2017 with worldwide syndication of the show, on paper I was well into eight-figures in my personal investment account. Now with an IPO in play for Dragul Enterprises, "the Em-Barrister" and "Hambulance Chaser," as Gracey alternately called me when our paths crossed in those early years, I could be joining the billionaires club any moment and definitely before the end of 2018.

The coup de grâce came a few weeks back when Verdon-Glassmere's managing partner knocked on my door pitching services for Dragul Enterprises. The emissary was George Mission, "my buddy" from law school, who professed his innocence at any transgression toward me. Yes, he had been a member of Gracey's entourage, but took no active role. As a means of making amends for past offences, George says he and the other partners fired Gracey that morning.

This was not a magnanimous gesture on George or V-G's part. V-G, once a cornerstone of the Canadian establishment, was looking desperate. Globalization cast its cloak over Canada's blue-chip industries. It put them under, or turned them into branch operations, with top executives and key legal and financial advisors now occupying offices in the U.S., U.K., Hong Kong, Germany, and even the BRIC nations. Toronto's previously vaunted professional services firms were left to fight for the scraps that remained.

V-G's once Olympian stature was also taken down by its arrogance and huge mismanagement, illustrated by appointing incompetents like Gracey to partner. Gracey could no longer rely on the influence of his father after a major development failed, taking with it the family's business empire and ending Robert Gracey's life in a heart attack.

Would V-G be given a chance, some role no matter how small when the new company is formed, my long-time buddy George asks?

I'm not a particularly vindictive person. I've been down and I don't want anyone to have to live through what I did. Still, George and friends had never had to live through what I did. Even if V-G went under, no one need have a tag day for these guys. They may be forced to sell their Forest Hill mansions and move into $2 million condos; get rid of the Rolls and opt for a Lexus; and, horrors, give up one or two of their many posh club memberships.

I won't be a party to financing that lifestyle. I will offer them a small bump-and-grind role finding and defending legal tax loopholes with their fee based on a percentage of savings. Once I discover who among their junior staff is the talent behind our savings, I'll hire them directly. Win-win for Dragul Enterprises and the junior staffers. Not so for V-G.

It's strange being able to make these calls. I long believed that fate had foreclosed on my future but it was sheer, superb luck that changed my fortune. Our big success was the focus of a Time Magazine article, which accurately quoted me saying: "I owe it all to Mangorian." And as Mangorian told Time, "I owe it all to Hamblyn."

It was a relationship forged anywhere but in heaven.

Our partnership found its seed in a barren interview room in Toronto Police Division 52 five years ago, just after a whiplash case I worked on for more than a year was tossed out by the judge. The insurance company provided the court with a video of my client helping a buddy roof his cottage.

"Case dismissed," says the judge and with it went the $30,000 fee I was expecting to collect.

I needed the money to pay back rent on my office, lease payments on my car, last year's taxes, a first birthday present for Johnny Jr., my sole grandchild, and yeah, some decent grub would be nice too.

I was truly at the lowest point in my life when I first came across Mangorian. He was beaten, bloody, and wearing rags more suitable for life in Toronto's storm sewers where he'd been living for nearly 10 years. You might expect that anyone who had been hunted and survived the way Mangorian had should be in a pitiable state. No one who saw him would characterize him as pitiable.

The courts gave me the nod to represent Mangorian after every other lawyer suddenly contracted the flu. My esteemed colleagues may have been put off by Mangorian's piercing yellow eyes, his Grim Reaper-thin six foot, six frame, and his sickly white skin. Then again, it could be the wickedly sharp, greenish fingernails, or the fetid breath that polluted the room. Okay, let's be honest. Hands down, it was Mangorian's dagger-like fangs and his appetite for fresh human blood.

CHAPTER TWO

DRAGUL ENTERPRISES

The laughter dies and Chloe Castor motions to the necklace, a shimmering icefield that drapes her neck. It gives the cameraman an excuse to focus on the starlet's ample bosom for a full five seconds.

"This little thing is worth $3.7 million. It's known as the Marie Antoinette necklace – a gift from Louis the XVI to his bride," Castor bubbles.

Presumably when Marie Antoinette still possessed a neck, I mutter to no one in particular.

The producers of Marie Antoinette, the movie, believed that the grand necklace, featured in key scenes during the filming of this, the third remake of the tale of Royals' pain in the neck, would bring added attention to the starlet's appearance on Late Bite and, certainly, to her best assets.

"Let me give you a better look," Castor, at her coquettish best, says to Dragul, as she leaps to her feet.

The house band strikes up 2 Live Crew's classic, Hoochie Mama. Castor's booty and breasts ride the rhythm on a panoramic route across the stage before circling back to the other side of the desk. Castor then thrusts her bare neck and plunging neckline directly in Mangorian's face.

Precisely on cue, Mangorian bares his fangs, hovering above the actress' porcelain neck. The cameraman zooms in to frame fangs, neck, necklace and bosom for – one steamboat, two steamboats, three steamboats – before zooming out to catch Mangorian as he mugs to the camera with his patented shrug. Plucking a huge, blood-red, silk handkerchief from a pocket, he then uses exaggerated movements to mop his brow.

The audience roars with approval. Mangorian bows and Castor curtsies.

I glance to my left and there's Jonesey Mallory, the starlet's agent, literally vibrating on the spot over the prospect of the tabloid press carrying front page photos of Dragul with fangs hovering over her protégé's exposed jugular and bustline. "If the tabs are true to form, it'll be a big front page photo with something gimmicky like: "Castor eyes on this! or Dragul's Tasty Treat," she says in a Hollywoodsy glamour drawl that I thought disappeared with the likes of Jean Harlow. "Kim Kardashian has nothing over my Chloe."

On stage, Mangorian waves his arms and shouts, "That's all for tonight. Tune in tomorrow when we put the bite on Hollywood's new heartthrob, Freddy Mummy. He's going to whip up some blood pudding. Yum!"

"Hit theme song. Roll credits. That's a wrap. Good show everyone, especially you Chloe and Dragul," says our Emmy-winning director, Jim Phillips.

The live audience exits with one, out of every three, handing over small blood collection tubes in exchange for signed autographed photos of Dragul in full open-mouthed fang mode, alternately inscribed with "Fangs for the memories," "You have wonderful taste," "My fang club is the best," etc.

Pretty awful stuff, but I love it, and so does my wallet. The cornier we get, the more our demographic loves Dragul, and the bigger the audience.

As usual, I collect the box, half-filled with a hundred or so tubes of blood. "These are much handier than the usual panties and hotel keys that other celebrities get and they keep the boss very happy and healthy," I tell the staff.

I shouldn't pat myself on the back but it really was one of my best ideas to create a win-win for my golden goose and society. Fans are encouraged to come to a clinic an hour before the show to donate blood. All the normal blood testing is put in play. Toronto's hospitals get a huge infusion of blood, except for one 2-ounce collection tube from every donor that goes to Mangorian.

Score one more much-needed PR point for Mangorian because there remains a sizeable segment of society that views him as the devil incarnate.

There's the occasional dad whose daughter went missing, but the biggest headaches are the religious groups of all denominations that hold prayer vigils outside the studio demanding Mangorian's imprisonment and, in some cases, decapitation.

Momentarily, I toy with an idea for a news release. "It's nice to see we've been able to bring Christians, Muslims and Jews together in a common cause."

No, that would be a train-wreck, but it's funny to think about.

Tonight a dozen people stand on the sidewalk with placards that scream, "Death to the Beast," "The Great Corrupter," and "Dragul is the Devil."

One of them is shouting, "You fiend. Where is my daughter?"

It's Ben Saxon, the same guy whose face was plastered on the cover of Super Nova and a couple of the other tabloid papers. He claims that Dragul is behind the disappearance of more than a dozen girls in the last year.

I guess it was just five years ago when just about everyone shared that opinion, even me.

CHAPTER THREE

THE CLIENT

The message light is blinking on my phone, and there's a stack of registered letters piled on the desk of what, for-the-moment, I refer to as my home office.

One is from my landlord. No surprise there. A second envelope with a big red 'URGENT ACTION REQUIRED' comes from Ford Credit. The others are an assortment of demands for payment from the phone and utility companies, a couple of credit card agencies, and, of course, the tax man.

I look at a picture of my son taken 20 years ago when I was still part of his life. Rather than cheering me up, it makes me feel empty and sad. My face is reflected in the frame's mirror finish. I see an old, defeated man – pallid, bloated and balding.

I dig into the pile of letters and uncover a large bottle of no name aspirin – the kind with those extra strength pills. My head is throbbing so I take one and try to swallow it dry. It gets halfway down and then puts on the brakes. I gulp twice to wet my throat, and then pop a second pill in the hope it will push down the first. Success. It's the first thing I've succeeded at since god knows when. Maybe it's a sign I should take all of the pills. I empty the bottle into a heap on the palm of my hand, taking care not to spill any. Death by aspirin is supposed to be relatively painless but way too slow. I stare at the clumsy, white pyramid for ten full seconds before dumping them back into the bottle. No, not even the courage for that.

I focus back to the phone and go to voice mail. The first message is from Ford Credit. "Please let us know when you will drop off the car." The second message is from Regina Naylor, a law student in her final year at the Usher Law School. A few weeks ago I was in need of some free help so I asked Jerry, my old prof, for a student volunteer. He sent me Regina. She sounded smart and best of all she owned a car.

"I got your message that we're taking on the Mangorian case, . . . incredible," her voice message says. "I've already started some of the paperwork and, of course, I can pick you up at the courthouse. Uhhh . . . you don't mind if I just stick to the paperwork and leave all the client interaction to you? Bye for now."

I hang up and shuffle the pile of letters to one side, pick up the keys for what-for-now is my car and head to a Ford dealership that's the shortest walk to the police station. I should just declare bankruptcy. That way I could come down with the flu myself.

On my drive, all of the radio stations carry sensational reports that a suspect in the Toronto stalker attacks has been captured and that early reports say he is a vampire.

"You're hearing this first on Rock 1060. Confidential sources in Toronto's police department confirm the suspect in the stalker attacks is a vampire. And we can confirm now that all of his victims had their blood sucked out of them."

I switch stations.

"Police are rumoured to have the suspect in a special cell that has no bars so he can't change into a bat and escape."

Next station.

"We have a breaking news report from our reporter Melissa Doig at 52 Division. What's happening in this vampire case Melissa," says Dee-Jay Brad G. of the Brad All Morning show.

"Thanks Brad. Detective Buddy Ferino, the lead investigator into the Toronto stalker attacks, just held a news conference and has identified the suspect as Dragul Mangorian, age unknown, address unknown."

"Did Det. Ferino confirm that the suspect, this Magurry, is a vampire?"

"Not quite, but the next best thing, Det. Ferino will not deny reports that he is a vampire. Listen for yourself."

"Is it true that he's a vampire?" Doig asks breathlessly.

"I have no comment to that question."

"So you are not denying he is a vampire," she persists.

"I have no comment."

"So," says Doig, "There you have it, no denial."

"Hey folks, you heard it here first on AM 960, Detective Buddy Ferino is not denying they have arrested a vampire in the Toronto Stalker case."

I switch stations again to the usually calmer CBC because the publicly funded broadcaster doesn't rely on ratings for its existence.

"Reporter Janice Chakrabarti is on the scene for what's turned out to be a sensational development in the Toronto Stalker investigation. Janice, what can you tell us?"

"Hi Peter, I'm here at Toronto Police Division 52 where the lead investigator into the Stalker Attacks is just concluding a news conference."

"We're hearing some very wild reports about vampires, giants, you name it. Is there any truth to this?"

"Well, I think you should listen and make that decision for yourself. This is part of the news conference. The voice you're about to hear is that of Det. Ferino."

"At approximately 9:10 p.m. last evening, police received a report of an incident at 8874 Decarie Drive. When officers arrived on the scene they found a 32-year-old female who had been physically assaulted. Police canine units were dispatched to the scene and tracked a suspect to a storm sewer outlet in the Don River Valley. It appears the suspect had been living in the storm sewer system.

"The suspect was found and arrested after a three-hour search. The suspect resisted arrest and had to be physically subdued. Two officers were injured during the arrest and are reported in good condition in Westley Hospital. The suspect is being held in custody at 52 Division and will face numerous charges in court later this morning."

A dozen voices shout out questions.

"Janice, what is your question?"

"Det. Ferino, is this case being linked with all of the other stalker cases?"

"Yes, we believe this case is linked with all of the other stalker crimes."

"Can you elaborate on why you think they are linked?"

"The crimes scenes are similar and the method of attack is the same."

"And that method is?"

"The victim last night, and eight previous victims, all had two puncture wounds on the neck and all of them were missing a quantity of blood."

Twenty reporters shout questions at once.

"Melissa, your question?" Det. Ferino says.

"Is it true that he's a vampire?"

"I have no comment to that question."

Janice's voice comes back live on air.

"Peter, there you have it. Police have confirmed that all nine of the victims in the stalker case suffered blood losses during the attack and all nine had two puncture wounds on their neck."

"It's beginning to sound like we have a story about a vampire or somebody who thinks he's a vampire."

"It certainly does Peter. This is CBC Reporter Janice Chakrabarti on the scene at Police Division 52."

I flip the station again.

"That's right . . . a vampire, like Dracula but for real. A blood-sucking fiend. Big fangs and nine feet tall according to our confidential police sources. We have an unconfirmed report that the suspect changed into a giant bat."

§§§

A hulking 40ish cop, with three chevrons on his sleeve and a blond, military-style brushcut that mirrors his square jaw, greets me at the front desk of 52 Division. His nametag identifies him as 'P. Crampton.'

"You Hamburger?" brushcut says, revealing a set of amazingly big teeth.

"Hamblyn," I correct.

"If you're that vampire Mangorian's lawyer, you're Hamburger," he says, again unveiling his choppers in a smile that stretches from one cauliflower ear to the other.

I just can't escape the name-calling. Half-muffled guffaws from a series of cubicles erupt to the rear of a glass partition behind the front desk, which does nothing to ease my feeling of foreboding.

I consider protesting but I can't waste any energy or emotions on this moron.

"May I see my client, sergeant?"

"Sure, but you may wanna see Detective Ferino first.

I nod okay and he waves at a guy in a hat.

"He's kinda an oddball but a good detective," Sgt. Crampton says.

A tall, wiry guy with a long thin nose and horn-rimmed glasses approaches. He's about 30 years old but, incongruously, is dressed in a trenchcoat and fedora, like he walked straight out of a 1950s pulp crime novel.

"So, you're the lawyer assigned to represent Dragul Mangorian. Detective Buddy Ferino. I'm the lead investigator in the stalker attacks," he says offering me his hand to shake. I take it and he gives two quick pumps and adds, "I'm sure we're going to be seeing a lot of each other over the next several months."

"Uhh, Al Hamblyn. Nice to meet you."

I say nothing more because I'm not quite sure what to say. I haven't handled many criminal cases, certainly none like this, and I don't want to show any cards, especially when I don't know what they are.

"I asked the sergeant to direct you to me when you came in," he says, drawing conspiratorially close to me.

Almost whispering in my ear, he says, "I shouldn't be saying this to a suspect's lawyer but I got to tell you . . . Be careful with this guy. I don't know if he's a vampire or what he is, but he's not normal.

"We tasered him and, even flat on his back, he still took out two of our guys."

I feet my blood run cold and ask, "You mean he sucked the blood out of two police officers?"

"No, no, no. I mean he took them out. He threw them against a wall. They're pretty banged up but they'll live."

"Oh good," I say with relief for my sake, not the injured cops.

Det. Ferino gives me a penetrating look and says, "We got him in a locked room, not a cell, and we've got shackles on him. Don't be giving us any of this civil liberties crap about the shackles. They're going to stay on as long as we have him."

I simply nod in reply.

He signals Sgt. Crampton, who returns. The sergeant then motions for me to follow him through a series of desolate, concrete-block corridors, painted grey with uncaring brush strokes, until we reach a massive steel door. He presses a buzzer and stares up and to the right at a camera and says, "Open up Bobby."

A moment later there's a loud clack and the door slides open to a sublime symphony of sweat, urine and eau de mildew. We follow the scent down another hallway to a guard station where a cop with the nametag 'R. Simms,' 10 years the sergeant's junior, joins us for another 20 paces.

Constable Simms unclips a set of keys from his wide black belt and opens the door to, what the sergeant describes as, the interview room – a bleak, harshly lit box equipped with only a stainless-steel table and two stainless-steel chairs, all secured to the floor with knuckle-sized, nickel-infused, steel bolts.

"You have 30 minutes and then we have to take him to court," the sergeant says and then nods to PC Simms and leaves.

The accused is manacled hand, foot, and neck. The second cop, looking as nervous as I feel, gives me a long, hard glance as he heads toward the exit to give me time to confer with my client in private, as the law provides. Just before reaching the doorway, PC Simms pauses, turns to me and says: "I don't suppose I have to tell you to stay on your side of the table. He's chained to the floor so he can't get to you and there's a buzzer on the table. Use it if you need me," adding a reflexive pat on his holster. "We'll be watching as well," he says giving his head a slight upward twist toward another camera positioned above the door.

My return look says, please, please don't leave, but he's gone.

CHAPTER FOUR

THE SANGUINUS

I assess my surroundings. Other than the table, chairs and chains, there's only a dusty chrome clock facing me attached, slightly off-centre on a wall that likely acquired its institutional-beige finish from the same artisan assigned to paint the corridors. I watch as the red second hand sweeps to the vertical and I hear a distinct 'tick' that impels the minute hand to 9:00 a.m.

Dragul Mangorian stares straight ahead. No emotion. No acknowledgement of my presence. I feel him tracking with some otherworldly sense my every movement, my every breath, my every thought. I sit down facing him, but I find it hard to look directly at him. I feel the hairs on the back of my neck, my arms, my legs, hell even the ones in my ears standing straight up. A bead of sweat runs from behind my ear to the nape of my neck where it joins with other streams flowing from my face and the back of my head to form a Niagara that flows down my chest and, for now, is held in check by the waist band of my boxer shorts.

I do a 10 second meditation as one of those self-help tapes of my youth taught me – breathe deeply, get in touch with my spirit, release and then tackle the world.

'Tick.' Dammit. A minute gone and I haven't uttered a word. What am I afraid of? Those chains would hold an elephant. He can't reach me unless I go around the table to him and, by all that is holy, that isn't about to happen. Still this Mangorian guy or whatever he is, is a fearsome presence. I don't mind admitting he scares the living shit out of me. Even his breathing sounds menacing and his awful breath could cause a heart attack. I gather my nerves and use another arm-chair psychology technique, self-talk to motivate myself. "I need this job. I need this job," I repeat to myself.

'Tick.' Another minute gone. Got to get a grip. I shuffle some papers, pull out my notebook, and write at the top of the page:

Al Hamblyn
First Interview with Dragul Mangorian
Sept. 15, 2013, 9:00 a.m.

Then I begin to fake writing some additional notes. One step at a time. Just get some answers from him before we make our first appearance in court at 10 a.m.

'Tick.' I try to make an assessment of Mangorian based on observation rather than just my fears and find both tracks reach the same conclusion. His shirt and pants, repulsively filthy, and smelling of sewer water – really just a collection of torn rags – are the sugar coating for what lies beneath. The rips and gaps divulge a paper-white gnarl of muscle and sinew on bone like something translucent that crawls from under a rock but a something that emanates primordial, instinctive danger.

'Tick.' Get on with it. Get on with it, I tell myself. I take three or four deep breaths, clear my throat and, on my third attempt, words magically come out of my mouth. "Dragul Mangorian. My name is Al Hamblyn. I am your lawyer."

'Tick.' 9:05 a.m.

Progress. It only took me five minutes to tell him my name. Within me, I feel the tiniest spark of pride forming around my bravery until those yellow eyes lock onto me, sending shivers from toe nails to hair ends. Show no fear. Show no fear, I say to myself with zero conviction. Again my voice fails me.

'Tick.'

"The sound of the clock impels me to act. "I have been appointed by the court to represent you. You face nine charges of attempted murder, nine counts of assault causing bodily harm, and sexual assault on six women. You are also charged with nine counts of break and enter, resisting arrest, two dozen charges of criminal prowl by night, causing a disturbance, and vagrancy.

"You should be aware that the police say they suspect you of murder and they are now combing your living quarters in the sewers to see if they come up with any evidence you've committed other crimes," I say. I look for any reaction, a sign of guilt, anger, anything. His face provides no reaction, at least no human reaction but his eyes and voice . . .

"They won't find any bodies, if that's what you are implying," he says, as much with those probing alligator eyes as his mouth.

His voice is deep, authoritative, like an evil Lorne Green and every syllable is laced with menace.

'Tick.'

"I do not murder. At least I haven't in 100 years," he says matter-of-factly. "I feed on people's blood, but I commit no assault. I sexually assaulted no one. When I drink their blood, on occasion I tear off some of their clothing."

On occasion? What a strange phrase to come from his mouth. On occasion. It's like saying, 'On occasion, we go on a picnic.' 'On occasion, I wear my blue sweater.' But, on occasion, I tear off my victim's clothes, the better to drink her blood? That's something that falls outside any experience I'd ever imagined having.

'Tick.'

"As my lawyer, I want you to understand that I am not guilty. I am compelled to drink blood," he says, leaning closer to me, a move that literally freezes my blood.

"Each time, it is a matter of life and death. My life and death. Surely the court cannot deny a man the right to fight for his survival," he says as his veil of calmness lifts just enough for me to see a fiery rage inside.

"You . . . you are a man?" I stammer the half-statement, half-question.

"Yes, I am a man. Perhaps, not the kind of man you have ever met before but, indeed, I am a man who, through natural selection, evolved to feed on blood. I am part of what once was a great nation, a nation that warred over food with your ancestors for 30,000 years. My nation it seems lost and, because of that, I am the last of my kind. When I am gone, the branch of humanity I represent is extinct."

'Tick.'

He's hit me with so much information at once that it overwhelms me, opens a hundred lines of questions. I don't know quite how to proceed. I go back to my lawyer's playbook and the law.

"Mr. Mangorian, if all you were doing was fighting for your survival, why didn't you turn to the authorities for help?" I ask, shocked that my tongue could be so bold while my sweat faucets are still fully engaged.

"Help? For me? The only help your kind offered my people was death, and death in a thousand horrible ways, decapitation, a stake through the heart, burning to death, disembowelment. My species has been hunted and murdered to the brink of extinction. Who is the predator? Who is the victim?"

'Tick.'

I glance up at the clock and am surprised that it's now 9:10. With only 20 minutes left, I shouldn't be taking time right now to discuss anything but the charges but when a guy looks like this guy and my bladder is one hiss away from letting loose, well who's going to interrupt.

"As far as I know, I am the last surviving member of a branch of mankind, a splinter from the genus Homo Sapiens. My people named ourselves Homo Sanguinus, seeker of blood, because it was blood that sustained us. We departed from your direct lineage about 30,000 years ago, during the last ice age, when food, shelter, and human kindness were in short supply," he says in a non-stop speech that invites no interruptions.

"Although stronger, faster, and much longer-living than Homo Sapiens, Homo Sanguinus do not reproduce readily. Pregnancy among our women is rare and even then only one of 20 of our offspring survives pregnancy and childbirth. When our kind and Homo Sapiens were more closely related we could interbreed and our numbers maintained themselves, even flourished."

'Tick.'

He pauses to take a breath so I jump in.

"So, you don't create your kind – er . . Homo sag . . ."

"Homo Sanguinus."

"Yes, yes, Homo Sanguinus. You don't create more of you by sucking blood and . . ."

"For heaven's sake. It is a base insult to my people. It is an affront to me to characterize my existence and the rest of my people as being the result of some kind of Hollywood-fabricated STD. We are born and raised exactly the same way you humans are with the one exception being our diet," he says, slamming a hand on the table to horrifying effect because of the amplified force and sound of crashing chains.

"I apologize," I say, really meaning it because when this guy gets agitated I get the feeling people die. "So you are how old?" I ask.

"I am middle-aged, just over 200 years."

"You don't look a day over 40 . . . and that's not a joke," I add the last part because I realize what a stupid remark it was to a guy who is a vampire and would kill me as soon as look at me.

"As I said, I am middle-aged. In my experience with Homo Sapiens like you, we are either the object of a joke or the object of fear. We invoke the latter to survive."

'Tick.'

"The name Dragul Mangorian. Is that Transylvanian?"

"My God. Did you grow up on vampire books and movies? If you must know, it is my family name. My family originated in what is known now as the Ottawa Valley in Ontario. We lived the last several millennia around Warsaw, Ontario in caves that have now become a bit of a tourist destination. The native populations and we coexisted as well as any two groups of Homo Sapiens and Homo Sanguinus. They tended to stay away from us, fearing we were evil spirits. They named us the Wendigo."

'Huh', I think to myself. 'Maple syrup, hockey, and now vampires putting Canada on the map. Who woulda thunk it.'

"And how did you come to live in Toronto," I say trying to lighten the conversation.

"We lived in the area you now call Toronto hundreds of years before there was a Toronto or even a Canada but I'm getting ahead of myself. Let me start at the beginning."

I think I should interject before he launches into the full story of his ancestry. However, one look into those piercing yellow eyes tells me, 'It won't kill you to listen, but it might if you don't.'

'Tick.'

"You and I share a common ancestor but, for some reason, natural selection created a splinter sub species from Homo Sapiens. As I explained, we later named ourselves the Homo Sanguinus. For many millennia, Sapiens and Sanguinus co-existed, sometimes in peace but most times as warring factions, competing for whatever food we could hunt or gather.

"A prolonged period of colder temperatures, cold even for the ice age, caused the food supply to further diminish. This set our two species against each other, not just as competitors for food, but as food. Sapiens took to eating our flesh and, for reasons unknown, we took to drinking your blood. Outnumbered, we retreated underground for preservation's sake and to reduce the caloric requirements of living in freezing temperatures. We found that, over many generations, we developed the ability to go into hibernation for months at a time to outlast winter food shortages. This separation during our underground period broke the tenuous genetic link with Sapiens and, thereafter, we could only breed among ourselves. The result was our numbers dwindled with each succeeding generation."

'Tick.'

"So," feeling a bit bolder, I ask the million-dollar question on every reporter and prospective juror's mind, "Are you a Vampire?"

Mangorian heaves an almost human sigh, lacing his spidery green-tinged fingers together on the steel table.

"My ancestors stayed underground to keep warm and out of harm's way. Over the millennia this evolved into sensitivity to daylight but not the 'death-by-sunlight' popularized in your books and films about Vampires. Sunlight burns us because we lack the pigmentation that absorbs ultraviolet rays but it won't kill us unless we stay out in full sunlight for prolonged periods. The same exposure would be extremely unpleasant for a human like you. Exposure to sunlight will not cause us to spontaneously burst into flames although your ancestors often made sport of setting my ancestors on fire as a satisfyingly cruel way to put us to death.

"We don't turn into bats, wolves or smoke. As for holy water and crucifixes, as you Sapiens say, I can take 'em or leave 'em."

"But you do drink blood – human blood. You've said that," I say, as a horrifying slide show of pale corpses runs through my mind.

'Tick.'

"Unfortunately, yes. Through our wars with Sapiens, and through all the food shortages, we acquired a taste for blood. When my lineage split from the direct line of Sapiens, it was, perhaps, nature's way of helping both species to survive. What is that old nursery rhyme? Ah yes,

Jack Sprat could eat no fat.
His wife could eat no lean.
And so betwixt the two of them,
They licked the platter clean.

Now he's quoting kids nursery rhymes, I think to myself. Completely bizarre.

"Our metabolic systems developed to ingest liquids and yours to ingest solids. My canine teeth are hollow so they can pull blood directly out of a vein or artery and you have teeth that tear and grind to consume flesh. This should have been the perfect answer for our two hunter-gatherer societies to be able to share a kill without fighting over who gets the choicest pieces."

"Yes, that seems like the perfect situation for all. But it obviously didn't work out," I say.

"No. No it didn't. Call it hominid nature, but our two species couldn't share. We preferred to kill each other, and eat each other, rather than cooperate. Eventually your ancestors, the Sapiens, drove my kind, the Sanguinus, away from the best hunting grounds. We ended up retreating underground when a particularly powerful period of frigid temperatures all but destroyed our food resources.

"We survived for thousands of years in underground shelters that we created or found, sucking the guts of earthworms and insects and, occasionally, coming across a warm-blooded mole or vole or, praise heaven, a gopher or rabbit to feast upon," he says, chafing against the neck manacle. "Our anatomical systems evolved to take food in only liquid form and, for reasons we cannot fathom, blood, human blood became not just our preferred food but a food we literally cannot live without."

'Tick.'

CHAPTER FIVE

ASCENDANCY OF SAPIENS

"So you do prey on humans."

Mangorian gives an even larger sigh, this time emitting a huge breath so thick and putrid I swear that for an instant the air turned green. Certainly, my face did.

"Ten thousand years ago, we killed our prey, as did humans. Back then, many humans killed other humans and ate their flesh and drank their blood. Are we so dissimilar to man in that respect? After many millennia, modern Westerners adopted a taboo against cannibalism and drinking of human blood although you continue to eat the flesh of beasts and consume their blood in many forms.

"Being separate from humans, we did not adopt these taboos nor could we. But we did learn to tame our appetites so we could feed yet leave our meal warm and breathing much like your forebears found sustenance in milk and eggs rather than always slaughtering the animal."

Another pause gives me time to jump in with a question that had been gnawing at me since he first started speaking.

"Now I would like to clarify something. You say you are a little over 200 years old yet you are recounting things from thousands of years ago, well before the written word was invented."

'Tick.'

"I remind you, we are very long-lived and have listened to our elders relate these tales night after night. In some cases, the elders played a role in the story or were only a few generations removed from the events. This is not unique to my people. There are many examples from your world where writing isn't needed to pass on a story accurately. Many cultures used memorization techniques to preserve their histories, genealogies, and religious teachings. In the early days, followers of Muhammad committed every word of the Qur'an to memory when literacy was rare.

"There is, however, one significant ability among many of my people that has allowed our history to be passed on accurately. This same ability has been misrepresented and that misrepresentation has greatly added to the vampire myth. The tall tales say that we have the power to compel. This is not accurate. We cannot take over someone's mind or make anyone to do anything that they do not want to do. But to those who we are physically touching, we can project images and, sometimes, entire stories that create understanding. This has allowed us to pass on an historical record of our people to an amazing degree of accuracy."

'Tick.'

"But you also use it to compel . . . er . . . persuade your victims to let you feed on them?"

"When we have the time and opportunity, we use this power to explain our condition and create empathy so those we meet invite us to feed. This eliminates any savagery and allows us to feed without otherwise harming them. The ultimate decision to let us feed rests with the individual.

"If we are invited to feed, the experience and the blood is of high quality. If we savagely attack an individual, the blood can still sustain us but it is less to our liking, much like the gamey taste of adrenaline-infused meat when the quarry is not taken down cleanly during a hunt."

"But we have nine people who do not feel they invited you. They claim you assaulted them."

"If we are rushed or haven't fed properly we may do more damage than intended but that is rare. The transfer of images among Homo Sanguinus works very well but the minds of Homo Sapiens do not always synchronize perfectly with us. The images come too quickly and like dreams, even vivid ones, they can be quickly forgotten."

"So you are saying that all of your victims consented but then forgot they consented."

"That is precisely my point," he says with a satisfied look.

"I don't see it. Who but someone with some ghoulish outlook would agree to be your food?" I say, thinking this is going to be one hell of a tale to try to sell to a jury.

'Tick.'

"You present my position in such a gross manner that of course it sounds repulsive. In fact, human nature leans toward this type of generosity. Your blood services system in Canada is based on voluntarily giving your blood to a complete stranger. In other instances, you have databases so that compatible donors can provide bone marrow and kidneys to people who need them. A donation of blood to me seems a small thing compared to donating a kidney."

I surrender the point and move on. "So if your people are so powerful, why are you in hiding and we dominate the planet?"

"Individually, we are physically more powerful than almost any one of your people but en masse Homo Sapiens possess the ultimate power, the power to multiply and dominate every aspect of this planet. That is a power far beyond any we possess. In the last 100 years, our numbers diminished to the single-digit thousands while Homo Sapiens proliferated into the billions. We would have remained largely in our underground lairs living separately and hidden from you but mankind's population explosion made that impossible."

'Tick.'

The clock causes me to break from the story and assess myself. I'm surprised at how calm I've become after only a few minutes in Mangorian's presence. On the surface, he still looks menacing, but there's something else, on a parallel plane, whittling away at my fear. I find myself becoming more and more fascinated by his story about a world previously unknown to me.

"There's no corner of the planet that your kind has not ravaged. Your construction of mega projects like the St. Lawrence Seaway, the Hoover Dam, the Chunnel, and hydro channels you cut into Niagara Falls, Churchill Falls and hundreds of other locations flooded many of our colonies, killing thousands. When one of your geniuses invented lateral drilling and hydraulic fracturing, you exterminated thousands by injecting poisonous gases into our underground villages, all in your unbridled pursuit of oil and gas. Whether it was unwitting genocide or part of a secret plan by your governments, other colonies simply disappeared as mines, subway systems, rail and road tunnels, and mammoth developments destroyed one habitat after another."

'Tick.'

I'm reminded of recent revelations about the treatment of the peoples of Canada's First Nations and, especially, of their children, who were sent to residential schools to be 'civilized.' For many, it was open season on their bodies and their innocence and, for all, it was the genocide of their culture.

These shocking stories turned my understanding of the world I knew on its head. Mangorian makes me revisit those things I initially viewed as good and great and reveals the devastation and evil wrought on unseen, unconsidered others.

"The stragglers who survived took to the sewer systems of your cities," he continues. They were not our first choice. The sewers are not places we could raise children but we could survive. A sense of hopelessness set in and, over the past 50 years, our numbers have been devastated much of it through suicide or through self-imposed starvation after losing the will to live . . . I believe I am now alone, perhaps the last of my kind. I have seen no other member of my species for more than 20 years."

'Tick.'

I look to the clock. It's 9:22 a.m.

"Uh Mr. Mangorian. You've raised many points that will take much time to prove and I really need to prepare for court. This is first appearance court so, considering the seriousness of the charges and the fact you are a flight risk, you will be held over without bail. Do you understand the charges before you?"

"Of course I do. I may have been living in a sewer but my very survival has depended on my understanding of your world. I know enough of your world and its laws to know that by having the consent of those I'm charged with attacking means there is no assault and, on all other charges, I cannot be held responsible for my actions."

"What do you mean 'not responsible'."

"I don't trust police. They are monitoring our conversation," he says, motioning toward the camera. "Come closer so I can whisper what my defence should be."

"Uh, I'm supposed to stay on this side of the table."

"What am I going to do? I'm shackled hand, foot and neck. You're my lawyer. I need you. Why would I want to hurt you."?

'Tick.'

I inch a bit closer reaching the side of the table when Mangorian says, "Oh come on. I don't bite. Actually I do, but I'll forego the pleasure this time."

"Ha, ha, ha, ha." Again with the maniacal laughter.

"Sorry. A bad joke. I need you to believe me. I need you to understand me."

"I believe you."

"No you don't. You believe that I've done everything the media has speculated about. You believe that I can turn into a bat and that I have weekly chats with the devil. You are frightened of me. Therefore, you cannot give me a proper defence. How will it look in the courtroom when you refuse to sit beside your client?

'Tick.'

"Let's get this over with right now. Bring your chair and sit next to me. I told you earlier that I will only drink the blood of those who invite me to do so. Are you going to invite me to drink your blood?"

"No."

"Then I promise that until you give me that invitation, you'll be perfectly safe. It's now 9:24. You have just six minutes and then the next time we meet will be in court. You need to have the knowledge necessary to defend me and win my case, or you need to find me another lawyer."

There may have been another time when I was more afraid than now but I can't think of anything that comes remotely close in this lifetime or any of my past lives, if I had any. Still, I really need this case. So, I do as he asks and I stand next to him, mostly because I fear what he'll do if I don't.

Mangorian raises his arms and then says, "I want to place one of my hands on your temple. It's vital to my defence. Let your mind go blank. I will be able to transfer my thoughts. You will absolutely and completely understand me."

If he could understand my thoughts right now they would be centred at the puddle forming at my ankles.

What the hell. My life is a complete mess. Just a half hour ago, I came close to downing a bottle of aspirin. If he kills me, I have a small insurance policy that, for the first time, will give Rosalie and my son and his family a little something from me. No one will miss me.

I hold my breath and nod my consent.

Mangorian reaches out to touch my quivering face. My mind does an internal somersault and the room starts to go fuzzy.

'Tick.' The last thing I see is the clock. It's 9:25.

CHAPTER SIX

THE UNDERSTANDING

I SEE LIGHT, then blurry shapes, and slowly everything comes back into focus. I'm in another time and place. It's a cave that goes straight underground, but we are a party of six moving toward the surface.

We emerge into the sunshine and are immediately blinded and feel a burning heat on our bare skin from the blistering ball of fire in the sky. We are dressed like cavemen. We hold animal hides above our heads with spears to block the sun, Cro-Magnon parasols if you will.

We run quickly and effortlessly across a savanna feeling the occasional lash of sunlight on skin and eyes when the protective hides fail to fully shield us. One of our number points to tracks and when we reach the top of a rise, there's a herd of gazelle or antelope ahead. We give chase. Despite the long legs and great bounds of the animals, we overtake the herd and, in practised coordination, our party outflanks one of the slower beasts. Our spears pierce the antelope and it goes tumbling down. At once, we are upon it. Our spears cut into arteries in the legs and neck and then mouths and teeth latch onto the gushing wounds.

Suddenly, there is a cry from our left side. We stop our feeding to look around. It's hard to see with the sun so bright. Twenty men holding spears and large stones come at us in a run. We turn to face them and ready ourselves for battle when another cry comes from behind. Thirty men charge at us with spears in their hands and the sun at their back.

The six of us stand back-to-back when the first wave of rocks comes crashing upon us from our sun-blind side. Our leader takes a large stone to the back of his head and falls heavily. More rocks fly and I feel a crack as something snaps in my left shoulder. We pick up the stones and hurl them back but for every one that we throw 10 are returned.

We are down to three still standing when a dozen men charge at us. They thrust with spears at us and our coverings to make the sun an ally in their attack. I feel sunlight cutting my skin like a hundred razor blades but I manage to deflect a spear thrust. I grab my foe's arm, pull him to me and rip out his throat with my fangs. I suck in the blood madly and a fiery strength courses through my entire being. I fling his body at two other assailants and sink my fangs deeply into the carotid artery of another. A stone-tipped spear rips into the same damaged shoulder. With a howl, I burst through the enemy line with the only other member of my pack, who's still on his feet, right behind me.

We are faster than they are. They do not pursue us. Instead they vent their anger on our fallen comrades whose lives end in a rain of rocks and spear points.

Wounded and severely sunburned, we make it back to our cave opening without the prize we so greatly needed to feed our families. That night the rumbling of empty stomachs vies for dominance over the wails of sorrow.

The world begins to pulse and spin again and then nothingness, an endless white void that begins to take shape like pieces of a jigsaw puzzle falling together. I am walking on a field stained red with bodies of fallen soldiers. I am wearing the battered and bloody armour of a knight with a large cross on my shield.

My comrades, also disguised as Crusaders, kneel over the dead and dying as if administering last rites. Instead, in practised stealthy steps they find a choice opening in a dying soldier's armour and drink deeply. There's an agonizing hunger within me. My heart and veins are pumping acid, an internal assassin searing every part of my being. I want to tear out my eyes, rip off my ears, wrench my arms and legs from their sockets and smash my head on the rocks to stop the pain. But there is another way. Raging through the agony, I part the armour shielding the neck of a shivering Crusader who's been sliced down the middle. I see a weak pulse in the jugular vein and my fangs sink deep and I drink.

The acid burning in my veins is instantly transformed into a cool, delicious liquid energy that infuses my cells with renewed vitality. I catch my breath just as the soldier coughs out his last. I end the suffering of six more before I am satiated. I stop to fill a helmet with the blood from two soldiers of Islam and head back to the cave.

Colours of the scene stretch outward in a spiral wrapping around the sun like yarn on a spindle moving faster and faster, faster and faster until all the hues blend together into a milky haze. Slowly a new picture emerges.

I'm standing at the back of a crowd, wearing a hood and cloak, so no one can see my face and to shield me from the sun. The crowd is chanting, "Witch, Witch, Witch."

I see one of the women from my community tied nude to a post in the village square.

Her skin is raw, blistered and peeling under the noonday sun while villagers pile branches and logs around and under her.

"The witch is going to burn! The witch is going to burn!" children sing while laughing, and chasing each other around the square.

A man in a black hood approaches with a fiery brand that terminates in a glowing 'W'. He walks up to the woman and stabs the brand into her bare chest. For an instant, I hear only the sizzle as brand and flesh become one. Then the woman's screams and sobs fill the air, followed by the villagers' cheers and laughter.

"With this brand, I have first ensured this blasphemer will carry the brand of the Witch with her for all eternity into the 9th circle of Hell," he shouts.

"The Court of Oyer and Terminer for the Village of Salem has found this creature guilty of the foulest of crimes. She has consorted with the Devil. She has practised the dark arts of witchcraft, casting evil spells on our townsfolk. She has committed blasphemy against our Blessed Lord by drinking human blood. She has cast our Village onto the road to damnation."

The hooded man walks a few feet and picks up a flaming torch.

"I now carry out the sentence of the Court and Magistrate – death at the stake by the cleansing power of fire and, thus, erase this affront to God."

The fire roars to life amid the woman's screams and the crowd's jeers and shrieks of laughter as the scene blurs like a spatula scraping across a wet painting.

I'm back at the police interview room, the chrome clock and beige wall stare at me as does Mangorian. He nods. "Now you understand. Now you can be my lawyer."

CHAPTER SEVEN

COURT APPEARANCE

The courthouse for first appearances is in Toronto's Old City Hall, a sandstone block edifice built with large arched windows when access to sunlight was necessary to maintain indoor lighting levels. The building is four blocks from the police station, an easy walk, and there's a Giant Tiger en route where I pick up a cheap XXXL hoodie and big UV shielding sunglasses with my last $20 that I had been hoping to use to buy the week's groceries.

Hundreds of reporters, cameramen, photographers, and the curious are gathered. My name has been leaked to the media but, because of my current lower-than-low profile, nobody knows what I look like. Among the general citizenry, some read newspapers with headlines that scream: "Dracula captured," "Vampire jailed."

Dozens hold placards that more or less say, "Vampire killed my daughter," "Death to the Devil," and oddly a couple that say, "Vampire Love = Perfect Love" and "I want to bear Dragul's child"

I shudder not knowing which side is sicker.

I simply walk in like any other citizen. I have a special card that lets me bypass the crowds and gives me access to the police section of the garage where I wait for the paddywagon. The hoodie and sunglasses are for Mangorian – to shield him from stray bits of sunlight streaming through the windows as he walks through the corridors and into the holding cells. Once Mangorian is secured, I make my way to the judges' offices.

"I need to speak with Judge Batten and the court clerk before court is in session," I say.

It's a bit out of the ordinary, but word is passed on. I'm summoned to Judge Batten's chambers.

"Your Honour, I need you to make certain provisions in the courtroom to accommodate my client."

"Mr. Hamblyn, all of the accused are treated the same. We don't make special provisions."

"Please your Honour, hear me out."

"Very well."

"As you know this case was assigned to me by the court. It wasn't a very popular one and, in many ways, I would have preferred not to have it either. Nonetheless, I do have the case, and I must do my utmost to represent my client. My request is this: Mr. Mangorian has a severe allergy to sunlight. If we allow even the small amount of sunlight from the windows to shine upon him, he could have a very adverse reaction and that reaction will be reported and severely prejudice my client's chances of a fair trial. The alternative would be to keep him bundled up under a blanket. The media would have a field day with that, too."

"What's your solution counsellor?"

"I would like you to permit him to wear a hoodie and dark sunglasses and to switch the case to Courtroom 9 instead of 7. Nine has only one small window. If Mr. Mangorian keeps his head down and the sunglasses and hoodie on, that should afford him sufficient protection."

"And allowing him to wear a hoodie and sunglasses won't prejudice the proceedings against your client?"

"Perhaps a little, but nowhere close to the kind of negative feedback that would result from Mr. Mangorian's skin flaking and blistering in front of everyone in the courtroom, or him being wrapped in a blanket, or having the three large windows in Courtroom 7 so obviously blacked out."

"Very well," the judge says, turning to his clerk. "Make it so."

There's a bit of confusion, and a mad scramble, as the large crowd of media and the public lined up in front of Courtoom 7 is told Mangorian is appearing in Courtroom 9.

In the packed courtroom at the appointed hour, I stand before the judge with Mangorian shackled and muzzled like Hannibal Lecter, but a Hannibal Lecter wearing a hoodie and large sunglasses. He keeps his head bowed low so direct sunlight from the one small window does not strike him.

"Dragul Mangorian you are charged with the following offences," says the Crown Prosecutor who then reads the long list of charges that Mangorian is accused of committing.

"We plead not guilty to all charges Your Honour," I say.

As expected Mangorian is remanded in custody without bail until his trial. The judge also orders that Mangorian is to be assigned a cell far from any windows, the right to keep the hoodie and dark glasses, and permission to shift his outdoor recreation time to after sundown.

I ready myself to leave the courtroom and face the inescapable media onslaught, now that I've suddenly become visible.

"Is your client a Vampire?" Babs Holloway, the beautiful blond with the microphone asks, a well practised look of sternness applied to her face to help her transition to breaking news reporter from my favourite weather girl.

"There are no such things as vampires. Vampires are fiction. Mr. Mangorian is a man of supreme dignity and intellect who, by his nature, must act in certain ways, which we will outline, to the court. He is not responsible for his nature, and he is not guilty of any of the charges against him."

Cameras and microphones joust for position. Above the chatter of automatic camera clicks and a half dozen 'live on the scene intros' by TV reporters at the edge of the scrum, I hear someone mutter that this is going to be a continuing problem because, 'That Hamblyn guy is so short'. Another says his shot is bad because of the glare off the head of the vampire lawyer.

"Why did Mangorian plead not guilty?" one reporter shouts.

"Because he isn't guilty," I say with as much conviction as I can muster.

"Can he change into a bat?" asks a Toronto Sunrise reporter.

"If that's the level of the intellect in this group, this scrum is over," I say, as I hop into the passenger door of a Toyota Corolla owned by Naylor, my law student assistant who whisks us away.

"Do you really think he's innocent," asks Naylor, cute, blonde and all of 5-foot, 2.

"Innocent? Hardly. But I believe he is not guilty of the crimes he's been charged with. I think we really stand a chance to do something no one expects with this one. Ready to spend the next few months buried in precedents?"

"That's why I'm here."

As expected, the newspapers and TV news networks have a field day with the story. As the old saw goes: When a dog bites a man, that's not news, but when a man bites a dog . . .

I've got a client accused of multiple counts of biting more than a dog.

CHAPTER EIGHT

A MEDIA SENSATION

One month and one year to the day later, as expected, Dragul's trial is the hottest media ticket in the world.

More than 5,000 media representatives from more than 1,400 accredited news outlets – newspapers, magazines, and TV stations plus countless blogs and other web-based media from around the globe set up camp in Toronto.

"In the past decade, only the Olympics drew more worldwide media attention," crowed Toronto's larger-than-life Mayor Bobby Mercury, live on multiple TV channels and displayed on the giant screen in Dundas Square, the Canadian version of New York's Times Square.

Mercury, Toronto's one-man, questionable-publicity machine, seizes on the trial as an opportunity to out-vampire and out-party New Orleans.

"This is the centre of the universe for all things vampire and Toronto's going to show everyone how to party," the barrel-chested politician says to the media.

The Metro Toronto Convention Centre is now Media Central with a direct feed to the CN Tower for TV crews to make immediate and direct satellite uploads to their home audiences in Japan, India, Brazil, the UK, Abu Dhabi, South Africa – you name it.

"We estimate another 250,000 visitors are in Toronto to watch this case unfold," Mercury says, his large frame jiggling with excitement. "The National Exhibition Grounds have been taken over for GothFest. The Toronto International Film Festival Lightbox and nine other theatres are running a Vampire Movie Festival. Restaurants across the city are featuring blood pudding, blood sausage and goodness knows what else on their menus. One of the boutique hotels has renamed itself Hotel Transylvania during the trial."

Before leaving the scene, Mayor Mercury dons a cape and false vampire teeth and poses with anyone and everyone who wants a photo.

The trial established another landmark, this one in the Canadian courts. The question over having cameras in courtrooms has been long debated in Canada. Until now, the answer has always been no for criminal cases. In the past, it was always the media that clamoured for access, especially in high-profile cases, but the sheer demand by the media for accreditation and a seat in the courtroom for the trial made the Supreme Court Justices take a new, hard look.

Virtually all sides joined the media in wanting the trial broadcast – from victim rights groups, to civil liberties organizations seeking to protect Mangorian's human rights interests, and an environmental group called SAR – Species At Risk – that demanded to have its position heard. Even fringe religious groups, Goth covens and Dragul groupies sent letters to the Supreme Court.

"In the end it all came down to Dragul and me," I would later write in No Crime, No Time, the book about Mangorian's trial. "The Justices wanted to know if we felt the tsunami of media attention would prejudice the case against Dragul. We submitted that televising the proceedings could not possibly prejudice the case compared to the prejudice that already exists, and would continue, because of lurid TV and sensational newspaper and tabloid reporting. We pointed to some of the tabloid stories quoting "eyewitnesses" swearing they saw Dragul turn into a bat. If Dragul is acquitted, he could never hope to walk the streets in safety because the public would not have heard directly why he was acquitted. It would be solely through the filter of reporters, who want to continue to promote fear to sell their products. We said that the only way for Dragul to get a fair hearing was to allow the public to witness the trial themselves and that outweighed any other considerations."

I confess that all of this was a very good thing for me. The publicity put my law practice on a completely different level – no fewer than seven major law firms wanted me to come aboard as an associate with one offering a partnership, win or lose, within six months, as long as I didn't blow the case in too embarrassing a way. It was, after all, a foregone conclusion that Dragul would be convicted and locked up for life, which is a pretty long time when you live as long as he does.

Best of all, while I'm still working on a barebones budget provided by Public Legal Aid, this case has put my life back in order thanks to a $250,000 advance from Dark Publishing for my story once the trial is over.

And that's only for starters. Barry Rosemore, Toronto's top-end men's clothier, calls me directly and says it would not do for the city to have the lawyer at the centre of a case the whole world is watching to be under-dressed. He sends his top tailor to take my measurements and one week later I have five incredible Italian designer suits, a pair of Alden Ravello Wing Tip Boots and a pair of Cole Haan oxfords, gratis. "I'll call you in a couple of months, if the trial's still running, and we'll fit you with a couple more suits. Just mention where they came from, if anyone asks," he says with a wink.

The same thing happens when I go to show off Rosemore's sleek black suit to my ex, Rosalie, our son Johnny (now John), his wife Jenn and their son Johnny Jr. by taking them to Toronto's poshest steakhouse, Le Sauvage. At the end of the most incredible meal I'd had in my life, restaurateur Harry Sauvage asks if everything was to our liking and then explains that it is his privilege to have us as guests and there is no charge. He and his chef then pose for a picture with me giving a thumbs up.

To top off the night, Luxury Limousines Inc. picks us all up and takes us back to our respective homes. 'Limo Larry,' the owner, is supplying me with free 24-hour, seven-day a week limo service for the duration of the trial "as long as the noose cameras keep catchin' us droppin' youse off and pickin' youse up at the courthouse."

"You got it." Things are definitely lookin' up for old Al.

When the limo drops off Johnny, Jenn and Johnny Jr., they smile at me in a way they never have before. Then Rosalie says she isn't ready to go home yet so we take a long spin around the city along the lakefront, up the Don Valley Parkway, through posh North Toronto neighbourhoods, and then head back downtown along Bayview Avenue while we sip champagne and laugh about the past.

I first met Rosalie after she was in a slip-and-fall accident. She was one of those hot, auburn-haired, Russian beauties who left a hard life and harder people for a better life in Canada and ended up working as a stripper at Gold's Gentlemen's Club on Richmond Street. One day, as she's stepping off the stage, some idiot grabs her ass. She reacts by trying to take a swipe at the guy and ends up falling off the stairs and ripping her knee and damaging her shoulder in the process.

Her boss fires her because she can't bump and grind with a bum knee and shoulder and so she calls me after seeing my ad pinned on a laundromat bulletin board.

In the weeks we spend putting her case together, Rosalie and I talk a lot and hit it off. Turns out the guy who grabbed at her was a big-shot corporate exec who wants the thing hushed up. I cut a deal for her that gets her $50k less my $15k cut.

Turns out she's looking for a new place and so am I, so we figure we'll put the $15k back with the rest of the bankroll and move in together. I was a lawyer and, at the time, I still had most of my hair; so for her, it's a win. For me, hell, she's an ex-stripper. Even with a bum leg, she's really, really hot and, in the beginning, what I was hoping for didn't require her to be standing.

Six weeks in, we got married in Vegas. and, a year later, she gave birth to Johnny. How I loved her. Turns out as well as being a knockout, she was an incredibly caring woman and a great mom. I love Johnny but somehow the role of dad, someone he could look up to, has never come easy for me. I really didn't know my dad. So, I sort of orbited around Johnny and only interacted with him when Rosalie told me what I should be doing.

Still, life was better than I imagined it could be. I had a son, a woman I loved and who loved me. With a bit of physiotherapy, Rosalie's leg and shoulder healed perfectly and she picked up a part-time waitressing job once Johnny turned two.

Surprisingly to other lawyers and the judges, I'm pretty effective in the courtroom, too. I put together strong arguments and win most of my cases that come to court. Trouble is, I'm not very good in the getting-clients department. I don't think a short, pudgy, balding guy emanates waves of confidence. My work is unexciting and gives me a mid-scale, blue-collar income but we had what we needed. For the first few years of marriage, we were happy together.

On June 16, 1994, everything started to unwind.

Beatriz Alvarez, a 72-year-old widow, was a fiery, fireplug of a woman. She emigrated from Portugal when she was 28 to marry Antonio, a distant cousin who was 20 years her senior. She and Antonio sold produce out of a storefront in Little Portugal on Dundas Street West near Ossington Avenue for 25 years until Antonio's death. Thereafter, she ran the business for another 10 years before retiring at age 63 to her semi-detached brick home in Little Portugal where she fervently worked at keeping her accent by exclusively watching Portuguese programming on Toronto's many ethnic TV networks.

Unlike U.S. cities, Toronto's core never lost its rich mix of neighbourhoods, wealthy and poor, traditional and new immigrants. Like many of those older residential neighbourhoods, Little Portugal was undergoing an urban resurgence.

Mrs. Alvarez was oblivious to all of this. Her home was hers free and clear and she expected that's where she'd live for the rest of her life.

That's why she was astounded when she received notice that the mortgage holder was foreclosing on her home.

Seven months earlier, someone impersonating her took out a mortgage for $240,000 and then disappeared. The impersonator paid the initial three payments and then stopped. With no further payments, the lender started the foreclosure action.

Mrs. Alvarez was filled with anxiety and fear for the future when smooth-talking V-G lawyer Tim Gracey approached her on behalf of Empire Estates. Empire Estates, it turns out, was planning a development in the area and, given the scam that ensnared Mrs. Alvarez and some of her neighbours, Empire was proposing a win-win opportunity.

"Mrs. Alavrez, you probably can sue and eventually win, but at what cost. You may be forced out of your home in weeks and how many years do you want this hanging over your head?" Tim Gracey said with all the sincerity he could muster.

"We will pay you the appraised value of your house – less the $240,000 mortgage. We will pursue this case for you, at our cost, and, when we win the case, we will release the rest of the money due to you. Best of all, you get to keep living in your home for another year free while the development gets in place. Otherwise, you will be foreclosed on and be out on the street while you're still fighting the battle," he explained.

"If you sign with us, we will go ahead with the development, pay off the mortgage holder while continuing to sue on your behalf until the money is released. Meanwhile, you will be free to lead your life as you wish.

"Oh, and by the way, because of a variety of legal and confidentiality issues it will help us deal with the bank if they are not embarrassed. You need to sign an agreement guaranteeing you will discuss these terms with no one," Gracey added.

Mrs. Alvarez agreed. It took 10 months, when all of her neighbours began to move out of their homes before she began to smell a big, smelly rat.

Was there collusion among the scammers and the lenders and the lawyers? It was abundantly clear, but proving it was another story.

Once Empire won the case, in a suspiciously easy slam-dunk, and paid all of the homeowners fair-market value for their homes, none of them wanted to spend a nickel to battle even though they knew they had been conned. Some of the victims tried to get the police to lay charges but V-G was too well connected. The amount of work required to nail fraudsters like Gracey was far beyond the ability of police, who have few resources to pursue white-collar criminals. As the gruff superintendent in charge of Criminal Investigations explained, "No one is really out any money."

But Mrs. Alvarez was not like everybody else. As the owner of a produce store for more than 35 years, she haggled every day with the wholesalers and then haggled with her customers. This was a woman used to going to the wall.

Eleven lawyers turned her down because, 'How much could the home-owners and, by association, their lawyer receive?' considering everyone got fair-market value for their homes.

Mrs. Alvarez tried a 12th lawyer, and then a 13th and a 14th and then she knocked on my door.

Normally, I'd have turned her down, too, but when I heard that Empire was a subsidiary of Gracey Developments and that Tim Gracey was the lawyer who signed the deals, I was hooked.

Given Mrs. Alvarez's poor financial state, I agreed to be paid a flat fee of $2,000 a month plus 30 per cent of any court award. We sued for $3 million for mental anguish, loss of enjoyment of the family home, and fraudulent misrepresentation.

Call me naïve, but I thought V-G and Empire would do anything to avoid a stain on their reputations, and we could get a quick out-of-court settlement. Failing that, I figured I could push this through the courts within a year. I did not understand that, in the world of dirty double-dealing, its denizens do not lie and cheat but once. It is a pattern they stick with to ensure a bitter end.

Backed by V-G's army of researchers and associates, Gracey was able to delay the suit for three years by invoking an unending series of motions contorting the rules of procedure with every possible ugly tactic to stall, stall, stall.

While V-G often got an earful from the judge, its team was very skillful at staying on the right side of being held in contempt of court for dilatory tactics.

The case became an obsession with me. I spent all of my time researching and going over the motions. At $2,000 a month, my personal trajectory was bankruptcy. The thing about being an ambulance chaser is, it's not so far from the truth that you actually have to chase ambulances. It is a case of opportunity – showing up when a likely case comes up. Too often, I shut myself in my office researching some esoteric legal point or missing the early morning discharges from emergency after spending an overnighter with my face in the books.

Three years, two months, and twelve days after launching the suit and another day of beating down yet another BS motion, Mrs. Alvarez's son Clemente called me.

"Hello, Mr. Hamblyn."

I was about to ask him how his mother was when I suddenly went cold. He never called me before and there was something ominous in his voice.

"My mother died this morning. It was a heart attack."

She looked fine a week ago and even extended an invitation to come for lunch in two weeks to celebrate her 76th birthday. I was speechless as Clemente explained details of the funeral arrangements. My internal organs began to twist in all directions. A question burned on my tongue and I wanted to spit it out. Did her son want to continue the case? Then my brain invoked sense and discipline.

How do you sue for misrepresentation when the person who was misrepresented is dead? How do you sue for loss of enjoyment when the person who lost the enjoyment is dead? How do you win over a jury emotionally when you don't have the person who was betrayed to look them in the eye?

It was over, really over.

I replaced the phone slowly and silently. I couldn't face Rosalie. I didn't tell her that night it was over but she'd guessed as much.

Throughout the case, Rosalie had pleaded with me to let it go or, at the very least, put less of myself into it to salvage the rest of my legal practice. One day, she looked at me with a seriousness that I'd never seen in her before.

"There is another way to settle things for Mrs. Alvarez, 'the Russian way,' she said. "You've heard me talk of my friend, Alexei. He is in Russia but he can get things done anywhere."

I knew Rosalie grew up in a harsh environment, worse than I did, but this was a hard side to her that I'd never seen before. My holier-than-thou moral code and my incredible stubbornness stood in the way. "I am a lawyer. I use the law to fight my battles. Otherwise, I'm no better than Gracey."

I was a horrible father and husband during this period. I had been obsessed with being on the side of righteousness and getting even with Gracey on my terms.

I still had to go through the motions of unwinding the case. The Graceys, true to their nature, wouldn't let us off the hook and said they wanted to keep fighting. Empire sued for costs and won against Mrs. Alvarez's estate, although the judge knocked back the amount to the minimum.

Times like these, maybe Rosalie and Shakespeare were right: "Let's kill all the lawyers."

Financially, I had dug a huge hole in our family finances. Despite never being much of a drinker, I went on a cheap gin binge, slept in the office and in the same clothes for three days. When I returned home, Rosalie acted like nothing was wrong and cheerily chattered non-stop about her and Johnny's day. I didn't speak for a week.

For the first month, I didn't wake up before noon. I'd try to work for an hour or two but got nothing accomplished. Worst of all there was no income other than from Rosalie's minimum wage salary and tips. We had already re-mortgaged the house during the case so there was nothing left in the tank.

We sold the house and moved to a one-bedroom flat. Six months later, we divorced, not so much because we fought but because there was no fire remaining in us. I had no passion, no spark, no fight left in me and began sleeping on the couch. Rosalie always presented a happy front but, when I stood outside the bedroom, I could hear her crying herself to sleep. She was a caring, passionate woman and I was a dark, empty space disguised as a man. Life with me was killing her. So I left.

Rosalie was only on the market for a few months when she started dating a really nice guy, a plumber named Fred. From what I could gather, he treated her well and after a while they moved into Fred's house. He raised Johnny like his own son. They lived happily for another seven years until Fred died of a heart attack. I called Rosalie to see if she was okay and, true to form, she was working through it like a champ. I asked if she'd be okay financially, not that I would be much help. She told me Fred named her as his beneficiary for the home and an insurance policy. It wasn't a king's ransom but it was enough to pay off the mortgage with a bit left over to send Johnny to university and help him through law school.

Luckily for Johnny, he inherited his mother's looks and my brain for academics. He went into law but he couldn't have been following in my footsteps. I was no role model. He had no problem getting an articling placement with a small but established law firm, not close to V-G's stature but not bad.

CHAPTER NINE

THE TRIAL BEGINS

The trial before Justice M. R. McGregor of the Ontario Supreme Court starts today – Wednesday, October 15, 2014 – with a packed courtroom, tens of thousands in the streets and millions watching on TV. What an absolute freak show.

The Crown Attorney has selected its most successful prosecutor, Alicia Patullo. Patullo is mid 30ish, slim with jet black hair in a pageboy cut that suits her well. If she could lose the scowl that's permanently etched on her face, she might pass for pretty. I don't think she cares one way or another. She possesses a special ability to connect with juries and a habit of leaving defence counsel in tatters. With her is a team of four assistant prosecutors.

I am assisted by Regina Naylor who has served in that capacity since my initial connection with Mangorian, first as a student volunteer and then as my articling student for the past seven months. Her marks at law school suffered greatly because of the hours she put in the case, but the profile she's gained will land her a job with any law firm once the trial is over. We have enlisted help from Jerry Hennesey who's come out of his four-months of retirement to help. Jerry is the one law professor that I respected completely. We have added a second articling student Theresa Davis to expand our research reach and, sometimes, I bounce ideas off Sally Wiseman, my old articling mentor who, at a fiery 61, really has her hands full taking on the rest of the world. And that's it by choice.

Given the case's profile today, all those flu suffering lawyers have miraculously recovered, and knock daily on my door offering to act as co-counsel or in any support position I desire, pro bono. That same stubborn vanity that cost me so much with Rosalie and Johnny is still there. I turn down all of the offers even though I know it's insane. Patullo and her team are a pack of Dobermans. I hope we have enough legal muscle to keep them on a leash.

One of the people always popping up in the media is Ben Saxon, the self-appointed vocal avenger. Thirty-one months ago, at age 18, his daughter Rachael disappeared smack in the middle of the time period the prosecution says Dragul was most active.

I feel genuine sorrow for the 50ish ex-dad whose wizened frame and emaciated face make him look 70.

As Jerry, Regina and I make our way into the courthouse, Saxon blocks our way.

"Excuse me, please," I say, not giving any indication I recognize him from the tabs.

"Do you realize what you are doing?" he says with an hysterical, wide-eyed grimace. "Do you realize who you are defending? He is the devil. He is the great deceiver. Nothing that he says is true. He lies. He will betray you. He will destroy you in the end."

Reporters, photographers and cameramen cluster around, like hogs gathering at the trough, hoping I'll rise to the bait as I hear the whirr of rapid-fire shutters and feel two dozen microphones pressing close to my face.

I fake left and then step 45-degrees to the right so I'm do-si-do with Saxon. The crush of the crowd does the rest, and I'm free.

For a year, thanks to Saxon and the media's proclivity for the sensational, the public has been force-fed the most lurid details and worse by the tabloids and the explosion of new TV 'news' channels that never let facts stand in the way of a good story. All of that, I hope, is about to change for the better. On this occasion, the comments are about to come from Patullo, someone with actual knowledge. I expect this will shut down the ravings, hysterical neighbours, fanatical religious groups, or the all-too-common, know-nothing TV talking head interviewing his own microphone.

Patullo pulls no punches in her opening statement.

"Ladies and gentlemen of the jury, you have a vital task before you. The Crown will prove without a doubt that the accused is the individual who, in separate incidents, attempted to murder six women and three men in savage attacks where he actually drank the blood of his victims."

By the time she's done outlining a tale of terror ripped right out of a horror novel, many members of the jury are visibly shaken, with a few scarcely able to conceal their complete revulsion.

The emotional battle is already lost. Will logic alone be able to sway the jury? I have two jurors, a physics professor and a structural engineer, who I hope are rational thinkers. A third juror is active in the civil liberties movement and there's a fourth, who seems overly happy at being on the jury. Call it intuition, but I don't think her pleasure comes from the zeal of public service. The double lines of dark eyeliner she's wearing today hint of this homemaker's Goth past or a continuing love of the macabre.

Now it's my turn. No time for self-doubt but, wow, am I ever out of my league. I've never done a criminal trial before and every word I utter will be broadcast across the planet. Get a grip there Al. Time to chuck in a few curveballs to see if I can throw Patullo off her game.

"Members of the jury, you have heard the prosecution's remarks. My client does not dispute drinking the blood of the individuals named as victims," I say in opening. No one in the jury blinks. The reporters' pens move in a frenzy. "However, we will prove to you that, for Mr. Mangorian, the drinking of human blood is not a matter of choice but a necessity of life. Secondly, we dispute that any assault has occurred. We will prove that the so-called victims voluntarily agreed to provide their blood to Mr. Mangorian and, therefore, my client has not attempted to murder anyone."

There's a hush when I finish that last statement that gives way to excited whispering. I have their attention.

My opening statement took about two minutes so far. The prosecutor spoke for 20.

"An opening statement should be short and clear," Dr. Jerome Hennesey – Jerry – told me all those years ago in law school. Despite working mostly as an academic, Jerry took on interesting pro bono cases in the summers. He had a 1.000 batting average.

I recall Jerry's words almost verbatim. "You have to give the jury a clear road map so they can see where you're going and understand it when you get there. Make your point, be sure they understand it, and then sit down before they forget what you've told them."

I look at the jury.

"I know you will render a fair and honest verdict based on the facts. Thank you," I say and take my seat. Jerry gives me a wink.

Patullo doesn't miss a beat. Her pale green eyes and athletic body remind me of a cat as she springs to her feet. Her job is to erase my words from the jurors' minds. With all the importance of a Lord Chamberlain announcing a king's arrival, she says: "For my first witness I call on Police Detective Brigitta Bloom."

Bloom, a thin, take-no-prisoners looking, 39-year-old with dirty blond hair, thin lips and sharp features, goes through the usual swearing to tell truth routine and then looks to Patullo.

"Detective Bloom, can you describe your role in the events in question on Sept. 14 last year?"

"I was on duty in the sexual assault task force at 52 Division. A call came in about a woman assaulted in her home at 8874 Decarie Drive. Given the circumstances, my team was dispatched," she says in perfect cop speak.

"We found the victim Shelley Holland in a very distressed state. She was confused. Her clothing was in disarray and some of it was torn. The victim had dried blood on her neck and signs of bleeding from two puncture wounds over her carotid artery."

"And what did Ms Holland say happened to her," Patullo says while looking carefully at the jurors to signal them to pay close attention.

"She said she didn't know. She said the doorbell rang. She opened the door and that was the last thing she remembers."

"No memories at all?" Patullo says, emphasizing her surprise.

"None. She was shocked when we started to take an inventory of the signs of assault on her person," the detective explained, and then slowly, as Patullo had coached her to do, Bloom laid out the police procedure.

"Our forensic team collected several pieces of evidence – the victim's clothing, fingerprints, some dirty bits of fabric, blood, samples of various unknown liquids and they ran a rape kit," she says looking straight at the jury to further embed the steps.

"Did this scene remind you of any other crimes that you have investigated?"

"Yes. Personally, I have been at three other crime scenes that bear a remarkable resemblance to this one over the past seven months. In each case, the victim had bled from similar wounds to the neck, had torn clothing, and small bits and fibres from very old and very dirty fabric."

"In your opinion, as a seasoned police officer, what conclusions do you draw from this?"

"It is my opinion that the same individual was the perpetrator in all four attacks."

"You believe it was the same individual who committed all four attacks," Patullo repeats for emphasis while pacing toward the jury.

"Yes, that's what I believe."

"That's all the questions the prosecution has for this witness," Patullo says with a triumphant strut to her seat that proclaimed the case had already been won.

"How many years have you been a police officer," I ask Detective Bloom during my cross-examination.

"I'm coming up to my 20th anniversary on the force."

"And, in that time, how many assaults have you investigated?"

"I couldn't guess. Lots. Several dozen at least."

"Did any of those assaults occur inside of a building as did this one?"

"I guess a dozen, maybe more," she says quizzically.

"Can you describe what you would typically find at such a scene."

"Well, an injured victim, torn clothing, blood."

"Would you not expect to see some damage to the furnishings – say a knocked over table or chair, a broken lamp, things tossed about the floor?"

"Uh, I suppose."

"Well let's not suppose. Think of the last assault case you handled that could in no way be linked to this one. Got it?"

After a momentary pause, she answers: "Yes."

I place my right hand against my temple, a Jerry trick to subliminally guide jurors to imagine along with me. "Now use your mind's eye and describe what you see."

"The victim is bleeding from a gash to the forehead and there are a number of welts and bruises all over her body. There is a broken dish and magazines on the floor. A section of the wall is caved in where it looks like someone was slammed against the wall. There's a crack in the TV screen and the whole screen has been turned sideways."

"And defensive wounds. Did this victim have defensive wounds?"

"Yes."

"Can you describe them?"

"Along her arms there were bruises and scrapes consistent with trying to block blows."

"Bruises and scrapes on her arms to block blows, is that correct," I repeat the phrase to reinforce the mental image for jurors.

"Yes it is."

"Would you say that scene is more common than not when there's an assault?"

"Yes," the detective answers, showing a bit of concern for where my questions are leading.

"Now describe the state of the house and furnishings at 8874 Decarie Drive when you investigated that evening."

"The victim's condition was the only sign that there had been a struggle."

"By victim's condition you mean the two puncture wounds on her neck, some tears in her clothing and her state of confusion?"

"Yes."

"And defensive wounds?"

"We examined the victim and found she had no wounds that could be characterized as occurring in defense of her person."

Cop speak again. I translate.

"So, unlike the vast majority of the assault investigations you've been involved in, the so-called victim appeared to make no effort to defend herself? Why would that be?" I say making sure I look directly at the physics prof and the structural engineer on the jury so they follow the logic.

"I cannot speculate."

"Could it be that the victim felt no need to defend herself because she was not assaulted?"

"That wasn't my conclusion."

"But it is a possible conclusion?"

"Uh . . . " Bloom looks to Patullo for direction.

"Is it a possible conclusion?" I ask again.

"I suppose but in my experience it is highly unlikely," Bloom says, her cheeks now giving illustration to her name.

"In all of these other cases that you believe are linked, were the circumstances similar to what you found at 8874 Decarie Drive – neck wounds, some torn clothing but otherwise no damage to the furnishings or walls and no defensive wounds to the victim?" I ask, in a slow meter to ensure the jury, especially the dark eyeliner lady follows, my point.

"That is correct."

"And can you describe the neck wounds. I believe they punctured the external carotid artery."

"Yes they did."

"Now, you'll have to explain this to me. My understanding is that carotid artery is a very large artery that takes oxygenated blood to the brain."

"That's not my area of expertise but I think that's correct."

"Now as a blood donor, I know that when I give blood, a large needle goes into a vein in my arm. When the needle is withdrawn, I have to put pressure on a pad for 10 minutes to stop the bleeding. Sometimes 10 minutes isn't enough and the blood starts spurting from my arm. Is it the same for an artery?"

"You'll have to ask a doc for sure but in my experience, yes."

"Now suppose someone created those neck wounds you testified about. I presume they were larger than a needle?"

"Yes sir."

"My question is, Why didn't Ms. Holland bleed to death?"

"The wound had scabbed over. It had healed enough to clot so there was no more bleeding."

"Would a puncture the size of Mr. Mangorian's fangs scab over naturally?" I say, once again glancing intensely at the eyeliner lady.

"I'm not a doctor. I'm not in a position to say."

"Fair enough but surely you've been on the scene many times when someone is bleeding badly."

"Yessir."

"Then tell me. Have you ever seen a major artery or vein that was punctured that simply stopped the blood flow on its own?"

"No, not without help."

"So what kind of help are we talking about? Did the perpetrator actually take time after wounding Ms Holland to place a compress on the wound and keep pressure on it?"

"I shouldn't think so. He wouldn't have had the time."

"So how did the blood stop?"

"It appears some sort of chemical was used to help clot the wounds."

"Now considering your last statement, can you see any grounds whatsoever for a charge of attempted murder when the perpetrator actually did something to stop the bleeding."

"I can't answer that."

"Let me rephrase the question. If you saw someone taking measures to prevent someone from dying, is it logical to charge that person with attempted murder of that same person?"

"I suppose not."

"One last question. The Crown raised the fact that you ran a rape kit. Was the victim raped?"

"No, there was no sign the victim had been raped."

"Thank you. Those are all the questions I have for this witness."

I look at Jerry and he gives me a big smile. No attempted murder, no rape – boom, boom, just as Jerry planned.

Patullo examines and I cross-examine two of the other cops involved in investigating incidents and then the court adjourns for the day.

As much as I was expecting a huge, crazy mob and a sea of media, I could scarcely believe the scene outside the courthouse. Police closed the streets surrounding the building to traffic and transformed it into fenced areas for the thousands of the curious and a huge parking lot for dozens and dozens of media trucks flying the colours of every network from ABC to India's Zee TV.

Mayor Bobby Mercury has again inserted himself in a crowd-control/media-control/promotions capacity literally to prevent all hell from breaking loose while, simultaneously, launching a tourism boom and paving the way for his personal re-election. Who says politicians can't multi-task?

Reporters, who had been in the courtroom, and those in a nearby auditorium watching the proceedings via television, are not allowed to create a scrum wherever they want on the pretext an uncontrolled crowd poses a safety risk. The reality is Mayor Mercury wants a publicity platform in front of the largest audience possible.

Mercury's team borrows from the playbook of rock concert promoters and erects a huge stage in front of the courthouse. The script calls for Patullo and me to address our comments to the world media from this pop-concert-style platform complete with rock band speakers positioned front, back, left, and right. And if that isn't enough, a jumbotron (do they still call them that?) on each side of the platform will give magnified visual life to our every pronouncement. The only thing missing is Mick Jagger and his geriatric buds.

Mercury takes to the stage and, with his own permission, acts as emcee. Signaling for silence, Mercury then shouts into the mike: "I know all of you have questions, but we have to have some order here. Assistant Crown Attorney Patullo and Defence attorney Hamblyn are seated behind me on the stage to answer your questions. As we explained in our news release, we will not be taking verbal questions from reporters or the public. You must tweet questions to me at: @askmercury. A panel of our best known journalists to my right will select the best questions and give them to me to pose to our guests.

"First question, and this is an obvious one for Mr. Hamblyn, is your client a real vampire?"

The crowd goes wild, hooting, whistling and participating in conflicting chants that drown each other out. When the din dies a little, I respond: "There's no such thing as a vampire – at least not the kind in books and movies. The only thing he has in common with the fictional vampire is his need for human blood for sustenance."

Again the crowd breaks into conflicting roars and screams.

"Question #2 is also for Mr. Hamblyn. How can you assert that your client is not guilty of assaulting nine people when he has pretty well admitted to taking their blood?" Mercury says.

"We will provide ample evidence to demonstrate that there was consent requested and given," I say as the crowd, now settles in to a largely unanimous chant of "Blood! Blood! Blood!"

"Supplemental to that last question," says Mercury. "How can you state this when all of the victims have stated their blood was taken forcibly and without their consent?"

"You'll have to wait and see how that comes out," I say.

Despite Ontario's strict drinking laws, it's clear most of the crowd is hammered and doesn't give a whit about the questions or answers. A vampire on trial is the trial of the millennium and to the majority of the city's residents, that's reason enough to have a beer or 12.

"This next question is for Ms Patullo," Mercury shouts importantly, as if anybody is actually listening. "If the attacks on the victims in this case was as savage as you have stated, why isn't there any signs of a struggle at any of the crime scenes?"

Patullo's truly a good sport. Even though her boss and her boss's boss, a close friend of Mercury, has insisted on this freaky sideshow, she delivers her comments with dignity.

"Mr. Mangorian is physically very powerful. He stands 6-feet, 6 and has super human strength and speed. When you're facing someone with that much of a physical advantage, how much of a struggle could there be? How much of a struggle and furniture breaking would happen in a fight between an adult and a two-year-old?"

With that, Mercury concludes the questions by saying, "Folks, we have to leave some surprises for tomorrow. Please help me thank Mr. Hamblyn and Ms Patullo for their presence. They have a lot of preparatory work to do before court resumes."

With that Mercury starts to clap and the crowd responds with two-handed thunder as a thousand paper bags tilt their liquid contents into happy partyers.

"But don't go just yet," Mercury says. "We have Tony James, star of the hit cable TV show Zombies On Steroids who will be your emcee for an evening of music and entertainment. This will show the world Toronto knows how to party."

The mayor is roundly booed but keeps the usual silly grin on his face as he wades into the crowd and samples the contents of a paper bag handed to him.

"Sheesch," I say, ducking between media trucks – Do you believe it? – from Abu Dhabi TV and Al Jazeera. I guess the good side of this is that even terrorism and clashes in the Middle East are taking a day off to watch the "vampire trial."

That night, I pick out the grey striped suit for day two of the trial. During court, it will be covered by my legal robes. It will look good for the TV interviews afterward, I think to myself. "Oh God," I say aloud. "I'm getting sucked into this, too."

CHAPTER TEN

TRIAL, DAY 2

Thursday, October 16, 2014

Back in court, the Crown starts the day by calling on the Forensic investigator who gathered evidence at the crime scene.

"Dwijendra Gupta how long have you been an investigator with the Toronto Police Forensic Investigation Service ?"

"I've been a police officer for 10 years and, because I hold university degrees in chemistry and forensics, I've been assigned to the Forensic Investigation Service for the past nine years."

It's apparent the short, bespectacled, slightly chubby investigator in his pin perfect Savile Row blue suit is all about the facts, having misplaced his personality on the way to court.

"Did you attend a crime scene at 8874 Decarie Drive about 13 months ago and gather evidence at that time? "

"Yes I did," replies the investigator in a precise Oxfordian English accent.

"Constable Gupta, was there anything unusual, anything dramatically different about the evidence that you gathered at the scene?"

"Yes, there were some things that were highly unusual. The first was some of the DNA samples we collected were different than anything we had ever seen before. The second thing that we found that perplexed us were several hand and finger impressions on the scene that, again, were like nothing that we had previously encountered," he says.

"Constable Gupta, can you enlighten us about how these samples were different than what you would normally expect to find? Please start with the DNA."

"It's common knowledge these days that DNA, among other things, defines the boundaries among species. You may have heard discussions that Homo Sapiens and chimpanzees are closely related. Studies of both the human and chimpanzee genome prove this. They show that 96 per cent of the genetic blueprint is common in both species and give further evidence to the thinking that we share a common ancestor."

Constable Gupta delivers all of this in a monotone while seated with perfect posture, and fingers interlaced before him, the absolute gold standard for teacher's pet.

"When we tested all of the samples that potentially contained DNA, we divided the results into three groups: DNA from Ms Holland; DNA from Ms Holland's friends and family; and DNA from persons unknown. What we didn't expect was a fourth category. DNA from a subject who was not quite human."

"Not human? Can you explain?" asks Patullo.

What I'd like explained is how Gupta could deliver that last line still in a monotone.

"As I mentioned earlier, chimpanzees share 96 per cent of their genetic code with humans and they are the closest species to humans that exist. Biochemically, any one human, regardless of race or where he comes from, is 99.9 per cent similar to any other human on the face of the Earth. The DNA that created our fourth category was 99.0 per cent similar to human beings."

"In other words, the DNA came from someone who was not quite a human being as we know it," says Patullo, now using her engagement skills on the jury.

"That is what we found. I had my work checked and rechecked by my colleagues. We sent some material for outside opinions from the two foremost forensic laboratories in North America, the RCMP's Forensic Science and Identification Services Laboratory and the Virginia State Crime Laboratory. Scientists at both facilities confirmed our findings."

"Now, Constable Gupta did you have occasion to take a DNA sample from the accused?"

"Yes I did."

"And what did you do with that sample?"

"We sequenced it and discovered that the sample from the accused was not quite human," he says, wide-eyed and finally releasing a tiny hint of a smile to show that he is human.

"By not quite human, do you mean that biochemically it was 99.0 per cent similar to humans?"

"That is correct and, moreover, it was a 100 per cent match with the Category 4 samples we recovered from the crime scene."

"In your expert opinion, would you agree that this DNA evidence clearly places the accused at the scene of the crime?" Patullo asks, emphasizing every word to alert the jurors to pay close attention.

"In my expert opinion, yes, the accused must have been at the crime scene."

"Now for the fingerprint evidence. You mentioned that this also presented some unusual findings."

"Yes. We started by lifting as many fingerprints as we could from the crime scene. Then we started the process of elimination. First those of the victim were set aside. Any prints of her mother, her brother and two closest friends were filed away. Eventually we came down to one set of fingerprints that we couldn't identify. Frankly they mystified us," he says, emphasizing the enormity of his surprise by removing his glasses and cleaning the lenses.

"Why is that?"

"I call them prints but in fact they were finger impressions and not prints as we know them, just a flat regular impression of the shape of fingers but with no ridges."

"I take it this is unusual," Patullo notes for the jury's sake.

"Yes. In the field of dermatoglyphics – that's the study of fingerprints – there have only been four families worldwide that have displayed this condition known as adermatoglyphia. No member of any of these families currently resides in or has visited North America in the past two years."

"Could the fingerprints have been surgically removed?"

"It's possible but there would be clear signs of surgical tampering, such as the profile of the finger being flatter than normal."

"Was it possible the individual was wearing gloves."

"No possibility, whatsoever. Fingerprints are caused by the secretion of sweat. These sweat beads provide the fluid that define the ridges of the fingers. We found the sweat beads but they were applied in blobs, no visible ridges. The sweat patterns also lead us to believe that the owner of the finger patterns did not have adermatoglyphia."

"And why is that?"

"People who have adermatoglyphia also have much fewer sweat glands on their fingers than the regular population. In this instance, the unknown subject had the normal amount of sweat one would expect."

"Well then, can you explain this phenomenon?"

"Not in a human."

"Please explain that comment," the prosecutor says to ensure jurors are prepared to follow the logical trail.

"The ridges that form fingerprints are an evolved feature that helped humans develop fine motor skills to manipulate tools. The ridges provide an extra level of grip just as the treads on a car tire help grip the road better."

"Are fingerprints unique to man?"

"Gorillas have fingerprints, too, but strangely, not chimpanzees."

"So are you saying a chimpanzee left these prints?"

"No, we found no indication a chimpanzee or anything other than a person left these impressions. But that person has no prints."

"You said no person with adermatoglyphia is in North America."

"We discovered an individual who does not have adermatoglyphia and has no fingerprints."

"Do you see that person in the courtroom?"

"Yes I do. It is the accused," Constable Gupta says, pointing to Mangorian.

"And you fingerprinted Mr. Mangorian yourself?"

"Yes."

"The results?"

"He had no prints and he did not exhibit signs of adermatoglyphia," Gupta says as proudly as if he had discovered cold fusion.

"To your knowledge have there been other criminal cases where this same phenomenon – no prints and no adermatoglyphia – has been found?"

"Yes. We found six more crime scenes with similar circumstances – an assault, the taking of blood – where unsmudged finger outlines were recovered that displayed none of the characteristic ridge patterns we call fingerprints."

"What, in your expert opinion, would you say the odds are that the same person, the one without fingerprints but with normal sweat patterns, attended each scene?"

"The science of dermatoglyphics has determined that fingerprints are unique to each person, even more unique than DNA. For instance, identical twins have identical DNA but they have different fingerprints. It has been calculated that there's less than a one out of 64 billion chance of any two people having the same fingerprints."

"And with the population of the Earth being just over seven billion . . ." the prosecutor's voice purposely trails off.

"Yes, the odds are almost impossible that two people have the same fingerprints."

"Now in the case of no fingerprints do the odds remain the same?"

"In my opinion, with the exception of adermatoglyphia sufferers that's even rarer."

"Thank you. I have finished my direct examination."

"Constable Gupta," I say as I approach the witness. "You testified that chimpanzees have no fingerprints, yet gorillas and humans do. Why is this?"

"I'm not an expert in zoology so I don't know."

"Would it be fair to say that evolution treated these three branches of the primate family differently, providing two of them with fingerprints and one with none."

"Yes. That would be my expectation."

"Is it possible that the accused, Mr. Mangorian is actually not a human being – a Homo Sapiens – as we know it and, therefore, is a member of a species that does not have fingerprints?" I ask.

"Objection. Constable Gupta has no expertise as a geneticist."

"Objection sustained. Constable Gupta you do not have to answer the question."

"Okay, let me rephrase that," I say. "If Mr. Mangorian is not a Homo Sapiens and in fact is of a different species, might that species, like chimpanzees have evolved without fingerprints?"

"It's logical if you take all those 'ifs' into consideration," Constable Gupta says.

"Following that logic, if Mr. Mangorian is a member of a species other than Homo Sapiens and members of that species like chimpanzees do not have fingerprints then blank fingerprints are worthless in terms of identifying a suspect."

"In that hypothetical case, it would be true."

"Not so hypothetical. He has no prints."

"True."

"One more thing Constable Gupta. Did you have occasion to determine the amount of blood Ms Holland lost?"

"Yes, the medical report states that Ms Holland received 1.7 units of blood through transfusion. She had low blood pressure when she was brought into the hospital."

"Is 1.7 units a lot? I mean, would someone die because he or she lost 1.7 units?"

"A unit is roughly a pint and, no, a person would not die from the loss of 1.7 units of blood, barring any other complications. She would be weakened, and may get dizzy, but likely not suffer any long-term health issues because of the loss of 1.7 units of blood. When you donate blood, you typically give one unit."

"Just for perspective's sake, how much blood would you have to lose to die?"

Gupta goes into a long, overly scientific explanation of blood and its role in the body. Finally, he says that an average person weighing 180 pounds has about 10 litres of blood. If an individual lost 40 per cent of his blood supply, roughly four litres, his life would be in peril.

"And for the sake of clarification for the court can you confirm that there are about two units or pints of blood to a litre?"

"Roughly so, yes."

"So if my math is correct, taking two pints of blood would be equal to one litre or about 10 per cent of an average person's blood supply."

"Yes."

"Enough to weaken them but not do grave or lasting damage."

"Yes."

"Would you say that if someone consistently took two pints of blood from different people that this would be tantamount to a pre-mediated attempt to murder?" I say, trying to corral the point.

"No, it seems to me such an act would indicate quite the opposite," says Gupta who, grasping my logic, now seems eager to run with it. "The suspect was taking the blood but by restricting the amount to less than two pints. There seems to have been a conscious decision to avoid causing lasting harm or death."

Patullo directs a steely look at Gupta who averts his eyes after realizing what he's done. I got the point I needed on the record so it's time to shut down this witness.

"Thank you Mr. Gupta. I've finished my cross examination."

"The witness is excused. Court is adjourned and will resume at 10 a.m. tomorrow," Justice McGregor says.

§§§

Immediately after court adjourns, Mangorian and I conference for a brief recap of the first two days of the trial.

"You are doing very, very well Al. I have no doubt we will win the case."

"We have a very long way to go but so far so good. Do you have any additional thoughts for tomorrow?"

"The police evidence will be the police evidence. There's nothing to dispute. I was in her home and they will prove it. It is the testimony of the 'victims' that will prove my innocence. They will not lie."

Mangorian is truly an amazing client. He agrees with almost every one of our strategies, never refuses to provide clear, honest answers and even provides insight on how to interpret his actions in a way that will evoke empathy. Considering the spotlight on him, he is upbeat and perfectly confident in the outcome. He's nothing like the fearful character that I had first imagined.

Still, from time to time Mangorian manages to remind us that he is something other than human. In the lead up to the trial when Patullo interviewed him in the presence of Regina and me, she mocked his story about the horrors that Sapiens inflicted on the Sanguinus.

In that instant, Mangorian began a transformation that scared the three of us to our very core. His fingernails and canine teeth seemed to grow longer, sharper, more deadly, but my heart really jumped when I looked into his eyes, twin yellow flames that ignited so fiercely, I swear I could feel the heat. Then it was over, as fast as its onset.

During another interview, Mangorian also expressed displeasure with police tactics.

"We'll be cross-examining the police who captured you."

"Yes the police," says Mangorian, suddenly sounding fearsome and his eyes seemingly radiating an amber heat. "That's a score I'll have to settle. Eight of them shot me with tasers and then knocked me senseless with their clubs. It is the old feud between Sapiens and Sanguinus. It is in our blood. Kill or be killed. Our species are mortal enemies. We were meant to die at the hand of the other."

Under normal circumstances, I might ask my client if he is kidding. I know better with Mangorian.

The same officers are on the stand tomorrow. I'm hoping the unalloyed hatred I saw that day doesn't make a return visit.

CHAPTER ELEVEN

TRIAL, DAY 3

Friday, October 17, 2014

On day three, the prosecution's first witness is the leader of the canine unit that led police to Mangorian.

"Sergeant Kennedy, can you describe the circumstances on the night of September 14, 2013 when you attended the scene of an assault and subsequently came upon the storm sewer channels that empty into the Don River?" Patullo says.

"A neighbour called 911 and reported seeing a suspicious character leaving 8874 Decarie Drive. When she looked in, the door was ajar and she found the victim unconscious with her blouse torn open. I got the call about 9:15 p.m. and as the night shift supervisor for the canine unit, I took our best dog Hero to the scene of the assault and he followed the vampire's scent from there."

"Objection your Honour. The term vampire is unduly prejudicial to the accused," I say.

"Objection sustained. The witness will refrain from using the word vampire."

"As I was saying, Hero followed the scent of our suspect from the home of our victim into a small gully that led to the Don River. Officers on the scene perceived a large storm sewer outlet where the access grate had been removed."

"Before you give the details of the search. Can you describe the scene outside the sewer," says Patullo.

"It was pretty muddy. We had a tough time walking down the slippery ravine. It had rained pretty hard the day before and the river was high. If you know the area, the ravine drops pretty sharply, maybe a drop of 200 feet from top to bottom."

"Now tell us what happened after you found the sewer grate was not secured," Patullo says, to quicken the pace.

"We contacted the city's works department and in minutes a supervisor was dispatched to the scene. He brought along a laptop with maps of the sewer system. We put out a bulletin on all media, Facebook, Twitter, you name it, asking Neighbourhood Watch and the public in general to park cars on storm sewer grates and manhole covers in their neighbourhoods. Our officers were dispatched to send teams into the sewers to block off the major access points in a five-mile radius and then we started into the sewer with Hero leading the way."

"That's pretty amazing work and done so quickly," says the assistant Crown attorney.

"That was Det. Ferino's doing. The Vam . . . I mean, the suspect eluded us in the past and so, this time, we were ready. Ferino was working with Neighbourhood Watch so members already knew to park their cars on sewer grates. We just had to tell them where."

"And then you discovered the accused?" says Patullo.

"Yes m'am. There were actually six teams that went into the tunnels, two of them with canine support. Most of the rest were Tactical guys. When the tunnels branched, even though our dogs pointed us in one direction, we would leave two officers to secure that branch just in case.

"After moving through about four miles of tunnels, Hero and the other dog Sebastien became extremely excited. This usually means the scent is very strong, very fresh. We turned a corner and there he was glaring at us. It was a good thing we couldn't see him in the dim light as well as I can see him now. What we could see was scary enough. The bunch of us on the scene stopped dead in our tracks. He was so tall and thin, like a walking skeleton but one with these yellow eyes that glowed in the dark and breath worse than the sewer gas."

"And at that point you arrested him?" Patullo says cheerily, a statement she knows is false.

"No. No. He was, is a very scary, intimidating character. We kept our distance. I don't mind telling you that I've been in a lot of dangerous situations but this really scared the crap out of me. I was really glad we had our Tactical guys with us. They're the best, all tough and great with weapons. But even some of them were nervous, especially when he hissed at us and bared these incredibly long claws and fangs," he says.

'That's when Det. Ferino ordered the canine units to back off and the Tactical Squad to move in."

"In your opinion, do you feel that Hero tracked down the same person who had fled from the crime scene?" Patullo asks.

"Hero is our best dog. If he led us to the accused, at the very least, the accused was on the scene."

"Thank you Sergeant. Those are all my questions."

I approach the witness box carefully for my cross-examination. He's so wired, the last thing I want to do is make him jump.

"Sergeant Kennedy, I would like to go over something you just said so there's no mistake. You did not say that Mr. Mangorian was the perpetrator of the events that night," I say.

"Yessir, I didn't say that."

"So to clarify, Hero led you to Mr. Mangorian because Mr. Mangorian, in your opinion, had been in that house. However, in no way are you alleging that Mr. Mangorian committed any crime."

"Yessir. It was just our job – mine and Hero's – to follow the scent."

"Now how did it come about that Hero picked up the particular scent that led you to Mr. Mangorian."

"The victim was wearing a shawl when she was attacked and we took it as a sample for Hero to sniff. He picked up the scent immediately."

"Can you be certain that if Mr. Mangorian's scent was on the shawl that the scent came from Mr. Mangorian's presence that evening or is it possible that Mr. Mangorian had left his scent on another occasion?"

"It's possible."

"In fact, isn't it true that a good dog like Hero can detect scents for a year or more?"

"I'm not sure about a year, but I believe that Hero can pick up scents that are several months old."

"The prosecution also brought up the point about it raining the day before. Please tell me if rainfall would impair Hero's ability to follow a trail."

"No, it would not impair following a trail."

"Is it not true that, in fact, a rainfall or moistness can increase Hero's ability to track?"

"I believe it would, and that has been my experience."

"So to make a long story short, if my client had gone to Ms Holland's house two days prior to the alleged attack, or even two months before the attack, with or without rainfall, there's a good chance Hero would still follow the scent."

“That’s correct.”

“Now of all possible scents for Hero to follow, why do you suppose he followed the accused’s scent? We have heard that at least 10 other people had been in the house in the several weeks leading up to the incident. Why did Hero follow Mangorian’s scent?”

“Mangorian’s scent was on the shawl.”

“How did you know that?”

“I could smell it myself. I figured if I can smell it, it will be a piece of cake for Hero.”

“Ah, so you directed Hero to follow that particular scent.”

“Not exactly. He followed the scent that was on the shawl.”

“But it was you who gave him the shawl to sniff.”

“That’s true.”

“Did you give Hero any other materials to get scents from?”

“Look, we arrived at a fresh crime scene. A neighbour saw something and reported it. The victim was wearing the shawl. The shawl was pulled away from her neck. It’s logical that who ever bit her on the neck touched the shawl. We knew we could catch the perp but we had to act fast. I did what I did, and we caught the accused,” he says in an irritated voice.

At that, I’m finished with the witness. Next up is Det. Buddy Ferino.

“Detective Ferino, you were the arresting officer of the accused on the night of September 14, 2013?” says Patullo.

“Yes I was.”

“And as the lead investigator for what’s been publicly called the Toronto Stalker assaults, do you feel that you apprehended the right suspect, for not just the call that evening, but for the additional eight assaults that were committed previously?” Patullo says.

“Yes m’am I do.”

“What brought you to the conclusion that all nine cases were linked?”

“Let’s put it this way. Never before have I had crime victims who had their blood sucked out of their necks.”

“I would like you to describe the events on the night of September 14, 2013 that led to the arrest of the accused.”

“I got the call at 9:25 p.m. First responders reported they believed it was the work of the Toronto Stalker so, as the lead investigator in the case, I got the call and showed up at 9:45 p.m. One look told me that it was the Stalker all right. That's when I put my plan into action.

"By the time I got to the crime scene, the dog units had just tracked the suspect to the storm sewers that empty into the Don River. We expected this location because we searched the area before after two previous attacks but came up empty both times.

"This time I had a plan that I worked out with Neighbourhood Watch to get their members into action. I sent a text to NW's head, Ben Saxon, that described which area we needed to control. Within minutes, we had the ability to get more than 3,000 block captains in the area around the Don River Valley to mobilize their neighbours to park cars on manhole covers and storm sewer grates.

"Once we knew the suspect had nowhere to go, we moved in from five different directions, tightening the noose around our suspect.

"At 11:31 p.m., our canine unit led me and a group of eight officers from our tactical team to a large chamber within the sewer system that acts as a reservoir to slow the flow of water and prevent flooding. That's where we discovered the suspect Dragul Mangorian. I ordered the suspect to surrender, but he remained belligerent, snarling, and spitting some kind of foul saliva."

Ferino is now fully into the story, telling it not like a cop might but more like the scene from the kind of crime novel he clearly loves.

"Once I knew we had him surrounded, I ordered the canine units to back off and had our ETF, that's the Emergency Task Force squad, move in. The suspect didn't like that. He came right at us, so fast I was frozen in place. Two members of the ETF squad fired their tasers and hit him square in the chest. It didn't slow him much but enough so the other six tactical officers could fire their tasers as well."

Ferino is now talking so fast he's clearly reliving the experience and probably verbatim to how he told the story to other cops and their families. The thought crosses my mind that he might even be planning to write a book.

"Once he fell to the ground," Ferino continues, "we tried to cuff him but even on his back he grabbed two of our guys by the legs, and tossed them against the sewer wall like they were toys."

Definitely a novel in the making, I muse.

This colourful narrative is starting to have a negative effect on my case. I see Patullo happily leaning back, watching the horrified reaction of the jurors.

"Then everybody got into the act and started firing and reloading their tasers and used their clubs on him. After a few minutes, he seemed to be unconscious. We carefully used every cuff we had to restrain him hand and foot and called for reinforcements to bring the really, heavy-duty shackles before trying to get him out of the sewer."

Ferino scarcely takes time during his description of the scene to catch his breath.

"Not one of us was interested in moving him when he was wearing just plastic handcuffs, no matter how many we used," he says, mopping a sleeve across his sweating brow.

Patullo steps back in to keep the energy and tensions high.

"So you had the suspect in custody and that was it."

"No way. Even with him being unconscious – maybe – and even with 50 of us at the precinct, none of us felt safe. Someone found a couple of those old style hardened steel manacles, like the ones he's wearing today and, just to be sure, we doubled up by putting two sets on his arms and two sets on his legs. We hooked another chain onto a collar around his neck. Then we put a muzzle on him to prevent anyone from being bitten."

Det. Ferino looks as if he's close to having a stroke and that's precisely the image Patullo wants the jury to remember as she quits her examination of the witness.

"Det. Ferino, you mentioned that the accused injured two of the arresting officers when he resisted arrest," I say in my cross-examination.

"Yes, that is correct."

"And can you describe how these officers were injured?"

"We tasered him until he fell to the ground and when we went to cuff him, he grabbed two of our Tactical guys by their ankles and smashed them against a wall."

"When he was down, did you tell him he was under arrest?"

"No, that didn't happen until after we had the cuffs on him."

"So he's on his back on the ground and your men move in to cuff him."

"That is correct."

"And at no time, while the officers were attempting to cuff him, was there another taser shot or did anyone hit him with a club."

"No sir."

"According to a written report by one of the officers on the scene, tasers were used throughout the entire time until Mr. Mangorian was securely handcuffed."

"They were used at the beginning and again when he resisted arrest."

"Could it be that Mr. Mangorian wasn't resisting arrest but merely trying to protect himself from further tasers and club hits?"

"I didn't see it that way."

"Given what you said about the accused's ability to protect himself with long claw-like fingernails and long sharp teeth, wouldn't it have made sense to use these to fight back at the officers?"

"I really don't know."

"But no officers were cut, or even scratched, by his nails or teeth, were they? In fact, neither of the officers, and I quote you, who were 'tossed against the sewer wall like they were toys' suffered serious injuries and both were back on the job within a few days."

"That is correct."

"I put it to you, that, if the accused were truly trying to resist arrest, wouldn't he use all the weapons he had available?"

"I couldn't say."

With that I wind up my cross-examination of Det. Ferino and because it's 4 p.m., I request an adjournment until Monday, which the judge grants.

CHAPTER TWELVE

ALONG COMES SALLY

The nine alleged victims are scheduled to testify next week so I've set aside time with Mangorian to go over our strategy again.

"You know if the victims all call you a devil that things will go very badly. It's one hell of a risk to press them," I say.

"I understand the risk but you must trust me and trust yourself. Trust what you feel," says Mangorian. "You remember the level of trust you gained in me when I touched your mind? The same is true of these so-called victims. If you press them, some may remember, if not the actual thoughts and memories, at least the emotions."

With the victims testifying next week, I'm in for a busy weekend poring over their statements and evidence gathered by police. There is one duty, however, that pulls me away from the research. The Parkdale Community Legal Clinic is holding a fundraiser to keep its operations afloat and I'm the guest speaker.

My new-found celebrity has helped fill the ancient Masaryk Hall to its maximum capacity, 25 tables of 10 and instead of the usual $50 tickets, the price tag this time around is $200 a seat.

"Al, I want to thank you so much," says Sally, her raging red hair now grey but no tamer than a quarter century ago. "This will really make a difference." We hug and I introduce her to my date Rosalie, which prompts that familiar squeal from Salvo Sally.

"You guys are back together? Incredible."

"Incredible? Yes, she is," I say winking at Rosalie, who in a rare moment blushes.

Then I reach into my breast pocket and pull out a thick envelope chock full of cheques I solicited from top law firms, judges, the publishers of all the local media, and even a certain assistant Crown attorney.

"There's enough to bring on another associate so you can stop sleeping at the office," I say. Sally gives me a thumbs up in return.

After chowing down on our chicken dinners, I launch into my speech as the tables are being cleared. Everyone expects that I'm going to talk about the trial or my illustrious client but, instead, I talk about the toughest lawyer I've ever known – Salvo Sally.

"That's right, I called her Salvo Sally, but never to her face until now," I say, as audience members familiar with Sally's doggedness laugh and applaud.

"And I called you 'dumbass' to your face," Sally responds.

I shrug and bow in surrender.

I cut off my speech after the sixth David vs Goliath tale where Sally – win, lose or draw – always left with her head held high while her opponents slithered away after exploiting their arsenal of loopholes aimed at denying widows, orphans, the sick and the disabled their cash entitlements.

"Thank you, thank you, thank you," Sally says at the evening's close, planting a wet one right on my kisser. "Hiring you was the smartest thing I ever did."

"And firing me was the second smartest thing you ever did."

"I didn't fire you. You quit."

"I consider it being fired when you offer me a job with no pay."

When Rosalie and I jump into the limo, she squeezes in tight and says, "You know Fred was a very good man. Very good to me and to Johnny. But I never married him, never wanted to give up your name, even after the divorce. I have never loved anyone except you. What you did tonight makes me understand why."

CHAPTER THIRTEEN

TRIAL, DAY 4

Monday, October 20, 2014

On Day Four, the first of Mangorian's alleged victims is called to testify, Shelley Holland, a mousy-looking woman with light brown hair braided in the back.

"Ms Holland you reside at 8874 Decarie Drive in the Castle Frank area of Toronto and you lived there on September 14 of last year."

"That is correct."

"Now, in your own words, can you describe the events of the evening of September 14."

"I was just cleaning up after dinner and was about to settle in to watch one of my favourite TV programs, Downton Abbey, when someone came to the door."

"Can you describe, in as much detail as possible, what transpired next?"

"Actually, I can't. I remember the doorbell ringing, going to the door and opening it, but after that, it's a complete blank. I can't remember who was there, or anything else, until I suddenly became aware that I was surrounded by police and ambulance attendants."

"Would you look at these photos taken at the time of the assault and tell us how you feel?"

Patullo shows photographs showing two huge blood stained gashes in Holland's neck along the carotid artery. She's wearing a blue, flower-print dress that's torn on one side revealing the neck and a bare shoulder. She appears to be in shock. Another photo depicts Holland being swarmed by EMS attendants who have partially placed a large bandage over her neck wounds.

"I feel disgusted and violated," she says with a look of horror mixed with despair – put there, no doubt, by Patullo and her team.

"What were you feeling at that moment?"

"I was confused and afraid. I didn't know what was going on."

"What about your physical condition? Were you in pain? In discomfort?"

"I was really afraid. I didn't know what happened to me but the cops kept pointing to my neck and, when someone mentioned the possibility of rape, I guess I went off the deep end."

"Now, I would like to go over this last part again, very carefully. You do not remember who assaulted you?"

"No."

"You gave no consent that night for anyone to touch your person, wound you, or take your blood?"

"Absolutely not."

"No more questions."

Patullo smooths her gown as if signifying that, with Holland's testimony, she had ironed out all the wrinkles and erased all doubt about the case.

I take a few moments before standing up for my cross examination – a dramatic pause as Jerry describes it – to appear flummoxed, all the better to indelibly etch what would happen next in the jury's collective mind.

"Ms Holland, when I listen to the information presented by the Crown and its witnesses, it presents quite a frightening picture, doesn't it?" I ask.

"Yes, yes it does."

"Is it fair to say that when police and the Crown attorney presented you with the facts, it deeply troubled you?"

"That is absolutely true," she says, emphasizing her answer with several nods.

"However, you say that you personally do not have any such memories," I say in my best Perry Mason voice.

"Yes, police explained how I was assaulted and that really upset me. That's how I learned what happened."

"Ms Holland, you testified that you live at 8874 Decarie Drive, Toronto, where the alleged assault occurred just over a year ago."

"Yes."

"Does it bother you to live in the same house where the alleged assault occurred?"

"No . . . it doesn't. I like my house. It's my house. Actually, it never really occurred to me," she adds with unspoken new thoughts percolating through her brain.

"It never occurred to you? I would think that if such a horrendous event happened in your house that you would have a hard time living in the same place. That's a normal reaction."

"Now that you bring it up, maybe I should be upset. I'll have to think about it," she says, confusion written across her face.

"Just as you had to think about being upset when you were first told you had been assaulted?"

"I guess. I didn't remember anything," she adds looking even more perplexed.

"Now Ms Holland can you open your collar a little so we can see the marks on your neck?"

"Objection your Honour. Do we have to further traumatize the witness?" Patullo says.

"Your Honour, the Crown has shown photos that portray the incident of September 14, 2013 in very violent terms. I would simply like to show the jury the lasting scars."

"I'll allow it," says Justice McGregor. "Please open your collar so we can see the scars."

"There are no marks on my neck," Holland says.

"No marks?" I gasp, dramatically, and aim a mock look of surprise at the jury. "From the photos they look like horrendous wounds to your neck."

"I know but, after a few days, they healed and even the scars faded away," she says almost apologetically.

"They faded away after just a few days?" I say in simulated astonishment.

"No, the wounds healed in a few days. It took a couple of weeks for the scars to disappear."

"I stand corrected. The wounds healed in a few days and scars took two weeks to vanish."

"That's right," she says, satisfied the error has been corrected.

"Ms Holland have you ever had an instance like this before where a terrible scar healed amazingly quickly?" I hold my breath as Holland pauses and seems to be hit by an unexpected thought.

"You know, I did. Now that you mention it, I noticed two big punctures on my neck a few months before the assault."

"Two punctures on your neck in the same place?"

"Objection your honour. The defence is bringing up information that has no relevance to the charges before the court," says Patullo, anxious to block the new and unexpected direction the evidence is heading.

"Your Honour, I believe this evidence will provide a much fuller explanation for the events of September 14 last year."

"I will allow this line of questioning."

"Ms Holland, you were talking about the two wounds on your neck that happened three months before the incident that brings us to court today?"

"Yeah, I don't know why, but I only remembered them when you asked me about them, " she says with a confused look on her face. "I didn't know what caused them. They were gross at first. Big scabbed over blotches that oozed a bit. I kinda thought it might be AIDS but I hadn't slept with anyone since my husband left me three years before that."

"And what did you do about these wounds?"

"I called my doctor to get an appointment. He was busy and his secretary booked me in to see him in two days. But, the next day, I looked at the wounds and the scabs were gone and the scars weren't that bad. So I cancelled the appointment and, somehow, I forgot about them until now," an expression of bewilderment etched on her face.

"You testified that it doesn't bother you to keep living in the house where the alleged assault occurred. How much does it upset you to think about the events of that day? Do you have nightmares or recurring thoughts that upset you?"

"I don't have any nightmares and I don't think about it because I don't remember it."

"But you said you were upset on the day of the event but you didn't remember it then either."

"I was kinda numb actually. The woman cop kept asking me about the wounds on my neck, but I couldn't see them and I didn't know anything about it. She asked me whether I had been sexually assaulted, raped, and then I got really frightened. I heard about that rape drug, you know, the one that knocks you out and you can't remember . . . so it really frightened me. That's what I thought happened," she says, now completely befuddled.

"The issue of the rape kit has been raised by the Crown," I say. "What was the result?"

"It was negative. I wasn't raped."

I pause for a moment and glance back at the defence bench. I look directly at Dragul and he gives a slow nod.

"Now, Ms Holland you know that my client Mr. Mangorian is charged with assaulting you."

"Yes."

"Can you look at him and see if in any way you recognize him?"

Holland scans his face carefully, seems to think about it for a second and then looks again.

"Uh, there seems to be something familiar about him, but I can't place him."

"Does that familiarity upset you?"

"I don't know what you mean."

"Does it make you anxious, or frightened to look at my client? After all, he's accused of attempting to murder you. Besides, he doesn't look like your average man."

"Well," she says thoughtfully, "he certainly is unusual looking but he doesn't frighten me."

A look of complete bewilderment comes over the Patullo who appears ready to leap out of her seat.

"Can you dig a bit deeper and tell us when you look at him exactly what emotions you are feeling?"

"Uh . . uh . . . " Holland appears completely baffled and so I press on.

"Tell us, what emotions are you experiencing when you look at him?

"It's strange but I kinda feel warmly toward him."

Whispers ripple through the courtroom. Patullo stares in wide-eyed shock.

"Warm? As in friendship?" I say.

"Uh . . . yeah . . . very strange but I do feel a sense of . . . of . . . I guess friendship."

Gasps of surprise burst out everywhere, even in the jury box. Patullo's team is visibly stunned.

Justice McGregor allows 10 seconds for the buzz to die but, when it doesn't, he bangs his gavel twice and says, "Hear, hear. Order,"

I resume my questioning: "Friendship! You have a feeling of warmth and friendship toward a man you don't remember knowing and who is charged with attempting to murder you and causing harm to you. These are very serious charges."

"Yes, I know. I'm feeling really confused right now. I can't explain it but I want to tell the truth," says Holland who seems to be falling apart before my eyes.

Patullo is visibly vibrating in her chair, still looking for grounds to object.

"And how would you feel, if Mr., Mangorian were sentenced to life imprisonment for crimes he's alleged to have committed against you?"

"Uh . . . uh . . . uh . . ."

"This is a very simple question. How would you feel if Mr. Mangorian were sentenced to life imprisonment?"

"Objection your Honour. Ms Holland has been through an extremely upsetting situation. The defence is trying to take advantage of her obvious good nature to get her to say something she doesn't mean."

"I disagree," says Justice McGregor. "We often allow victims to tell the court of the impact a crime has had on their lives and to allow them to say what the punishment should be. I'm curious to hear what this witness has to say. Proceed, Mr. Hamblyn."

"Ms Holland, how would you feel if Mr. Mangorian were sentenced to life imprisonment?

Directing her comments to the astonished prosecutor, Holland says, "I'm sorry. I'm really sorry. But I have to tell the truth . . . It would make me sad to see him imprisoned."

The courtroom erupts in a hundred conversations, this time many at full volume.

"Order or I'll clear the courtroom," says Justice McGregor. When the courtroom settles, he adds, "Please resume your cross examination."

I pause, look at every individual in the jury, as they each replay Holland's last statement in their heads, and ask, "Miss, I'd like to change the topic a bit and ask whether you have had other wounds on your body that didn't heal as quickly as the neck wounds and have left scars on your body."

"Objection. I do not see how other wounds have any bearing in this case," an unnerved Patullo says, again afraid where my questions were leading.

"Your Honour, if you would grant me some latitude, it will become apparent, in a few moments, how this has a direct bearing."

Justice McGregor, now full-on curious, is not to be swayed. "I'll allow it."

"Ms Holland, I apologize if this upsets you, but it is important. In reviewing some of the other photos taken by police, I noticed scars on your wrists. Can you explain them?"

"Yes, and it doesn't bother me to discuss them anymore. After my divorce, I went through a very bad time. I was deeply depressed, and attempted suicide three times."

"And when was your last suicide attempt?

"It was last year, on May 2. A girlfriend found me, and I was sent to emergency. I nearly died."

"You seem to be much better these days. Were psychiatry or support groups helpful?"

"Actually, I had therapy after my first and second suicide attempts, but it didn't help. After my third attempted suicide, I was scheduled for it, but I never went. I didn't seem to need it. I felt happier than I had in years. I even started cooking from scratch again and going out with friends. Everybody remarked how much I had turned around my life."

"And this turn-around started in May of last year. Can you tell me the exact date when you noticed the first marks on your neck and also the date when you felt happier?"

"I remember seeing the marks for the first time and thinking that, if I had AIDS it would end my problems, and that upset me because I realized I didn't want to die. It happened within a week of my suicide attempt probably the day after I got home."

"So the marks on your neck and your new found zest for life happened virtually simultaneously."

"Yessir."

"Do you have any idea how the marks got on your neck back in May 2013?"

"No, but I would guess that if Mr. Mangorian was responsible for the marks in September that he was also responsible for the marks in May. They looked identical."

"I know you can't absolutely answer this next question but I would like you to express any feelings you have about the relationship between the wounds in May 2013 and your improved outlook on life."

Patullo is about to object but Justice McGregor catches her eyes and shakes his head.

"I think somehow those wounds helped me, made me want to live again."

The courtroom again erupts for a full 10 seconds before Justice McGregor makes any move to hush the crowd. When the courtroom is quiet, Jerry rotates his index finger, my signal to wind things up.

"Thank you, Ms Holland. Those are all the questions I have for you."

With the end of my cross-examination, the judge orders an adjournment until the next day.

As I leave the courtroom, reporters are instantly on me with two burning questions.

"How is it possible the victim feels friendship for the accused?"

"Are you leading the victims to say they all gave their consent but don't remember giving it?"

My response to both questions is: "Wait and see."

On the limo ride from the courthouse I see mobile food trucks hawking 'blood sausage on a bun' and 'fang fries' for $5. It is a strange, strange world.

Tonight, I get together again with Rosalie. We've been out several times since the case started. I expected to hit a homerun in court today, and I did. I wanted to celebrate. It had to be special so we made dinner reservations at the Obisidian Club where chef Henri Bonnier and its new sommelier Nathan Sherlock have become the culinary sensation of the city and, maybe it's just hype, but some say the world. With all the celebrity around the case, the board of the Obisidan Club took the unprecedented move to invite me to be a member. The House of Petrocelli paid my first year fees on top of the $100,000 stipend a year simply for wearing Petrocelli suits exclusively supplied, of course, by Barry Rushmore.

The dining experience was spectacular, everything we heard about and more. When the limo arrives at Rosalie's house, she invites me in.

At 46, Rosalie is an amazingly attractive woman. I have never fallen out of love with her and, despite all the crap I put her through, it appears she feels the same about me. We share a drink and then wordlessly go into the bedroom. For the first time in more than 18 years, we make sweet, wonderful love that lasted into the wee hours of the morning.

I rise at 6 a.m. and, despite getting little sleep, I feel incredibly happy and full of energy. I congratulate myself for being smart enough to have tucked a complete change of clothes, including a fresh Petrocelli suit with a crisp shirt and tie in the limo, when I hoped might happen, did happen.

I kiss Rosalie goodbye and she wishes me luck in court today. "I know you really don't need luck. You are still the handsomest, smartest man I ever met."

Other than Rosalie's obvious vision and perception impairments, she is perfect.

The limo weaves through the crowd to the courthouse parking lot and I hotfoot it to a back room to don my gown. When I enter the courtroom, there's Patullo staring daggers at me. Her slam-dunk case definitely got slammed yesterday.

"Mr. Hamblyn . . . more tricks up your sleeve today?"

"Just a couple," I say giving her a wink. A wink? Have I become that cocky now? I've never given anyone a wink let alone a striking, powerhouse lawyer like her. I half gulp as I walk away, fearing she will use the slight as inspiration to really take it out of my hide.

CHAPTER FOURTEEN

TRIAL, DAY 5

Over the next three days the prosecution brings forward more alleged victims.

Five of the witnesses, Eleanor Kreiger, George Beauchamps, Jenna DiAngelo, Samia Adjaye, and Naomi Carter, gave statements to police indicating they had no memories of the attacks. When police informed them of the nature of their wounds, each said they were afraid, angry, outraged and stunned to learn they had been assaulted and deprived of two pints of blood.

Tuesday, October 21

Kreiger, the first witness called to testify on Tuesday, tells the court she was at home alone on the evening of August 7, 2012 when she blacked out and then awoke to find herself surrounded by police. A friend, worried she didn't answer the phone, visited her house and saw her lying on the floor after she checked the windows.

Police and EMS workers noticed, and documented, blood along the collar of her torn blouse and two ugly wounds on her neck that appeared to tap into her jugular vein.

During my cross-examination, Kreiger's story stirred more than a few echoes of Holland's tale.

"Ms. Kreiger can you explain your role in the Canadian Armed Forces, particularly the events that led to your honourable discharge?"

"I served as a lieutenant in a combat unit in Kandahar Province, Afghanistan. During a regular convoy run on November 2, 2010 a local truck drew along side the convoy and then exploded, killing the terrorist and three Canadian soldiers in the closest armoured combat vehicle. I was in the next vehicle and suffered wounds, as did two other soldiers in my truck."

"Were these wounds serious?"

"Serious enough for me to be sent home and receive an honourable discharge."

"You seemed to be able to function here today."

"Yes, physically, I'm okay, not as fit as I was, but okay."

"Lt. Kreiger, you suffered other wounds that are not as apparent, did you not . . . psychological wounds that led you to seek professional help?"

"Yes, I was diagnosed with PTSD in 2012."

"PTSD, that's post traumatic stress disorder."

"Yes it is."

"Can you describe the effects you experienced as a result of PTSD?"

"Well, often I had memory lapses. I would forget even basic things, but the old, dark memories would never go away," she says, her visage coloured by sadness.

"And those old dark memories are . . . "

"Uhhh," she winces as some of the thoughts come to mind.

"Take your time Lieutenant."

"Well, uhhh. Bad stuff . . . uhhh . . . that happened there . . . Uhhh . . . Sights and sounds, even smells of my friends dying . . . uhh . . . like I was there again. Explosions, fire, people screaming. I feel the heat of the blast. My wounds ache."

"And what effect would these, can I call them flashbacks, have on you?"

"People always said I was the toughest person they knew. I was self-assured, physically fit before I went to Kandahar. When I returned even though I knew it was irrational, I kept thinking that they had planted a bomb in my house, in my car, and sometimes even inside of me."

The jury is deeply engrossed and waits on Lt. Kreiger's every word.

"I would wake up in the middle of the night and tear my apartment apart looking for a bomb. Then I'd go to bed and get up again in an hour and do it all over again. I lived in a constant state of fear. It made me sick and angry. I felt so powerless, so hopeless. I was overwhelmed by thoughts of suicide on February 5th, 2012 and again on June 19th, 2012. The second time, I even put the muzzle of a gun in my mouth. Instead, I called my sponsor in the support group and she talked me down."

No sound breaks the silence as Kreiger regroups her thoughts and then resumes.

"On June 25th, I woke up with an incredible thirst. I downed four glasses of water and then had an overwhelming desire to go biking. I hadn't done that since before Kandahar. I was an accomplished cyclist with top 10 finishes in three local road races so getting back on the road felt great. I was really steaming along for a couple miles. Then I started to feel faint, so I took it slow back home. My mental health has been really good ever since."

It's time to pop the big question.

"What happened that caused this healing?"

"I don't know, it just happened."

"Can you recall anything unusual about your physical appearance at that time?"

"No, I . . . Maybe . . . It's starting to come back. I remember feeling tired but great after the short bike ride so I took a shower. When I finished, I looked in the mirror. Oh God! I saw two really big, ugly marks on my neck. I touched them and they felt like small calibre gunshot wounds that had healed over," she says in astonishment at her owns words.

"The wounds didn't hurt and weren't bleeding. For some reason, they didn't seem important to me. So I left them for the time being because I had a doctor's appointment within a couple of weeks. I never raised the issue with the doctor because the marks were gone. I was elated that the doc told me I was doing great, physically and mentally."

"Since that day in June 2012 have you continued to have flashbacks and suicidal tendencies?"

"I'm still disturbed and saddened by the memories, but that's only when I think about it. But it's under my control. Not like before when I couldn't separate my flashbacks from reality."

"Now that you remember the original neck wounds, can you compare them with the marks on your neck that led to the charges my client is facing?"

"They're the same," she says, as the concept begins to solidify in her mind. "Oh my God. They're the same."

"So you think there's a connection between the first time you found marks on your neck and your improved mental health?"

"I hadn't thought of that but, yes, it was exactly the same time. I keep a diary and I know they happened at the same time."

"Will you please look at the accused? Is he a potential killer in your mind?"

Kreiger takes a long, thoughtful stare at Mangorian and then looks at me and says, "I know killers because of my time in the military and, despite his ferocious look, no, I just don't see him as the killer type."

"You told the prosecutor that you did not grant permission to the accused to take your blood. Do you still stand by that?"

"I don't know. I don't remember. Maybe I did."

"Did what?"

"Maybe I did give him permission, but I don't know for sure."

George Beauchamps, a former high-flyer who lost his vice-presidency at a major financial house to an insider trading allegation, and his wife and kids to his crack habit, was the next to take the stand.

He testifies in my cross that he had twice tried to commit suicide. About 14 months before he was allegedly assaulted, he noticed there were two scabbed-over holes by his carotid artery that punctuated the rope-burn marks on his neck.

"From that moment on, I was a changed man," he says.

He started to work again, at the bottom, as a financial planner and began volunteering as a coach on his daughter's soccer team.

Under my cross, Beauchamps says, "I don't know if the accused had anything to do with my recovery but I am willing to give him the benefit of doubt and I hope the jury will do the same."

I'm sensing a real shift in how the jury sees the case. They aren't glaring at Dragul like he's a monster," I say at O'Reillys after court has adjourned for the day. "Three prosecution witnesses in a row – wham. Patullo can't be happy about that."

"When Beauchamps asked the jury to give Mangorian the benefit of doubt, I expected Patullo to faint," Regina says. "But you've got to give the lady credit. She showed zero emotion, like what he said wasn't important. The lady deserves an Oscar."

"Or at least a seat at a million-dollar poker game," I add.

"You've done great work," says Jerry, "but the race is still in progress. The finish line is still a long way off and we can't be sure the other witnesses are going to be nearly so helpful. I'm sure Patullo's team is working overtime to make sure of it."

Six blocks away, Patullo sits stone-faced while 'Stormin' Norman Sutherland, ex-army colonel and now Crown Attorney for York Region, lives up to his nickname.

"What the hell is going on?" he says, stomping back and forth in time with puffs on his cigar. In his steel-grey pin stripes, he resembles an antique steam locomotive with its boiler pressure riding the red line.

"How can you blow a case when all the evidence says Mangorian did it?

All the victims' wounds can only have been inflicted by Mangorian and even Mangorian has admitted to taking their blood. This is a slam-dunk. You're blowing it, Alicia. You have had a remarkable career up to now. You don't want your reputation as a prosecutor to take a nosedive."

"I know, Norman. We're working on it but it's tough to get to the witnesses on the eve of their testimony. Our tactics could be called into question, and we could be accused of coaching our witnesses."

"You're a smart lady. That's why I hired you. Stick your foot right on the line and get those witnesses back on side."

"It's too late for much more than the brief chats we had with Naomi Carter, Kofi Adjaye and Jenna DiAngelo because all three testify tomorrow. We have long interviews scheduled with Micculetti and Kmerza. I've dropped Beers, the high school student. My team thinks he's too risky to call."

"Okay, but just remember, if you lose, YOU LOSE. Catch my drift," Sutherland says. "Now get out. You've got lots of work to do."

Patullo nods courteously and leaves.

Stormin', making threats and blowing smoke up yer arse, she thinks reverting to her Italian via Sudbury roots. Somebody should report him to the tobacco police. Imagine, a high official like him breaking the law by smoking cigars in a public building.

CHAPTER FIFTEEN

TRIAL, DAYS 6 & 7

Wednesday, October 22, 2014 - Thursday, October 23, 2014

The next morning, Patullo calls on Jenna DiAngelo, a blonde, blue-eyed, all-Canadian girl who spins her wheelchair next to the witness stand.

"Were you assaulted on the night of January 6, 2013."

"Yes I was."

"Can you describe the nature of the assault?"

"The actual events are a blank. I can't remember what happened. One second I'm doing my physiotherapy exercises and the next moment my house is filled with police and people in white coveralls."

"Can you tell me what happened next?"

"The forensic people take samples from cuts to my neck, examine me for other damage, and they take a rape kit."

"Were you upset that you had been assaulted?"

"Of course. How would you feel when somebody breaks into your house and assaults you. I'm disabled and live on my own, so I'm pretty vulnerable. That's why I've taken extra precautions in case of an accident, health issues or crime. But that all didn't seem to help."

"And these extra precautions, what are they?"

"I have all windows and doors on alarms. The front and back entrances have video cameras to record would-be intruders and deliver a voice warning that the intruder is under surveillance. All doors have double-bolt locks and the windows are automatically locked down every night."

"And on the night of January 6, 2013, someone got by all of these extra precautions to assault you. Do you know how?"

"I have no idea and neither does the security firm. The videotape of the grounds during that time-period is blank so the video would have been turned off, but that's impossible, because it can only be done from inside of the house. On top of everything else, none of my neighbours reported hearing the intruder-alert warning."

"Your security system, and the company that provides it, are the best in their field, I understand."

"That's also my understanding."

"So if the system is so good, and everything was working, would you say it would take someone with extraordinary abilities to get past these measures, perhaps a truly extraordinary human being?"

"That would be my guess."

"So on top of everything else, you must have felt very vulnerable when all the extra precautions you took had no effect."

"That's true. It really upset me."

"When police told you that you had been assaulted, how did that make you feel?"

"Not very good, not very safe."

"Now in a statement given to police, the accused, Dragul Mangorian admitted to taking blood from you but he claims that you gave it to him voluntarily."

"That's just not true. I've never seen him before in my life."

"Let's be clear here. Did you, or did you not give the accused permission to bite into your carotid artery and suck out two pints of your blood."

"Of course not."

"Thank you. Those are all of my questions."

I grab photos of DiAngelo's home that were entered into evidence and show them to her.

"Is this your home?"

"Yes it is."

"And you own the home yourself."

"Yes I do."

"This looks like a very expensive house and it obviously has a lot of sophisticated surveillance equipment in it. How does someone as young as you, I believe you are 26, afford a home like this?"

"I paid for it with money from an insurance policy."

"That's some insurance policy."

"I was one of the world's top snowcross snowboarders. I finished in the top three at the X Games three years in a row, including winning gold in 2009. As part of our sponsorship package, all of us get an insurance policy thrown in just in case the worst happens . . . As it did with me."

"I understand you severed your spine in a horrible crash when another competitor landed on your back with the tip of her board."

"Yes. I was in the hospital for the rest of 2010."

"That must have been painful."

"Very," she says, showing some annoyance.

"Were you taking a lot of painkillers, heavy-duty painkillers?"

"Of course." Her responses now take on a distinctly hostile tone.

"And did you subsequently get hooked on these painkillers, specifically oxycodone?"

"Your Honour, where is Mr. Hamblyn going with this?" Patullo interjects.

"Mr. Hamblyn?"

"As with one of the previous witnesses, I ask the court's indulgence in order to establish that there was, indeed, a relationship between Mr. Mangorian and Ms DiAngelo, whether she can remember it or not."

"Very well, but I need to see the connection quickly," the judge says.

"Did you get hooked on oxycodone?"

" . . . Yes," she says softly but with contempt in her voice.

"And being an addict, is that a problem for you?"

"It was a terrible problem. Once my prescriptions ran out and my doctors wouldn't renew them, I had to buy it on the streets. You say that I seem wealthy for a 26-year-old. Well, that wasn't going to be true for much longer."

"Is an addiction to oxycodone difficult to kick?"

"It's virtually impossible."

"And yet you have kicked it, haven't you?"

"Yes I have," she says with a look of astonishment.

"And what incredible treatment do you credit for getting you clean?"

"That's the thing. I don't know. I woke up one morning and the urge wasn't there."

"Do you recall the date when you went cold turkey?"

"It wasn't cold turkey – not in the normal way – because I just stopped, no fuss, no muss."

"And the date?"

"Oh, just before Nov. 3, 2012, my mother's birthday. I remember taking the money I was going to use to buy drugs and splurging on a necklace for my mother."

"Was there anything physically different about you when this happened? Perhaps some wounds on your neck?"

DiAngelo's mouth drops open.

After a long pause, she says: "Yes, yes. I don't know why I didn't remember it until now. But now that you say it, there were these two ugly . . . They . . . "

Suddenly her mouth falls wide open again.

"They were just like the marks on my neck later on, on, on January 6. That's it, isn't it? They were the same as the marks on my neck on January 6."

Patullo looks on with disbelief. The rest of her team crumple in their chairs.

"And, again, you saw these wounds and immediately your addiction to oxycodone vanished?"

"It did. It really did. I don't know why I didn't remember it until now."

"Hypothetically speaking, what would you have given to be rid of your addiction?"

"I'd have given anything, absolutely anything . . . I guess what you're asking is, would I give Mr. Mangorian two pints of blood? The answer to that is yes."

The courtroom erupts.

Under my questioning that day and the seventh day of the trial, the testimony of Naomi Carter and Kofi Adjaye, echoed that of Holland, Krieger, Beauchamps and DiAngelo. Carter admitted to thoughts of suicide that ended about the time she found strange marks on her neck, marks that were precisely the same as the marks that led to the charges. For the sixth alleged victim, Adjaye, suicide had been constantly on his mind until the day he discovered the marks in his neck. None of the witnesses received professional medical attention for the earlier neck wounds because they healed and then disappeared in short order.

In total, six of the eight testified in response to my direct question that they would be saddened to see Mangorian remain in prison.

Two witnesses, Joyce Micculetti and Helen Kmerza, admitted they had long-standing substance abuse problems, booze for Micculetti and percocet for Kmerza. Neither remembered seeing fang-shaped wounds on their necks prior to the alleged assault.

"My sister came to my house and woke me that Sunday morning. When I got to the door, she screamed when she saw my neck and rushed me to the hospital. Police interviewed me in the emergency ward and told me I wasn't the only victim."

She testified under Patullo's examination that she remains angered over the assault in her own home. "I did not give permission. I wouldn't. It's sick."

Kmerza also testified that the neck wounds she suffered during the assault were a first. She heard a knock on her door and thought it was the limousine she ordered to catch a flight to Miami. That was the last thing she could recall until she awoke with police and EMS attendants around her.

"The limo driver rang the bell and when there was no answer, he looked in the window and saw me sprawled on the floor."

In answer to my question whether she was certain she didn't give permission for her blood to be taken, she replies: "What kind of wacko would agree to that? No way."

Despite the final two witnesses, Team Dragul certainly seemed to have captured the momentum by the end of my cross-examinations. Patullo and her team sat stoically, showing no emotion throughout.

Thursday evening, Jerry, Regina, Theresa Davis and I decide to kick back and have a few beers and leave the books alone for one night.

"My question is, why did the last two witnesses Micculetti and Kmerza not have the same bond with Dragul as the others?" asked Regina.

"That's a question we'll probably never be able to answer, " I say, taking a huge sip of my beer." Dragul visited them only once and it may take multiple visits to create that bond. Maybe, they just didn't sync with him as much as the others. Who knows?"

"It doesn't really matter. Patullo must be going crazy. The victims' testimony was supposed to be her grand slam but now her whole case is a mess," says Regina, a wide smile planted on her rosy-cheeked, cherubic face.

"In the pre-trial interviews, all of the so-called victims said they were outraged and felt violated," she says. "Not one said anything about previously having bite marks. Talk about Miss Perfect getting cold-cocked."

But I argue for caution: "She's going to come back with the argument that despite what Mangorian testified, and regardless how the victims feel now, we can't prove permission was given. Mangorian told police, and will admit in court that he took blood from all of them. De facto, that's assault causing bodily harm, regardless how you cut it."

Theresa looks over the witness list and says, "Patullo's final witnesses are two psychologists. She's dropped the ninth victim, the high-school senior Jonathan Beers. I guess she's had enough."

"I wonder if it could be more than that," Jerry muses. "Teenagers are pretty rebellious. They tend to over-react when any adult tries to control them. I just don't see him being as accepting of our position. Something's going on here."

"Patullo's not going to call him so what can we do about it?" Regina asks.

"I suggest we call Beers as our witness," Jerry replies, a wicked smile hinting at the potential for mischief.

"Didn't you tell me in law school that you never ask a question without knowing what the answer will be?" I say.

"True, but we've been purposely breaking that rule all week, so that we wouldn't be telegraphing our punches. This is just more of the same, except we are calling Beers as our witness."

Regina agrees: "None of the other witnesses hurt our case and if she's trying to keep him away from us, perhaps there's a memory there where he grants consent."

"That's a risk," I say.

"Yes, but a small one," says Jerry. "If he had anything really damaging, Patullo would be using it. As it stands, all the sympathy is on our side."

CHAPTER SIXTEEN

TRIAL, DAY 8

Friday, October 24, 2014

The next morning, the Crown puts her final two witnesses on the stand, Dr. Joyce Chen and Dr. Duncan Horst.

"Dr. Chen, you are the psychologist with the York Detention Centre where the accused was held for about a year while he was awaiting trial?"

"That is correct."

"And during that period you had an opportunity to meet with the accused on several occasions?"

"Six times."

"What are the conclusions that you reached when you examined the accused in terms of his personality and his view of events such as he is accused of committing?"

"The accused does not react to violence the way we expect a normal human being to react. In detention, even hardened criminals have fear for their personal safety and, at some level, are disgusted by the worst violence."

"And the accused is not?"

"I'll give an example. There was a brutal murder in the prison. An inmate's throat was sliced ear to ear. There was blood everywhere. I should mention that Mr. Mangorian was in another part of the prison. He had nothing to do with it. It was my job to try to calm the inmates; so, I held meetings with many of them, especially those who were new arrivals. Mr. Mangorian was among them.

"Most of those I interviewed wanted to talk about it and be assured that they were safe."

"But that wasn't the accused's reaction?"

"No, not at all. He seemed to be obsessed with the details, whether anyone saw the moment of death. He wanted to know if the inmate was in agony when he died and asked many questions about what we did with the blood and the blood of all people who might be murdered in prison.

"His reaction is clearly that of a psychopath. He sees everything only in the context of what will benefit him with no concern whatsoever for anyone else. A man was murdered and his sole concern was what happened to the blood. I do not believe the accused can be trusted. In many ways, he does not view human beings on an emotional level. Any concern he has is like that of a farmer for his livestock."

"Dr. Chen, have you ever examined another member of the genus Sanguinus?" I ask in my cross.

"I have not."

"You know that the Sanguinus consume only blood for their sustenance with human blood as their principal food?"

"I am aware of this."

"The meeting you described having with Mr. Mangorian took place about two months into his incarceration and up to that time his diet consisted 100 per cent of cow's blood?"

"I believe that is true."

"You testified that he was obsessed with the blood of the victim and the death of the victim and not concerned about the welfare of the victim himself."

"True."

"I put it to you, how would any of us react if our food source was severely restricted for two months and we were, literally, starving? Would not the human reaction be to fixate on the food above all else?"

"Perhaps, perhaps not."

"Are you familiar with Maslow's Hierarchy of Needs?"

"Of course, it is one of the first things you learn in psychology 101. "Do you prescribe to the theory."

"All psychologists do."

"Maslow says all living things must first satisfy their physiological needs, the physical requirements for survival. These needs are air, water, and food followed by clothing and shelter and then a sexual instinct to reproduce and maintain the species. Do you agree with this?"

"Yes I do."

"I suggest that Mr. Mangorian was in a different situation than all other prisoners. With the exception of access to sexual reproduction, all other prisoners had their physiological needs attended to. Would you give your opinion whether the prison was meeting Mr. Mangorian's physiological need for sustenance? Was he not literally starving to death?"

"That's a matter of interpretation. He was supplied with whatever quantity of cow's blood he needed."

"And what would you suggest the other prisoners' reactions would be to a brutal murder if for two months they were on a diet of stale bread and water?"

"I'm not in a position to say."

"Surely, you can come up with a better answer than that."

"Objection your Honour. Defence is badgering the witness."

"Objection sustained. You asked your question and received the answer. Move on counsellor."

"Those are all the questions I have for this witness."

Patullo calls her second psychologist of the day, Dr. Duncan Horst, a specialist in legal insanity.

"In your expert opinion, Dr. Horst, does the accused meet the criteria for someone who was unaware of or did not appreciate the nature or quality or wrongfulness of his acts?" asks Patullo.

I turn to Regina and wink. As we expected, the prosecutor is shutting the door on any possibility we will play the temporary insanity card. It's a necessary move on her part but a moot point since we have no intention of raising the argument.

"I interviewed the accused twice and it was absolutely apparent that Mr. Mangorian was completely aware the acts he committed are considered wrong in law and by custom. It is my professional opinion that in no way could the accused claim to be cognitively insane."

"Dr. Horst, you have heard the claim by the accused that he is a Sanguinus and, by his nature, he is compelled to drink the blood of humans. Would you say that this compulsion is an irresistible impulse that qualifies him to a claim of volitional insanity? In terms the jury can understand, it means a compulsion so strong that it overwhelms all sense and understanding of the consequences and is, therefore, a form of insanity."

"Again, in my professional opinion, the accused does not fall into this category. Someone with volitional insanity would have no control, whatsoever, over his actions. There would be no planning, no stealth. To suffer from this form of insanity, the accused would have been on a rampage with no rationality involved. For instance, the accused took about two units of blood from each of his victims, not enough to cause lasting health issues. If he were suffering from volitional insanity, he would drain his victims to the last drop. I suggest that the decision to stop at two units was an extremely rational decision."

When Patullo completes her examination of Dr. Horst, she announces that the prosecution has completed its case.

"Your Honour, I would like to submit an amendment to my witness list," I say.

"I hand over a copy of the new list to both the judge and Patullo.

"I object Your Honour. Jonathan Beers was never named by the defence as a possible witness."

"That is true Your Honour, but the witness was on the prosecution list. My esteemed colleague cannot claim she is unprepared to question the witness."

"I agree. The defence may call Jonathan Beers as a witness for the defence when court resumes next week," Justice McGregor says.

CHAPTER SEVENTEEN

TRIAL, DAY 9

Monday, October 27, 2014

When court resumes on Monday, I open the defence case with psychologist, Dr. Gregor Amos.

"Dr. Amos, you have had an opportunity to spend time with Dragul Mangorian with the express purpose of assessing, to the extent that it is possible, certain unusual capabilities he possesses."

"Yes, I have had a total of eight sessions with him over the past 12 months and can verify that, as difficult as this may be to believe, he has the ability to create a mental link with a person's thinking processes."

"Then he can read your mind?"

"No, I don't believe he can, nor do I believe he can read anyone else's mind."

"Then, just how does he connect with your thoughts?"

"In some way that I cannot fathom or begin to explain, Mr. Mangorian has an ability that no human I know possesses. I have witnessed it directly through personal trials and, indirectly through my assistants. He is able to touch people and convey images and emotions into their minds."

"What specific images are you speaking of?"

"It's not as easy as stating a specific thing. It is more like creating an entire contextual environment where an individual's own feelings and desires create a story. That story helps the person come to terms with himself and his desires. The story allows the subject to visualize a better future.

"We try to do something like this at a much less complex level when we train an athlete to visualize winning the gold medal. If the visualization is strong enough and complex enough, it will enhance an athlete's ability to perform. All of the world's elite athletes do this.

"The same theory is the basis in hypnosis to help smokers quit. Even here there is debate about how exactly hypnosis works. Some believe that when a person is hypnotized, he is able to relax and concentrate, and becomes more receptive to suggestions, such as giving up smoking.

"When an individual is in a trance during hypnosis, he is not unconscious and may be fully aware of the surroundings. It is well established that under hypnosis a subject cannot be made do to anything against his will. In fact, brain tests performed on patients during hypnosis show high neurological activity.

"Through hypnosis, smoking-cessation programs create imagery where the patient is directed to imagine unpleasant outcomes brought on by smoking. The hypnotherapist may request the patient imagine that smoking leaves him with a dry, unpleasant feeling in his mouth, or that smoking emits fumes that are highly offensive to both the smoker and everyone around him. One respected program has the patient focus on three specific ideas: Smoking poisons your body; you need your body to live; you must protect your body to survive.

"So in my opinion, Mr. Mangorian creates a more powerful form of hypnosis because, in addition to providing suggestions, he conveys images directly into the brain. This action creates an environment where the personal feelings of an individual can play out a positive scenario. It is through this scenario that the person overcomes his psychological demons – substance abuse, depression, self-doubt, fear – and moves forward in a more productive way by visualizing a better life and then following that pattern in real life."

"And how did you come to this conclusion?"

"For something to have any scientific weight behind it, you need a blind study. We didn't have the scope – meaning not enough subjects – for a true blind study so I did the next best thing. I told you, Mr. Hamblyn, of a series of things I would like to improve about myself and asked you to have Mr. Mangorian, at some point without telling me, help me with one of them. After the fourth session while I was walking my dog, I realized that we had happily walked more than a mile. It just seemed so natural. Our usual walk was around the block but since then, it's always been a mile or more.

"Among the things I had mentioned to you, Mr. Hamblyn, was that I needed to exercise more and lose weight. Even though I suspected Mr. Mangorian had inspired this, I had a desire to keep walking. The next day, I walked up the stairs to my office on the eighth floor without even thinking about it. It seemed the natural thing to do and is now part of my daily routine. For the first time in my life, I found myself doing calisthenics while watching television news, something that I continue to do today.

"We all know that the best way to lose weight is to combine exercise and controlling calories. I found I was eating less and eating things that are better for me. I'm now 20 pounds lighter than I was a year ago. I feel incredibly fit, even though I don't belong to a fitness club or follow any kind of exercise regime. Millions of people have a weight loss goal, too, but don't achieve it even when they join fitness clubs, hire personal trainers or buy workout equipment. I'd say, without a doubt, that my weight-loss experience was directly attributable to Mr. Mangorian."

"Did Mr. Mangorian take blood from you?"

"No he did not. I specified at the outset that I denied consent for him to take my blood, plus it would have been difficult for him to do it in prison under the guards' watchful eyes."

"So, in your professional opinion, would you conclude that an encounter with Mr. Mangorian could be beneficial for people?"

"Yes. If he were in full-time practice, we psychologists would see a sharp decline in business as would fitness instructors and self-help gurus."

"After this kind of positive experience, do you think that some people would voluntarily comply with Mr. Mangorian's request for blood as repayment?"

"I know that I have profound respect and deep feelings of friendship for Mr. Mangorian and not just because he helped me lose weight and become healthier. It goes a lot deeper than that. If he really needed my blood to survive I would be happy to supply it to him."

"We have had other witnesses tell us they felt warmly towards Mr. Mangorian even though he is charged with their attempted murder. The baffling part is why none of them can remember meeting Mr. Mangorian, nor why they feel friendly toward him. Because none of them remember him, they also have no recollection of consenting to have him take their blood," I say.

"I tried to puzzle this myself and the only way I can frame it is to look at it like a dream. Sometimes we have very vivid dreams but when we wake up or within minutes, what we dreamed of vanishes. We know we had a wonderful dream or a horrible nightmare but that's it, no details."

"Has Mr. Mangorian provided you with an explanation?"

"He did. He said that these images are transferred much more completely from Sanguinus to Sanguinus so they are able to pass on their history from one generation to the next but less perfectly so between a Sanguinus and Sapien. On very rare occasions, a Sanguinus finds a Sapiens who is very compatible and the memories remain intact. The Sapiens remembers everything or mostly everything."

"Thank you Dr. Amos. I have no further questions."

Prosecutor Patullo's steps forward to cross-examine Dr. Gregor Amos.

"Dr. Amos, you have told us quite a fanciful story but do you have any real proof that Mr. Mangorian can perform such amazing feats that help people step back from the brink of suicide or, in your case, help you lose weight?"

"I have no proof, just my observations and my professional opinion that people don't suddenly fix themselves, especially when they have problems as deep and real as we've heard from the witnesses. The coincidence of timing is particularly interesting."

"But again you have no proof, just your theory."

"That is correct."

"I have no more questions for this witness your Honour."

"The witness is excused. We'll pick up again tomorrow," Justice McGregor says.

Despite the big day in court tomorrow, I have something even more important this evening, date night with Rosalie. On the agenda? A DVD of To Kill A Mockingbird, a bowl of popcorn and ice cold bottles of Molson's Canadian beer.

"I've been watching the case. You are fantastic," says Rosalie.

"Yes, I know," I say, huffing on my nails and polishing them against my jacket's lapels.

"You're a scoundrel," she says, wrapping her arms around my neck and pressing her lips tenderly to mine.

So much for the evening's agenda.

CHAPTER EIGHTEEN

TRIAL, DAY 10

Tuesday, October 28, 2014

I've lined up Jonathan Beers, originally one of the prosecution's witnesses, to testify today. I'm a little terrified about what he has to say beyond what I learned when I interviewed him several months ago. Was this a trap that Patullo set so she could treat Beers as a hostile witness and lead him through doors he was reluctant to open on his own? Jerry thinks I'm just being paranoid but just because you're paranoid, it doesn't mean they're not out to get you.

Beers takes the stand and swears to tell the truth.

The 17-year-old senior at Wilton Road High School is chubby, 5-foot, 7 with unruly black hair and a reddish complexion, the tail end of an acne outbreak.

"What do you remember of the evening of June 6, 2013? What do you recall that was out of the ordinary?"

"I just seemed to wake up or something, in my bedroom. Just before midnight, eh. So like, everybody's yelling at me or at each other. Like, I dunno what was going on. My mom's crying in the corner. And . . . and so I say, like, hey what's going on, eh."

"Can you tell the court how you were feeling at that time?"

"Well the cops they were busy talking into their radios. I hear a cop say they're looking for somebody, somewhere. One of the ambulance guys is checking me over, I guess to see if I'm hurt somewhere. Then he starts cutting my new Anthrax T-shirt. "Hey," I say, "That T cost me 50 bucks."

"Can we get back to your mental state. How did you feel at that time.

"Like I said, I was really pissed about my T-shirt. Hey, if this guy gets convicted, do I get my $50 back?"

I'm beginning to understand why Patullo pulled him from the witness list.

"Mr. Beers would it be reasonable to say that you were also in a state of confusion about what had happened to you?"

"I'll say. One minute I'm listen' to a Behemoth album. Next thing some woman's sticking these clips on my fingers and these sticky patches on my chest. Actually, I didn't mind that part. She was a babe. The worst guy was a neighbour, Ben Saxon, I think. Kinda weird guy. He's screaming at the cops to get the guy. So I scream at him, 'What're you doin' in my room'. Like, what's everybody doin' in my room?"

"Okay, that's after the incident but do you remember anything before waking up and seeing the confusion in your room?" I ask.

"Nope, nothing."

"Let's start at the beginning. Can you go through your day, minute by minute until you come to a blank?" I ask.

"Well, I went to school. I came home. Went up to my room and that's the last thing I remember."

"Please bear with me. I need more details because something that you missed may be important. Let's start with what time you arrived at school."

"My first class is at 9; so, I got there at 9."

"Right at 9, not 8:55?"

"No exactly at 9. That's when I always go in," he says irritably.

"My notes indicate that your father said he dropped you off at school at 8:30 a.m."

"Uhh, yeah he did." At this, Beers' face turns noticeably red.

"So he dropped you off in front of the school at 8:30 a.m. but you didn't go into the school until right at 9 a.m. What were you doing during that half hour?"

"I dunno. Just hanging around."

"Were you hanging around with anyone else?"

"No, just by myself."

A thought comes to mind of my law school days and how I would wait until the very last minute to show up for classes to avoid Gracey and his gang. I puzzle over this idea momentarily. Beers, meanwhile, is looking about as comfortable seated in the witness stand as someone sitting on a beehive.

"Who were you trying to avoid seeing?" I ask.

"Huh?" says Beers.

"Was there someone you were trying to avoid seeing?"

Beers couldn't have been more shocked and just sat there staring at me.

"Who was the bully you were trying to avoid?"

Without warning, the floodgates, as they say, burst open. Beers breaks into uncontrollable, loud, and wet sobbing.

After allowing a minute to pass, Justice McGregor says, "Mr. Beers, are you able to continue your testimony?"

Between sobs, Beer nods and slowly regains his composure.

"I apologize for raising such obviously disturbing memories," I say. "Unfortunately, I would like to continue along this line of questioning."

"Objection your Honour," interjects Patullo. "It's clear that this is a very emotional issue for Mr. Beers. I do not understand how probing into what appears to be a clear-cut case of school bullying will shed any light on what the court is dealing with today. If there are charges that can be laid related to bullying they should be dealt with entirely separately."

"Your Honour," I say. "I believe these circumstances very much impact on these proceedings."

"I'll be very interested in seeing how. Objection overruled for now. Show me the connection."

"Mr. Beers, it appears that you were trying to avoid contact with a certain person or persons. Is that correct?"

"Yeah, a lot of people."

"And were you physically afraid to be in contact with these people?"

"Yes, but it didn't matter any more."

"It didn't matter?"

"No, I was going to fix things," he says fixing me with a stare for the first time.

"By fix things are you talking about going to the principal or a teacher?"

"No," he says maintaining his eye lock.

"So how were you going to fix things?"

"I had a plan."

"And just what was the plan?"

"It doesn't matter any more because after what happened that night, I forgot about the plan."

"By that night, you mean the evening of June 6, 2013?"

"Yeah, that's right."

"So after your parents reported that someone allegedly assaulted you in your room and the police investigated, you had no more use of the plan."

"That's right."

"What changed? Did you report the problem at school to police or your parents?"

"No, I just decided on my own that I didn't want to do it."

"Do what?"

"The plan."

"Again, what was the plan?"

"I don't want to talk about it and it doesn't matter because nothing happened," Beers says testily.

"Okay, okay. Let's get back to your day in school. You're in class at 9 a.m. Describe what goes on."

"It's Mr. Percy's class, chemistry. Mr. Percy is writing on the board, see, when a balled up scrap of paper, too small to make noise, hits me in the back of the head. I ignore it. In the next three seconds, eight more balls hit me in the back of the head and two more go whizzing by me. I turn around. Jeremy is holding a sign that says: 'How's Beers Belly today.' His buddies all snicker and point at me silently. The next two classes pretty well go like that – different characters, same abuse – until I hit the highlight of my day, lunchtime.

"So, I'm in the line of the cafeteria shoveling as much food in my mouth as I can because I know it's just 50-50 whether I can make it to a table before someone trips me. That day I actually made it to one of the front tables before Meathead – I don't know his real name – drops a partially dissected frog from biology class into my bowl of soup. 'Just a bit of protein for you Beers Belly.'

"I'm done; so, I grab my tray and get no more than three steps when somebody's leg comes out. I don't see it and down I go. I'm crying. I'm lying in soup, mushed up shepherd's pie, and the frog and a piece of Jell-O are on my lap. I just want to run but the whole cafeteria starts yelling: 'Pick it up, pick it up.'

"Mr. Bouchard, he was the teacher on cafeteria duty, looks at me on the floor and says, 'Well, clean it up. The sooner you do it, the sooner they'll stop that infernal chanting.' I use my bare hands to scoop most of the stuff back onto the tray and then I toss the tray on a counter and leave school."

"Mr. Beers, according to a statement you gave to police and statements made by your parents, you didn't arrive home until almost 5 p.m. What did you do and where did you go between, say, 1 p.m. and 5 p.m.?"

Beers looks at me, thinks for a minute and then says, "I went to the stockade."

"The stockade?"

"That's what some of the kids call it. It's an old factory. I think they used to make shoes in it but it closed way before I was born. It's been empty ever since. We get in by lifting part of the wire fencing around back. Some of the kids go there to drink and do other stuff. I found a door inside that still had a key in the lock on the inside so I made the room my own private place. I could lock it up so no one could mess with my stuff."

"And what kind of stuff did you keep there?"

"Well at first I had some comic books and, uh, some skin magazines. Later I picked up an old computer and hooked it up to a battery backup that I'd carry back and forth. It had enough power for me to use the computer for 20 minutes before it ran out of juice."

"So did you play on the computer that day?"

"No."

"What did you do?"

"I put together stuff for my plan."

"What stuff would that be?"

"I don't want to say."

"Why not?"

"It'll get me in trouble."

"Mr. Beers, you are not the one in trouble. My client is. Would you please look at Mr. Mangorian and tell me whether he should be going to jail for allegedly assaulting you?"

"He didn't assault me. He helped me."

"Helped you?"

"Yes, it must have been him. I had it in my mind that the next day I was going to carry out my plan. But after the police left that night, I just didn't want to do the plan any more, and today, I can hardly believe that I ever did."

"What was the plan?"

"I'll get in trouble," Beers says, no longer able to look me in the eyes.

"I assure you the trouble will be small, if at all."

Beers gives a woeful look to the judge and the judge nods to him.

"Okay, you have to remember I was really, really pissed off. All this crap from my first day in high school and it never, ever stopped. Nobody, no student, no teacher, nobody would help me. I hated everyone and I just want to get even. I wanted to show everyone that I am a person."

"Go on," I say.

"About a year before that day, my uncle Phil died in a car accident. My dad wanted me to help clean out the house. Because I was skipping school pretty regularly to get away from the bullying, I had lots of time by myself in the house. It was nicer than the stockade. I could watch TV. I could play music really loud. I was boxing up stuff in the attic when I found a long wooden box that had a couple smaller boxes in it and two heavy things that were rolled up in an old canvas drop sheet.

"I opened the boxes first and found they were both filled with bullets. The smaller box was plain brown but had 9mm marked on it so I guess that meant these were 9 mm bullets. There were 10 rows of 10 bullets, so 100 bullets in total. The larger box had a Remington logo and was marked .223. The bullets weren't in rows just a pile in the box. It said 200 on the box. I counted them and there were 182 bullets left. I picked up the big thing in the canvas. It was really heavy and because I had already opened the bullets, I guessed right that it was a rifle. The smaller package was also pretty heavy and there was a sort of a long pistol in it. Later when I Googled images of guns, I found that what I had were a 9MM Semi Automatic MAC-9 pistol with a 30-bullet clip and an AR-15 fully automatic .223-caliber rifle with a 40-round clip. I also found out that the AR-15 was the first design for what would become the M-16. I knew I had one hell of a weapon."

Beers pauses to breathe deeply but no one else in the courtroom, lawyers, the judge, spectators, jury or me draws a breath.

"I put the two guns and the ammo into an old hockey bag and I took them to my room in the stockade. I just left them there until that day, you know, June 6. I was really pissed at what happened to me so I unwrapped the two guns and practised firing them without any ammo in them. From my reading on the Internet I knew that guns have a safety. I looked for the safetys for both the Mac-9 and the AR-15 and practised switching them on and off. I figured the biggest challenge would be to hold the guns steady because of the recoil and because they weighed so much, especially after I put the ammo in them. I had it in mind to put the MAC-9 in my book bag slung over my neck and shoulder and go initially with the AR-15 because I could fire off the entire 40-round clip with a single squeeze of the trigger."

Beers pauses a moment, closes his eyes, and starts describing what seems to be a detailed picture he designed in his mind.

"I'd need to find a big crowd of people, like in the cafeteria at lunch, because my aim wasn't going to be too good. I thought the cafeteria would be a good place to start the killing, a good place for revenge. I loaded both guns and then left the remaining bullets in the boxes and put them into my book bag.

"The next day was Friday. I'd let dad take me to school but instead of going in, I would go to the stockade. Just before first lunch I would carry the hockey bag to school and hole up in a washroom stall. I would sling the book bag over my shoulder, check the guns one last time, and head to the cafeteria. It was a Friday. I thought it would be great ruining the weekend for all the pricks I didn't get to kill."

Beers stops speaking and there is a long silence as everyone in the courtroom slowly processes the gravity of his words.

I break the silence. "But you didn't carry out your plan."

"No. I intended to do it the next day, but the stuff you talked about happened to me that night and, afterward, I couldn't imagine ever doing it. In fact, the next day, the day I was going to carry out my plan, I put a big hammer in my book bag and when I got to the stockade, I used the hammer to smash the AR-15 and the Mac-9 to pieces."

"And you say Mr. Mangorian stopped you from carrying out the plan?"

"I don't remember it, but it must have been him. I look at him and I just know it was him."

I turn to Beers and say, "Thank you. It was very, very brave of you to give this testimony."

I turn to the judge and say, the defence has finished with this witness.

Patullo has thunder in her face. She confers with her three colleagues and after a minute says to the judge, "We have no questions for this witness."

"This has been quite the day in court. Perhaps one of the most astonishing days I've ever had as a judge," Justice McGregor says. "The defence will continue its case tomorrow at 10 a.m."

As much media hype and craziness over the Mangorian trial as there had been to this point, things now go stratospheric. The school board shuts down Wilton Road High School and orders anti-bullying sessions for all teachers and students. My Twitter feed goes crazy as the trial garners the top headlines in Italy, Serbia, Thailand, Argentina, India, Australia and every part between.

Mayor Mercury arrives breathlessly at the courtroom before Patullo and I have packed up our bags. "We need to hold another news conference today. Everyone's going crazy. We can use this to really put Toronto on the map."

Patullo offers a terse: "Not interested."

I add, "The lady speaks for both of us."

She gives me a nod of courtesy as we each plot our strategy to escape the throng of reporters.

That night, I ask Jerry if he has any last thoughts.

"We've played our hand perfectly. It is what it is," Jerry says. "It depends on whether the jurors are sticklers for process and rules or they have enough gumption to make a decision on their own. It only takes one juror to think on his own to stall everything and overturn the prosecution's case."

"Personally, I think the jury won't take an hour to acquit. After Beers' testimony today, there wasn't a person in the audience who would convict Mangorian," says Regina. "After the media has anointed Mangorian as the saviour of a school full of kids, not the would-be murderer of nine people, the charges look pretty lame. The jury would feel like Pontius Pilate, if they convicted him now. I don't think anybody's up for that."

"Ah, the views of youth," I say. "Once you've logged as many hours as I have with juries you know the one certain thing about a jury ruling is, that there is no certain thing about a jury ruling."

"Besides," says Jerry, "The real test is going to be when we put Mangorian on the stand. He has to persuade the jury that he is no murderer and he has to provide the motive for why he took blood from all these people and why it appears it helped all of them."

"First things first. We still have to get Dr. Ostrander's testimony in. He is the link establishing that Dragul is human, a different type of human but a human all the same. Patullo may not go there, but there are grounds, slim grounds, that if Dragul doesn't fit the criteria of being a human being that he may not be able to benefit from man's laws."

"She wouldn't dare," says Theresa. "The media would go mad."

"I don't think she gives a hoot about the media. Her case has taken a hell of a hit and she's just determined and ruthless enough to play that card. Let's just close that door so she can't go there," I say.

CHAPTER NINETEEN

TRIAL, DAY 11

Wednesday, October 29, 2014

At 9:55 a.m., the courtroom buzzes loudly as I walk in flanked by Jerry and Regina. Patullo and her team are already seated and they collectively glare at us as we take our seats.

The court clerk announces the arrival of Justice McGregor and we all rise until he's seated.

"Are you ready to proceed Mr. Hamblyn?"

"Yes I am Your Honour. For my first witness I call on Dr. Felix Ostrander."

A thin, grey-haired, grey-bearded man in a tweed jacket with large suede patches at the elbows ambles up to the witness stand and places his hand on a proffered Bible and swears to be truthful.

I step forward and ask, "Dr. Ostrander you are a professor at Trent University, are you not?"

"Yes I am."

"Can you tell us what your specialty is and how your skills interrelate with this case?"

"I am someone who has the long-winded title of paleoanthropologist. My field combines the disciplines of paleontology and physical anthropology in the study of ancient humans. We look for fossils and footprints of hominids, that's ancient humans, to reconstruct what they were like and what their lives were like."

"I have spent 20 years studying the evolution of man and his culture this way and put much of it in my book published in 2002 called, Mirror on Man. It wasn't much of a best-seller but it covers some of what you're dealing with in this case, if I'm not mistaken."

"Can you elaborate on what relates to this case?"

"In the book, I theorize about extinct subsets of humankind such as Homo Sapiens Idaltu and other subsets of humanity that didn't quite make it the way we Homo Sapiens did."

"These hominids you speak of, are they our ancestors?"

"Yes, they are. A good number of those human subsets are directly related to us and many in our population carry remnants of their DNA. For instance, I was able to sequence Mr. Mangorian's DNA and compared it with our DNA. The comparison shows Sapiens and Sanguinus mated with each other's ancestors and the proof shows up in the DNA of populations in North and South America, the Pacific Islands and East Asians. So the answer yes means there's a bit of Sanguinus in a large part of us and much of us in Mr. Mangorian's DNA.

"This is not so surprising because research by some of my esteemed colleagues shows that we Homo Sapiens lived together with the Neanderthals, Denisovans and many other Homo subsets in a sort of Lord of the Rings world with many different hominid species living and mating side by side. The Sanguinus is, obviously, one such species."

"Quite a colourful description."

"Colourful but not mine. I believe Mark Thomas, an evolutionary geneticist at University College, London came up with the phrase and the theory."

"So the important question before the court is this. In your expert opinion professor, is Mr. Mangorian a human being and therefore entitled to the protection of our laws?"

"Yes and yes," says Dr. Ostrander and then continues with a long technical description comparing Mangorian's DNA to other species and to humans.

"Mr. Mangorian's DNA is closer than anything we've seen. Neanderthals were 99.3 per cent similar to modern humans and the samples from Mr. Mangorian show his DNA is 99.7 per cent the same as what we consider to be human. So, Mr. Mangorian is substantially a human being, but a more appropriate question is whether he is a sentient being. The answer to that is definitely a yes."

"Thank you, Dr. Ostrander. That ends my questioning of the witness."

Patullo stands and says, "I have no questions for Dr. Ostrander."

"A wise move on her part," Regina whispers in my ear. "The jury is beginning to dislike her. Attempts to make Mangorian a non-human, especially after he saved those school kids' lives, would just make her the villain."

I stand up and address the judge: "Your Honour, my next witness is the accused, Dragul Mangorian. Perhaps it would serve everyone if we adjourned now and started fresh in the morning."

"I agree," says Justice McGregor. "Court will resume tomorrow at 10 a.m."

Tomorrow is the day that the media has been waiting for. The chance to hear evidence directly from the lips of Dragul Mangorian. Media numbers that had peaked at 5,000 and then dropped into the hundreds roar back into the thousands. It seems Mangorian has created a new industry and everyone is trying to cash in.

Mayor Mercury has left 15 messages for me, none of which I'll answer.

A dullish anthropological treatise on hominid sub-species largely ignored when it first aired on the Discovery Channel two years ago, gets a general redusting with the addition of a section on Homo Sanguinus for its airing tonight. More than five million viewers will tune in.

e-NEWS, normally the purveyor of Hollywood gossip and flogger of celebrity fashion trends, sets aside tonight's entire program for celebrity takes on: who might play Mangorian in a rumoured made-for-TV movie; Dragul-inspired fashions; and the best party-bars for watching Mangorian's testimony live.

The streets are filled with Mangorian followers who, via Twitter, are organizing a 'Vamp Walk,' starting at the courthouse and ending at the Canadian National Exhibition grounds. There's a final blowout concert on the GothFest Stage featuring newly renamed rock/metal bands Mummy Mia, the Zom-Bees, and Fang-Dangle.

"We have a half-million followers for @vamptrial and I'm predicting at least 20,000 people show for the Vamp Walk," says event organizer Melissa Smedhurst, giving the cameras a double peace sign, the salute signifying membership among Mangorian's minions.

CHAPTER TWENTY

TRIAL, DAY 12

Thursday, October 30, 2014

As the saying goes: The moment everyone has been waiting for has arrived.

"The defence calls Dragul Mangorian to the stand," I say. The thought comes to mind that my statement was pretty flat. I should have said it in company with a trumpet flourish.

An audible gasp escapes the crowd as Mangorian stretches to his full 6-foot, 6 height and strides majestically, despite the shackles, to the witness box. Although he's been cleaned up and is wearing a designer suit, by Petrocelli of course, Mangorian's paper-white skin, piercing alligator eyes, inch-long fingernails with chiseled points, and canines that protrude a half-inch below his lower lip create quite a spectacle.

"Mr. Mangorian can you tell me about yourself and your species, the Sanguinus," I ask.

"Mr. Hamblyn, let's not beat about the bush. People don't use the term Sanguinus when they refer to me. They call me a vampire so we might as well stick to what the people want rather than trying to be politically correct."

"I'm not sure that's in your best interests . . . "

"Mr. Hamblyn if you have an issue with your client, this is neither the time nor the place to have this discussion," says Justice McGregor. "The accused has made a statement under oath and you cannot try to persuade him to alter it. Resume your examination accordingly."

The judge is right, of course, and I expected the spanking. It was, however, a nice ploy to show Mangorian opening up beyond what a controlling lawyer wanted from him. So, he begins.

"People view the Sanguinus and vampires as being synonymous. As long as I refuse to use the 'V' word, that misunderstanding continues to perpetuate ridiculous myths. My belief is, if I use the term vampire, I can redefine what people think of vampires and, therefore, the Sanguinus. Ask me all of the questions you can think of, even some of the silly ones," Mangorian says.

"Okay, let's give it a go. So what are the differences between Sanguinus and the popularized version of vampires?" I say.

"Most of what the public thinks it knows about the Sanguinus is rubbish. We are not glamorous, wealthy aristocrats who travel the world preying on hapless humans.

"Most live lives of hardship, poverty, and starvation. Life is so hard that I believe I may be the last of my kind. True, vampires, if we want to use that term, live longer than humans. We live a rather youthful life until age 80 and move into adulthood. We are middle aged from 150 to 200 and then weaken and begin to age and die at about the same rate as a human when we near 250 years. Once a Sanguinus is about 300, he is not strong enough to feed and wastes away. Human blood resources regardless of what people think, are not that easy to get."

"Besides drinking human blood, do you exhibit any of the traits that we associate with vampires in the movies?"

"We have an extreme reaction to sunlight because of the millennia spent underground. We lost the melanin and other pigments necessary to block ultraviolet light. The effect is quite dramatic and immediate, but we do not burst into flames as in your lore. It is uncomfortable to the extreme and possibly deadly if one of us is stranded unprotected under a hot sun all day. The same exposure would be extremely uncomfortable for a human.

"The whole vampires and religion thing is baffling," Mangorian goes on. "As for us shunning a crucifix, holy water, Star of David or any other religious symbol or artifact, it's just nonsense. Some of my kind were Christians and Buddhists and followers of Islam and Judaism. They sought peace and sometimes they found acceptance among certain human religious covens and sects," Mangorian says, pausing for me to get in my next question.

"In terms of your mortality, Bram Stoker's Dracula tale describes destroying the vampire with a stake through the heart," I say.

"Yes, that would certainly do it, as would a bullet to the brain, a severe loss of blood, or any other trauma that would kill a human being. We are, however, amazingly resilient to human diseases such as cancer, pneumonia, malaria. I suspect we don't contract HIV. It's too new to be sure but, with all the blood I've consumed in the past 10 years, surely one of my donors would have contracted the disease and I'm none the worse for it. We do have our own diseases that humans do not get, for example, a type of virus that causes fever and death."

"How old are you?"

"I was born in 1807 in the area you now call the Ottawa Valley in Ontario Canada."

"Then you are Canadian."

"Not exactly. I am of the Sanguinus Nation, truly a First Nation. The Sanguinus do not recognize your governments because our colonies pre-date all of your countries."

I then look to the jury and say, "The next several questions relate to reports mostly in the tabloid press and TV equivalents but they are beginning to seep into the mainstream media. Mr. Mangorian I beg your forgiveness for asking these questions in the interest of setting the record straight."

"I am happy to comply," Mangorian says.

"Can you turn into a bat, a wolf or smoke?"

"Only tomorrow night . . . Halloween, if I have a costume," Mangorian says as giggles course through the courtroom only to be stared down by an unsmiling Justice McGregor.

Mangorian resumes: "I can no more do that than any member of the jury. Given the horrible life I've had over the past 10 years, I would have loved to be able to turn into a poodle and be able to sleep in a nice warm house."

More giggles.

"Are you stronger and faster than most of us Sapiens?" I ask.

"Yes, I believe so. I've never done any scientific testing but whenever I was pursued by Sapiens, I had no problem getting away on foot. As for strength, the few times that I've had physical encounters with even large men, I was able to out-wrestle them even two at a time."

"Did you commit the crimes you are charged with – physically assaulting and harming nine people, sexual assault on the six women, prowling by night and resisting arrest?"

"I deny that I sexually assaulted any of those women. I had their permission to touch them. I had their permission to disturb their clothing to take their blood. Perhaps, I did resist arrest, but my experience has taught me never to trust Sapiens, especially Sapiens carrying weapons. As for the other charges, I had permission for everything else. Permission from my donors to take their blood and be on their premises. As for causing bodily harm, I do not believe that what was given to me was much of a price for what all nine of these individuals received from me in return. All nine of them are at peace with themselves and lead much happier, productive lives."

"Is it fair to characterize this as a transaction," I ask, "literally payment in blood for services rendered?"

"That's a very harsh way of putting it. I do need the blood to sustain myself but it is also necessary for me to be at peak power to be able to furnish 'my services', as you call it, to the best of my ability."

"In other words, you need the blood to provide peace of mind for your friends. Without the blood, your ability to help them would be less effective."

"That is so."

"Thank you Mr. Mangorian. Those are all the questions I have for you."

Prosecutor Patullo has her game face firmly on and walks purposefully up to the witness stand.

"Did you, or did you not, take blood from all nine of the people you are charged with assaulting?"

"Yes, I have testified to that but . . ."

She cuts him off mid-sentence. "I just want a yes or no answer and I got it."

"Do you have any signed documents or other evidence that supports your claim that you had the victims' permission to take their blood and to be in their homes?"

"No, I just have their word."

"And none of the victims can remember giving their word."

"My donors do not remember. That's what I've been told."

"How convenient."

"But they did say they . . ."

"I did not ask for elaboration," she says holding up a hand again to cut off his words.

"So you admit you took blood from all of the victims."

"Donors. I took blood from my friends who willingly gave it to me."

"If that was the case, why then did you run away? Why didn't you stay put? You and your friends could explain the situation to police when they arrived? Why did police have to hunt you down in the sewers?"

"The history of my people suggests I could expect a less than benevolent and understanding reception from authorities. Whenever we revealed ourselves to man, we were systematically butchered."

"And your defence of this is . . . that it is you who are the victim. Is this really what you are claiming?"

"Yes. I am a victim of humanity and so were all of my kind."

"When the police found you in the sewers, you attacked them."

"I was defending myself. I felt my life was in danger."

"Have you ever killed anyone?"

"Objection. Your Honour, the accused is not charged with murder. If the prosecution has further charges to lay, we'd like to hear them. Until that time, the prosecution should refrain from any hint of wrong-doing outside of the current charges."

"I agree. The objection is sustained," Justice McGregor says sternly. "If the prosecution mentions or even implies that the accused has committed additional crimes, you will answer directly to me. That question was completely out of line."

"I apologize your Honour."

"Resume your cross-examination but be careful."

Patullo nods to the judge, pauses to collect her thoughts, and then says, "Mr. Mangorian, you say you have lived for more than 200 years and that your diet has consisted of mostly human blood."

"That is correct."

"How many people would you say you have received blood from?"

"Thousands. I don't know the exact number."

"And of all those thousands was every one of them a willing donor?"

"Objection . . . Your Honour."

"Ms Patullo, that's it. No more probing in that area. You must stick to the list of persons that the accused is charged with harming. You are very close to being held in contempt."

Jerry gives me a knowing look. Patullo knows that the judge would never let her raise this line of questioning but her purpose wasn't to go there so much as placing a little worm in the mind of each of the jurors. 'Could every one of those thousands of people who Mangorian took blood from, day after day, month after month, over 200 years have been a willing donor?'

Every vampire book, every Dracula movie, every blood sucker film and television series would play in their minds and with the rarest exception the scenes reeling through their heads would scream out violence, gore, murder.

Patullo continues her cross-examination.

"You testified that the Sanguinus have been persecuted, hunted down and killed by Sapiens for as many as 30,000 years.

"Yes I did."

"Yes, your history, your people. I have a question about that. You claim you are 200 years old but speak of things that happened 10,000 and even 30,000 years ago. With all the historical data we've collected, all the science and scholars we have available, none of my people or Sapiens as you call them, none of our historians and anthropologists with all of their sophisticated equipment can provide close to the kind of detail you profess to know. How do we know you aren't just making up the whole thing?"

For an instant, there's a flicker in those yellow-eyes. Regina grasps my hand. We've seen this before. We know that if Dragul goes Sanguinus on us now, and the jury sees it, our whole case could unravel. But the flicker doesn't repeat itself.

Mangorian is composed enough to reply: "I don't think I made up the fact that students and teachers are happy and safe at Wilton Road High School today."

Patullo flushes a deep red.

"My ability and that of my kind to pass imagery to others is an effective tool to pass on our history directly and accurately. Let me touch you and you will understand."

"You would like that wouldn't you? I am not about to subject myself to your hypnotism or whatever you call it."

"Objection, your Honour. The Crown is not on the stand giving evidence. Her outburst is inappropriate," I say.

"Sustained. Ms Patullo, you will stick to a direct line of inquiry and not add your personal comments."

She nods to the judge and then continues.

"Mr. Mangorian, you claim that all of your victims willingly offered to give you blood."

"Yes, that is true."

"Yet in many instances we see signs of struggle where the marks on the victims' necks were horrendous wounds and their clothing has been ripped away. If all you wanted was their blood, why not take a transfusion from them or extract blood with a needle?"

"And why do you not take your food in pill form or from freeze-dried packets like your astronauts do? Fresh blood to me is like fresh food to you."

"And the torn clothing? Does that demonstrate willingness on the part of your victims?"

"A willing donor with fresh, warm blood is exciting, almost intoxicating to me. It is so delicious, so rare, so exquisite. I confess sometimes I am overwhelmed, overly eager. And yes, on those occasions in my zeal, clothing may get torn. I'm certain that nothing like that has ever happened to any of you when you are in the heat of love making."

Snickers break out across the courtroom.

"Are you saying that you were making love to your victims?"

"I am using a metaphor to describe what I go through, how thrilling and empowering it is when someone willingly gives their blood to me. But in some respects, while not love-making, there is a deep, sensuous connection, an exchange of fluids, an aftermath of extreme serenity, and for me, a form of rebirth . . ."

Dragul's description strikes an emotional chord with the younger women in the courtroom, especially double-eyeliner lady, who might have swooned if Patullo hadn't jumped in.

"And what if, during this heat of passion, your victim changed her mind?"

"That never happens."

"Never? You are sinking your fangs into your victims and draining their blood and they never, ever say stop?"

"They never say stop, but I do stop myself before I take too much blood."

"And we are assured of this because?"

"Because your own witnesses testified that I took no more than two pints of blood from any one person, so their recovery would be swift and complete."

"All this control while you are in the throes of ecstasy?"

"Yes, I do exercise control over myself."

"But you would like to continue . . . continue the ecstasy?"

"But I don't."

"So you say. Your Honour. I have finished cross-examining this witness."

"Mr. Hamblyn do you have anything to add, any additional witnesses?" says Justice McGregor.

"No Your Honour."

"Mr. Mangorian, you may step down. Court will resume tomorrow."

We all rise for Justice McGregor's exit. As the prosecution team and the rest of the courtroom clears, Jerry slaps me on the back.

"One hell of a job you did."

"One hell of a job WE did," I say to him and Regina.

We retreat to O'Reilly's Ale House – 62 beers on tap – and wash down cheeseburgers and fries with many pints of Guinness sent our way by the crush of fellow patrons who give the two-handed 'V' salute, forever erasing the memory of Richard Nixon's swan song gesture. The double 'V' is now synonymous everywhere for Mangorian's acquittal, literally 'Vampire Victory'.

CHAPTER TWENTY-ONE

FINAL STATEMENTS

Friday, October 31, 2014

For her closing remarks, Alicia Patullo takes to the floor first facing the jury with all the dignity and confidence of a general addressing her troops: "You've heard some amazing stories in this courtroom: a man who has lived more than 200 years; a secret branch of humanity that has hidden from mankind for tens of thousands of years; miraculous cures. But I want to remind you that all you've heard from the defence is stories. None of it is backed by direct, hard evidence. It is full of opinion, theories, people's feelings, things people may or may not have done because they feel certain things may or may not have been done to them. In short, the defence's case fails because it fails the burden of proof. There is no evidence that exonerates Mr. Mangorian. However, the prosecution's case is backed by indisputable hard evidence. We have fingerprints – unique fingerprints possessed by no other person on Earth, and DNA that is distinct from anyone else, not just because it differs as it does from one human being to the next but because it is not quite human, at least human in the sense that we think of it.

"The defence will make great noises about there being no one to testify that they actually saw Mr. Mangorian commit these crimes. But the esteemed defence will then leap to the other side and argue that Mr. Mangorian did take blood from all nine individuals named as victims, but he did so only as a favour, as an act of generosity, as an act of kindness to create a link with them and heal their psychological wounds. And the defence will further argue that this was done, and only done, after the victims granted the accused permission to take their blood.

"To this I say, hogwash. There is not a shred, not a scintilla of verifiable evidence that corroborates Mr. Mangorian's story. Ladies and gentlemen, he took their blood because he wanted to, just as a rapist rapes because he wants to. Do not buy the argument that Mr. Mangorian needed fresh human blood to survive. From his own lips he described that his people were forced to live on only the liquid insides of bugs and moles and not just for a few months but for thousands of years. It was not their preferred food but obviously they can survive on things other than fresh human blood. Who among us has not lived a lesser life than we desired? But is this any justification for assaulting a person who has committed no wrong other than by being human?

"This man, or whatever he is, cannot be trusted. Dr. Chen testified that the accused did not respond to scenes of torture and death as normal people would. She described the accused as being a psychopath, willing to say and do whatever it takes to get what he wants and damn the consequences for anybody else.

"The accused testified that he caused the large wounds on the necks of his victims and tore their clothing because fresh, warm blood sends him into the throes of ecstasy. He further says that while in this state of ecstasy he maintains full control, drinks only the amount of blood that his victim can provide without suffering any long-lasting health impacts. I've heard remarks like that hundreds of times from drunk drivers who say they can control their drinking, and from drug addicts who say they can stop whenever they want.

"But you and I know, this is not true. When someone is in the throes of ecstasy, as the accused claims, who among us has the power to stop each and every time? The accused may not be responsible for any of the thousands of people who disappear every year, but who is to say that he may not slip up some time in the future, allow himself to be overwhelmed for 10, 20, 30 more seconds, until his victim is drained? Ecstacy is, by definition, a form of trance.

"I have one more thing for you, the members of this jury, to think about. Whether or not the victims gave their permission is irrelevant. We charge men for battering their wives whether the wives agree to the charges or not. To secure a conviction, all we need is the evidence of an assault. You have seen the evidence, and it is indisputable. The accused committed nine assaults."

Patullo then ends her remarks with the following impassioned plea.

"Mangorian is not human, certainly not human as you and I know it. He is also a psychopath. He has powers and strength beyond those of a human being. Bring all of those elements together and you have a terrible threat to society. You have all of the evidence you need to bring back a guilty verdict.

The question you have to ask yourself is this: How will you feel if the accused is acquitted and his next victim is someone close to you, a mother, father, brother, sister, or child? You have the power to ensure this doesn't happen. You have the power," she says. Head hanging down, she walks slowly to her seat.

Not bad, I think to myself. Patullo has hit all of the highlights and hammered them home in terms of a straight interpretation of the law. But that's why we have juries. I'm counting on the jurors seeing past the law. Jerry gives me a nudge of encouragement and then a wink.

"Ladies and gentlemen of the jury, you have heard much about this trial and my client, Mr. Mangorian. You have agreed to serve on this jury with an open mind and to base your decision solely on the facts. I urge you to do just that.

"I want to say at the outset, I agree with the position the Crown has taken about the burden of proof. Yes, the prosecution has proved beyond a reasonable doubt and, by my client's own admission, that he took the blood of the nine so-called victims.

"However, my question is this: Even if the Crown is 100 per cent correct and Mr. Mangorian did take blood from the nine alleged victims, is that grounds for charges of attempted murder?

"Let me answer that question with cold, hard indisputable facts – real evidence – as the Crown Attorney puts it. Number one. The wounds on every single one of the alleged victims had scabbed over preventing further blood loss and presumably death. Constable Dwijendra Gupta of the Toronto Police Forensic Investigation Service testified that wounds of that size to an artery are difficult to close, and the likely result from such an attack would be fatal blood loss.

"The amount of blood taken from each of the so-called victims was less than two pints, a quantity that the forensic expert testified would not endanger an individual's health or life. After nine such cases, I would suggest that the amount – two pints – was no accident. It was a predetermined amount so that Mr. Mangorian could take what he needed to survive with the assurance that his donors would recover fully and quickly.

"So I put it to you, ladies and gentlemen of the jury, is this the picture of someone driven through psychopathy, taking what he wants and damn the consequences for anybody else? Is this someone who attempted to murder these nine people? I think not, and I believe when you think about it, you will agree with my conclusion.

"On the charges of assault causing bodily harm, the prosecutor has developed a very narrow definition of the law. Assault causing bodily harm happens when a person is assaulted and suffers a physical injury. Did Mr. Mangorian take blood from these people and, in doing so, did he harm them in any way? The Crown says yes.

"Mr. Mangorian left large bite marks on the neck of all nine people when he drew out blood. This constitutes assault causing bodily harm in Ms Patullo's mind.

"The question is whether the marks truly constitute assault causing bodily harm. It cannot be the marks alone otherwise all of our surgeons would be in jail for cutting into their patients. The question then is, 'What's the difference.' I would suggest the difference is consent. If you consent to allow a surgeon to cut into you, there is no crime if the surgeon honourably executes his craft. If a person is accosted on the street and struck in the face, that is assault and, if in the process, he received a bloody nose, that's assault causing bodily harm. However, there are many instances where a man can punch another man in the face and no crime has been committed.

"That case is the willing participation of two people to fight each other on the streets or in a professional boxing ring. The two street thugs may be arrested for other reasons such as causing a disturbance but assault causing bodily harm isn't one of them.

"You have heard Mr. Mangorian tell you that he obtained the consent of all nine people he is accused of assaulting. Not one of the nine remembers giving their consent but all nine remember nothing at all about the incident. Seven of the nine feel warmth, even friendship toward Mr. Mangorian. Young Mr. Beers testified he felt grateful to Mr. Mangorian and, if asked, would be willing to give blood to Mr. Mangorian.

"Yes, feelings, but here are the facts. All nine were damaged, severely damaged in some cases. All nine were vastly improved, psychologically, after they found the wounds, which Mr. Mangorian says he caused and all of the so-called victims believe he caused. It stands to reason that if the wounds are clearly Mangorian's in the second incident, the earlier wounds are his, too.

"The fact is, attempted suicide and addiction are very traumatic in and of themselves. They are very difficult for people to get over. You heard the testimony of psychologist Dr. Gregor Amos that rarely do people who have attempted suicide get over it quickly and certainly not without considerable professional support.

"Yet we have nine people – nine people – all of whom have had issues and yet all nine for all intents and purposes are whole again. They aren't troubled by their demons. They don't dwell on the past where they might have gone wrong. They move ahead.

"The question is how? The prosecution tells us it is a coincidence. If so, it would be the coincidence for all time to have happened to all nine alleged victims. Isn't it more likely that Mr. Mangorian cured these people? And if, indeed, he has cured these people, has his role been more like that of a surgeon who does small harm in cutting open a patient to perform the greater good to remove a tumour or, in this case, remove the psychological illness besetting them?"

"As Ms Patullo told you, as members of this jury, you have the power. You have the power to convict, based on a strict interpretation of the law, as the prosecutor would have you do, an interpretation that even the majority of the alleged victims disagree with. Or you have the power to ensure that not only is justice done, but is seen to be done. Mr. Mangorian, as you have seen, is a being capable of immense good. You should . . . No, you must set him free."

I stare at all of the jurors, one by one to ensure my words have had time to sink in. Then I walk to my chair and sit down.

Justice McGregor addresses the jury: "You have been asked to sit in judgment of Dragul Mangorian on a wide range of charges related to the alleged attempted murder and assaults on six women and three men. The facts of the case are clear and not disputed by either the Crown or the defence. The central matter for you to decide and, truly, what will determine your verdict on the most serious charges is whether the accused did or did not commit the criminal acts he is charged with. In making this decision, you must weigh all of the evidence and decide whether or not, in your opinion, the accused did have or did not have the permission of the persons whose injuries are at the root of the charges. Further, if he did have their permission to injure, was this harm an acceptable harm given any benefit the accused's lawyer argues that his client provided to the victims. If you determine he did not have permission, he has committed a criminal act, your finding will be guilty, and he will be sentenced accordingly. If you determine he did have permission and the harm was an acceptable tradeoff, he has committed no criminal offence and will be released. You will now be taken to the jury room to begin your deliberations.

I can't read seven of the jurors at all. A retired teacher and a woman my team has dubbed, "the church lady" look like they're in a hanging mood. I stare at the physics prof and the engineer as they file out, and see their logical brains whirring. The one, I feel will fight for an acquittal, is double-eyeliner gal. Don't fail me now. "Oh Maybelline, please do what I need you to do," I sing to myself.

CHAPTER TWENTY-TWO

THE VERDICT

Jury sequestered for verdict – Friday, October 31, 2014, 4:30 p.m.

"It's all over except the waiting," says Jerry. "First round at O'Reilly's on me."

Jerry, Regina and I walk out of the courthouse, right into a thousand video and still cameras winking at us like we're centre stage at a cyclops convention.

"How do you think it will go?" asks a reporter with an English accent holding a BBC tagged microphone.

"Is Mangorian nervous?" a voice from the second row booms in broadcast baritone.

"If he gets life, could he spend 100 years in prison?"

I can't begin to answer their questions, but Regina comes up with the perfect, made-for-TV, response by raising two arms in the air with her fingers forming 'V's. Jerry and I follow suit and the crowd of reporters part to record the spectacle of the three of us marching defiantly, giving our best Tricky Dicky impressions.

§§§

"Who's Tricky Dicky?" asks Theresa Davis who joins us at O'Reillys for beers and burgers.

"Long story that leads to a longer story. Basically, Richard Nixon, 37th president of the United States, impeached for a cover-up and forced to leave the presidency. Google it," says Jerry.

"Whoa. 37th president of the United States. Only a former law theory professor would be able deliver that one off the cuff," I say.

"Not one to show off but – Lyndon Johnson 36th president, Gerald Ford 38th, Jimmy Carter Number 39, Ronald Reagan 40th."

"Okay smart ass – Lincoln," I say.

"16th."

"McKinley," says Regina.

"25th."

"FDR," says Theresa.

"32nd."

"Okay, we give up even though I suspect you're just making it up."

"Of course, after all I am a lawyer," Jerry says and we all crack up.

The four of us are celebrities in O'Reilly's but two unwritten codes protect us from reporter interviews and being mobbed by general patrons. Since the demise of the Toronto Press Club, O'Reilly's is the unofficial haunt of current and former newsmen. The code of all press clubs, long pre-dating the Las Vegas commercial, is, 'What goes on in the club, stays in the club.' The second code invokes the stoic nature of an Irish pub. Patrons take their drinking and darts as seriously as a heart attack. You don't disturb a man with a glass or dart in his hand.

Another round of Guinness arrives at our table, compliments of a big table of people giving us the double 'V' and sporting 'Vampire Victory' ball caps and badges.

"Boy somebody's making a fortune off Dragul," says Regina.

"You mean more than the Guinness Brewery?" I say and we all laugh until we're in tears.

Then my phone rings.

"Hi, Mr. Hamblyn?"

"Yes."

"It's Denny MacDonald from Muldoon-MacDonald. Just wanted to double-check our plans for the TT if there's a verdict tonight."

"No problem. Got it. The TT. I have you on speed dial."

"What's that about and what's TT?" Theresa asks.

"Toronto Triomphe. The city's only six star hotel. They're throwing us a party if . . . when the jury acquits Mangorian."

"Man, I love this case," says Theresa.

After the second round, we start passing the Guinness to the surrounding tables. We need to keep somewhat sharp if the jury comes back tonight, which is doubtful.

One of the patrons, with a voice the crowd agrees is, 'not half-bad,' and a guitar that, 'can play a tune,' is coerced to perform Song of the Mira after the crowd showed enthusiastic appreciation for his rendition of Danny Boy.

Around the third chorus, my phone rings again.

"Mr. Hamblyn, the jury's coming back."

I look at my watch. It's 7:43 p.m. The jury was out just three hours, including their dinner break.

"Hey guys, we're on," I say grabbing my jacket.

"Regina, call MacDonald. Tell him to get ready. TT's a go for 9:30."

Regina, Jerry and I file into the courtroom where we meet Mangorian who is still in chains. Patullo's grim-faced team is already in place.

Next, 12 men and women enter through a door at the back of the jury box and take their seats.

"Everyone rise. This court is now in session, Ontario Supreme Court Justice M. R. McGregor presiding."

Justice McGregor seats himself, makes a few scribbles on a piece of paper, and then addresses the jury. He asks whether they have reached a unanimous verdict and they respond that they have.

The jury foreman hands a sheet of paper to the bailiff who carries it to the judge.

Justice McGregor looks at Mangorian and says, "Will the prisoner please stand."

Mangorian complies.

"Mr. Foreman, on the first set of charges, nine counts of attempted murder, how do you find?"

"We find the accused, not guilty."

Regina grips my hand.

Nothing surprising there, I think. In Patullo's wildest imaginings she couldn't possibly have believed the attempted murder charges would stick.

"On the second set of charges, nine counts of assault causing bodily harm, how do you find?"

"We find the accused, not guilty."

The courtroom explodes with screams of delight. Regina is squeezing my hand so hard, it's beginning to hurt.

"Order, order. We still have business to complete," says Justice McGregor, banging his gavel repeatedly.

"Now Mr. Foreman, how do you find on the six charges of sexual assault?"

"We find the accused, not guilty."

No shock this time. If there was no assault there couldn't be sexual assault. Ah, Regina's grip is beginning to slacken. I can feel my fingers again.

"On the charges of criminal prowl by night, how do you find?"

"We find the accused, not guilty."

"On the charge of vagrancy?"

"We find the accused, not guilty."

"On the charge of resisting arrest, how do you find?"

"We find the accused guilty."

"Mr. Mangorian, the jury has found you not guilty on all charges save one count of resisting arrest. On that single charge, I sentence you to time served. You are free to go. Bailiff, release the prisoner."

The court erupts into thunderous applause as reporters head out the door clutching at their cell phones. The tumult drowns out the sound of the heavy shackles hitting the floor as Dragul tastes freedom for the first time in more than a year.

When Dragul, Jerry, Regina, and I leave the courtroom, we can scarcely move through the media phalanx with all questions and camera lights directed at Mangorian.

"What are your plans?"

"Where are you going to live?"

"Are you hungry?"

That last question hits us oddly, and we start to laugh, even Dragul.

His deep, strange, inhuman laugh – something my team is used to – catches everyone else by surprise and they back off, a step or two.

That gives me an opportunity to take control back. I nod to Regina. At five-foot, 2 and cute as a button, she looks pretty tame but one of her many hidden gifts is a pair of lungs that could blast rust off steel.

"ATTEN-SHUN", she shouts, startling the crowd with the power of her unamplified voice. "We will answer any questions you have at the Toronto Triomphe at 9:30 p.m. sharp. Be there or be square."

I love Regina. When she's got the stage, she really works it.

I'm fixed there, with video rolling and cameras flashing, and think what a strange, strange scene. There's me, a ruddy-faced, pudgy, 54-year-old at 5-foot, 8 and Hobbit-height, rosy-cheeked Regina Naylor flanking, 6-foot, 6 Dragul of the blazing yellow eyes, glistening canines and complexion of a corpse, all with our arms raised and fingers forming 'V's that point to the sky.

CHAPTER TWENTY-THREE

LATE BITE LAUNCHES

One thing you have to know about Richard Triomphe, he sure knows how to throw a party.

More famous for being famous than being rich, Triomphe, 'The Dick' to his critics, and a thousand by-last-minute-invitation-only guests greet us in the grand ballroom of Toronto's only six-star hotel.

Among the guests are Canada's most recognizable faces from the world of entertainment, business, politics, the arts, First Nations and the media. Front and centre is our Mayor, Bobby Mercury, one arm encircling a lovely and the other arm with a death grip on two bottles of Bud. He tries to give us the double 'V' salute, but stops abruptly, when he realizes both hands are full.

As promised by Regina, a short news conference, telecast around the world, starts sharp at 9:30. All the questions, and therefore the answers, are the usual pap.

Triomphe has laid out a celebration in a way that few others could even imagine and, in the process, is making it look like Dragul's victory is his victory. The ballroom is transformed into the courtyard of Dracula's castle with 50-foot high banners hanging from the parapets, proclaiming this day as, 'The V de Triomphe.'

"Where does he come off with that," says Regina.

"It doesn't bother me," says Jerry, who slides back an oyster on the half shell and washes it down with his third glass of Bowmore 18-year-old single malt. "After all, he is 'The Dick.' Besides, this party will cost him a lot more than Dragul's legal bill."

Dragul also appears quite content as a large group of women surround him, each passing him her room key and an invitation to relieve her of addictions and anxieties.

Later in the evening, I see Mayor Mercury seated precariously on one of the parapets, singing enthusiastically to Legalize It by Peter Tosh, a bottle of beer in each hand. Insiders have a nickname for Mercury. They call him Humpty-Dumpty, not because of his girth, but because they expect his antics and gaffes will result in a great fall. If he keeps drinking, and doesn't move from that parapet, all the king's horses and all the king's men . . . well, you know the rest of it.

Just then, Rosalie dips into position under my arm. For me, the night's complete.

§§§

The next day, Mangorian continues to be besieged by requests for interviews, appearances, endorsements and, how do I put this in a polite way, yet more women inquiring about his personal services. One hare-brained pitch comes from a dentist who offers Mangorian $100,000 to clean and examine his teeth as long as he can videotape the procedure and get an interview afterward to use in his advertising.

We turn that one down.

The book deal for No Crime, No Time becomes more lucrative when Mangorian agrees to add his personal narrative. We each get a cool $500,000 progress payment on top of the $250k advance. We hear that bookstore chains are clamouring for the yarn and have guaranteed orders that will ensure Dark Publishing's launch of No Crime, No Time will be a best seller.

The most intriguing pitch is $25,000 to shoot a pilot for a half-hour talk show with Mangorian as the host. If the pilot actually airs, he gets another $100,000 and $100,000 per episode thereafter.

It sounds good to me but it's Mangorian who has to say yea or nay.

"We've got an offer to audition for a talk show."

"What's a talk show?"

"You know like Letterman."

"You mean the postman?"

"No, no, no. You know, David Letterman on Late Night television."

"Television?"

"Aw, c'mon, it's television, you know TV, you sit down in front of it and they play dramas and other shows with guests that talk about things."

"Oh, yeah, I know what you're talking about now except back in the coven we used to call it radio."

"No, no – it's television ... TELE VISION . . . meaning you see the show. You see moving pictures."

"Get out of here."

"No, no it's true. I'll show you, I'll . . . "

"Just kidding. You think I spent a year in prison without ever watching television?"

I brace myself for that hideous laugh, but it never comes. Instead, Mangorian looks at me seriously and says he wants me to stay on as his agent because we make a good team. I agree because the Mangorian gravy boat looks like it's about to become a long-term luxury cruise liner. Then he pulls out a contract that makes me a 50-50 partner in everything. That means rather than just the 15% most agents get, my take is exactly the same as Mangorian's.

"It's too generous."

"I'd be in prison for the rest of my unnatural life if not for you. Besides how many houses can a person live in at one time? It's not like I have expensive tastes, just bloody ones. Ha ha ha ha."

Now it comes. I still can't get used to that laugh but I shrug, hold up my palm and he slaps me, considering my height, for him a low five.

I see the brass at Cable NEXT the following week to negotiate terms of a show they want to call 'Late Bite.' I cringe at the name and also over the clause that says Mangorian has to allow himself to exclusively be called a vampire during the show, no mentioning Sanguinus. I counter with our demands. I am the executive producer of the show. Dragul and I have veto rights over content. NEXT maintains distributership for all time, but Dragul and I own the show and all spin-off enterprises.

I offer Regina a job as my assistant, which she accepts, and Jerry, an honourary chairman's role, which he declines. "I'm really retired this time. Look me up when you get to Tahiti."

The first few shows are clumsy. The scripts are poorly written. The direction is off. The jokes are bad and we've got a lineup of second-tier acts from the Las Vegas strip and other quasi celebrities. Jack Ace, master of sleight of hand, and Bryce Hanuman, reigning Mixed Martial Arts champion, are our headliners for shows #1 and #2.

Jack Ace (Jack Ass to those who know him) performs the usual card tricks and vanishes and then invites Mangorian to try his hand. Mangorian puzzles over the challenge and, surprisingly to all, especially Jack Ace, is his ability to replicate the trick perfectly, once it's explained to him.

Whoever thought of Bryce Hanuman needs a roundhouse kick to the head. The guy's rambling, incoherent account of his many mixed martial arts victories, including nine title defences, is the dullest interview ever. It just isn't credible when the script has Mangorian talking about being afraid to get in a fight with him. The best part of the segment was Bryce Hanuman giving Mangorian lessons on how to use his trademark weapon, the Muay Thai clinch, and a series of Brazilian ju jitsu sweeps and judo armlocks.

The Muay Thai clinch is a move where a fighter faces an opponent and places both hands on the back of the adversary's head. The hands pull the head down to chest level or lower as the fighter shoots a knee up to strike the opponent's face.

Hanuman used the clinch to win three of his title defences but on this occasion, the MMA champ, at 5-foot, 9, came off the ground like a feather when he tried the clinch on the 6-foot, 6 Mangorian.

The judo and ju jitsu doesn't work either. Mangorian's super human flexibility leaves him invulnerable to armlocks and his incredible strength and balance denies the sweeps.

With the first six shows in the can, episode one goes on the air. The publicity surrounding Mangorian creates a huge audience but it's not until the end of the week that the numbers come in.

Show #1 gets 7.2 million viewers in North America and cracks the top 50 most watched shows, an incredible feat for a cable-released product.

Show #2 gets 11.9 million viewers in North America, tied for 25th place among all shows watched on TV.

Show #3 gets an astounding 13 million viewers in North America, good for 15th position, just edging out Monday Night Football.

Best of all for Cable NEXT, 2.4 million households call up their cable providers to subscribe to the network.

The network executives, the crafts, producers, directors, and top comedy writers now knock on our door. I meet with NEXT. We scrap episodes #4, 5, and 6 and announce a two-week break to write better scripts and line up Tier One celebs.

The first show with Emmy-winning director Jim Phillips and a hand-picked selection of the top production personnel takes on a more serious note. Although Mangorian is emcee, Public TV's Billy Tulip has been brought on as a guest, but a guest who does the interviewing, in exchange for a second and longer interview being made available for Tulip's talk show.

"How was your time in prison?" asks the debonair Tulip.

"I found it to be quite pleasant."

"Pleasant? You're joking," says Tulip, scrunching his face in surprise.

"Prison can be a frightening and deadly place for most people, but not for me, considering what I'm used to. For the first time in a long time, I had a bed. I was able to get nutrition without a struggle. Al Hamblyn, my then-lawyer and now partner, ensured I had an amended diet of mostly cow's blood. Most of the prisoners avoided me entirely.

"There was one very large fellow who ran the place through intimidation and worse. They called him 'the Boss.' I seemed to be a problem for him. One day, he and two of his lieutenants, all armed with shanks trapped me in a dead end corridor. As they started to move in, I bared my fangs to their full three inches, kicked off my shoes to unveil razor-sharp talons and then twisted my hands to reveal claw-like nails extending a full inch from my fingers.

"While they were recovering from the shock of my transformation, I leapt forward shredding the pants of two of the would-be assassins into orange hula skirts and landed heavily upon their leader. With the nail of my index finger, I carved the letter 'D' for Dragul on his forehead.

"Your show airs during prime time so I won't repeat the message that I gave to the Boss and his henchmen. After that, they would run in the other direction whenever I was around. It was a nice move for me, too, because dozens of the inmates now wanted to be part of my gang, some because they were afraid of me and others because they felt I could turn them into bad-ass vampires, which I can't."

"You became the boss in prison?"

"It all seemed pretty silly to me but everyone else was so serious. I guess that's because being in the wrong gang could get you killed. I took them on and, as their dues, each one of them had to donate some blood once a month. That made my life in prison heaven."

"Were they afraid to give blood to you?"

"It's not like inviting people to a Tupperware party. There were a few who wanted to be vampires and volunteered right up front. I told them it wouldn't happen, couldn't happen but they wanted to do it. After they suffered no ill effects the rest of them just lined up. Most said it was a lot better giving blood to me than giving up their cigarettes or being someone's date for the night."

"Tell me about the Sanguinus. How do they live?"

"As far as I know, they don't anymore. We went through some very bad times. Thousands died when your megaprojects destroyed our underground homes. The survivors migrated to your cities and sewer systems. It was very depressing. The suicide rate was extremely high. I've looked but haven't found another Sanguinus in 20 years. Just another species gone extinct."

"Wasn't there some way that Sapiens and Sanguinus could co-exist peacefully?" asked Tulip.

"I can say this today because we live in relatively civilized times, but the genus Homo Sapiens is the most ruthless and most deadly killer that ever walked the Earth. Homo Sapiens cannot live in a world where they face competition.

"There are many sub-species of whale, many sub-species of ape, many sub-species of every living creature on the Earth, save one. And that is man, Homo Sapiens. The fossil record shows a wide variety of hominid sub-species that once flourished – Homo Habilis, Homo Georgicus, Homo Erectus, Homo Ergaster, Homo Antecessor, Homo Heidelbergensis, Homo Neanderthalensis, Homo Floresiensis, Homo Sanguinus and Homo Sapiens.

"With the exception of me as the last living member of Homo Sanguinus, all hominid sub-species other than Homo Sapiens are extinct. You have to ask yourself the question, why? The answer is clear, Homo Sapiens do not permit competitors. You know this to be true. Even within your own species you exterminate those who are different. Witness Nazi Germany and the Rwandan Genocide."

CHAPTER TWENTY-FOUR

SALLY'S MISSING

Our show and Tulip's draw record audiences. Subsequent episodes prove we are definitely on the A-List with some of the top stars in Hollywood.

Georgie Downs the Third, GD III for short, is starring in his fourth Titanium Man sequel with its plot centred on the arrival of Titanium Man's evil twin. GD III is a notorious prankster so we want a gag we can play on him. We called in Replica Roy for the task. Roy Romanelli got his nickname, and a place in Hollywood legend, 15 years ago as the FX guy for a low-budget, almost straight-to-video film called Replicas. It was a stinker with a bad script, and the worst directing and acting. The total budget was less than $2,000,000. But Replicas topped its competitors for best visual effects, winning an Oscar over competition that spent tens of millions on the CGI alone.

Ray came up with a great idea, and one that would involve the whole audience.

The gag calls for GD III to be sitting down with Dragul when someone in a Titanium Man suit walks onto the stage. He sits next to GD III and takes over answering questions about the movie and keeps butting in to try to get under GD III's skin. When Dragul switches topics to compromising photos of GD III that the tabloids have recently published, Titanium Man starts screaming.

"It's all a lie. GD III would never do that. That's an imposter in those photos."

Then he flips up his mask to reveal . . . GD III or someone who looks just like him. The real GD III is speechless. He looks at the audience, mouth hanging open, and then does a double take at his doppleganger. He turns to Dragul who meanwhile has flipped down a mask to reveal another twin, or is it a triplet, for GD III, not quite as convincing but good enough to keep the laughter going. Pan right to a cameraman who also looks just like GD III and then zoom in on the audience who have all donned GD III masks.

"We'll be right back after these words from our sponsors," says Dragul.

Audience members were ecstatic. They all had a Titanium Man mask as a souvenir and each one could claim he or she was on screen. After all, who could tell?

There were high fives all around after the show.

"Not quite the oomph you got with Bryce Hanuman," says Director Jim Phillips, aiming a karate kick toward me and belting out a huge laugh.

Now, four successful seasons in, Late Bite is an established hit, syndicated around the world, and forms the anchor of our soon-to-be multi-billion dollar enterprise.

But all is not perfect. There's the incessant paparazzi, the nut patrol of religious zealots, protesters, another rant from Ben Saxon about 'the devil,' and one lawsuit.

"Alan Gregory is suing you," I say. "He claims he gave you $10,000 and allowed you to bite him on the neck and take his blood in return for turning him into a vampire."

"Alan Gregory has more money than brains and is quite frankly a pretty silly guy," Mangorian says with a wave of his arm. "Did he pay me $10,000? Did I drink his blood as he requested? Yes and yes. Did I promise to make him a vampire? Absolutely not. It's impossible and I told him that.

"He wanted to try it anyway and had this elaborate ritual he took from an Anne Rice novel where I drink his blood and he drinks mine and, voila, he's a vampire. I agreed because, quite frankly I was just out of prison and I needed the money. At that point, I didn't know how I was going to survive."

"So should we just give him back his money?"

"Absolutely not. He paid it to me unconditionally. However, I will donate $10,000 to the anthropology department at the University of Toronto as an initial investment in the study of the genus Homo Sanguinus."

Just then my cell phone rings. I see that it's Rosalie, another part of my life that is now going exceedingly well. About a year ago she moved back in with me, not to a little house like we had but to a big white Georgian style mansion on the Bridle Path. As a teen, I was a delivery boy for a pharmacy and drove an order to this very same house. When I first saw it, I thought it was a school, or the official residence of the premier. I couldn't fathom a house this size being occupied by only one family. I had it in my mind that if I could ever live in a house like this my life would be a success. The house and Rosalie to share it with. This is what success feels like.

I shove aside the pile of paperwork for the IPO and grab a notepad, ready to jot down whatever it is that Rosalie wants me to pick up on my way home.

"Al!" Rosalie's voice sounds urgent and distressed unlike her usual upbeat self.

"What's up?"

"Sally's missing. No one's seen her today."

"I know I told you Sally doesn't take any time off – ever – but she is nearly 60, maybe . . ."

"No, she's really missing."

"Has someone gone to her house, contacted the police?"

"I did. I'm here now. The police won't come because she's not officially a missing person for 24 hours. "

After the success of the fundraiser during Dragul's trial, Sally named Rosalie and me as patrons of the law clinic, whatever that means. Rosalie took the role seriously and continued to fundraise and act as a volunteer intervener with clients 'on the edge' against lazy, incompetent bureaucrats and bloodsucking, loophole-wielding insurance companies. Like soldiers who have fought side by side on a battlefield, Rosalie and Sally became best of friends.

"I called her last night and left a message," says Rosalie. She didn't call back, which is really unusual, so I called again this morning. Her voice mail was full and nobody's seen her at the office. I went to her house and let myself in. There's no sign of her, but it looks like she left in a hurry, groceries left on the counter, still in their bags."

I leave the office and make a beeline to Sally's house. I know where it is but I've never been in it, 'much like Sally', I muse with a bittersweet smile.

We go to the police station to file a missing person's report. I ask for Detective Buddy Ferino but we get the same answer.

"We can't act for 24 hours," Det. Ferino says.

"Is she the kind of woman who might meet a guy and take an extra long weekend with him somewhere?" asks Ferino, still wearing his trademark trenchcoat and fedora.

"Nine times out of 10, gals like this turn up in a few days, red-faced and broke."

CHAPTER TWENTY-FIVE

THE MURDERS

The late spring evening is just so perfect. The temperature hovers in the Goldilocks zone - not too hot, not too cold - just right. As if on cue, the clouds part like curtains revealing a spectacular show of cosmic lights. Shirley Ames, stretches out on a hammock, usually reserved by day for improving her tan but tonight helping her to thoroughly enjoy the evening tableau. She is in the private world she created for herself – just her, the stars, and her magnificent garden to be enjoyed with a fine glass of Amarone. Even in the dark, the lilacs' light, spicy perfume triggers an arena of lavender, magenta and white in her mind's eye.

Every glance at the sky is sumptuous and every breath dessert. Absolute perfection. This is her life. Doing whatever she wants, whenever she wants, now that she's rid herself of that two-timing louse, Harry. She has to thank him, however, for the Rosedale home and the monthly alimony payments, a tidy sum, that allows her to spend a small fortune renovating the house and garden and to live a life of leisure.

Ten years ago, when she and Harry married, she was by all reports 'a knock-out' and naturally so. No lifts or tucks. Expert application of makeup, thanks to her training as an esthetician, and regular workouts, enhanced nature's gifts, causing whiplash injuries among males whenever she passed.. The intervening years saw her slip, but not by much. She figures that as a 37-year-old she passes for 29 and still makes men's heads spin despite tipping the scales at 125 pounds, 15 more than when she married.

The lightly scented wind moves stealthily through the trees and gently touches Shirley's face and bare arms. Between sips from her wine glass, she hears the tiny fluttering of a thousand flowered petals dislodged by a shifting gust.

That's when Shirley senses as much as hears a hushed landing. It's something that feels big but scatters no more sound than a leaf tumbling across the lawn. The hammock places her in an awkward position to see what caused the momentary ripple in her perfect world.

A large silhouette suddenly blocks her view to the stars, causing her to emit a short, surprised scream and lose her grip on her wine glass, which shatters on the deck below.

In the next 60 seconds, Shirley returns to perfection, back to the same weight she carried as a 25-year-old, thanks to the loss of 15 pints of blood.

§§§

"That's odd," Mahir Batros thinks to himself, checking his list against the addresses on the line of buildings on Gladstone Road. The 26-year-old removes his red Pizza Palace ball cap to give his head a scratch while he puzzles over the situation. The list clearly states, 'Number 106B Gladstone Road. Ask for George'.

The houses on the west side of the street run from 2 to 102 and then pick up again at 110. The only thing fixed between is a dirt and salt-stained, yellow-brick commercial building that lost its last tenant on November 12, 2005, according to a faded eviction notice on the door. No number on it, but what other address could it have, he thinks.

On the northern end of the building, severing it from 110 Gladstone, is a shoulder-width walkway steeped in shadows. Mahir hesitates. He hates the dark.

The part-time teacher began moonlighting as a pizza deliveryman after he and Rana married last year so they could afford to buy a home and have a family. The home part is somewhere in the distance, but the family part kicked into gear with Rana's announcement last month that she is pregnant.

A wrong address? Maybe, but he suspects the customer is trolling for a free pizza. Pizza Palace guarantees delivery in 30 minutes or the pie is free. People with hard-to-find apartments try to pull off this ploy all of the time at the deliveryman's expense. Failing to meet the deadline means Mahir's wages for the week would be short the $1 an hour bonus and, with two late calls last month, could spell strike three, the loss of his job.

Pulling the pizza box marked 106B Gladstone from the insulated bag,

Mahir heads toward the darkened walkway but not before clicking on his fob to make sure the car doors are locked, another precaution founded when he returned from a delivery to find the other pizzas missing. Stolen pizzas mean working free for at least a week, maybe two, something the daddy-to-be can't afford.

Guided by the faint glow of his cell phone in one hand and balancing the pizza on the other, Mahir carefully makes his way along the walkway when a sudden shiver spikes through him. Something incredibly fast emerges from the gloom. Mahir feels hot, putrid breath on his neck and then nothingness. He is dead before pizza and cell phone hit the ground.

§§§

"Hello dad? Did I wake you up?"

"Hi Johnny, not a problem I had to get up anyway. Hey, did you see last night's show," I say.

"Yeah dad, it was great, cheesy but great. I want to thank you for everything. You really didn't have to buy us a new car, and a Jag at that."

"Listen Johnny. I really was a pretty miserable father when you were young. I was never there and, for awhile, I was half in the bottle. I'm just trying to make it up to you, your family and your mother."

"Dad, money was never the issue. I just wanted to spend time with my dad. Do you think you could come by? Johnny Jr. is anxious to see Grandpa. He's the envy of the neighbourhood now that he has a half-dozen ponies and his Grandpa is best friends with Dragul Mangorian."

"Not much sense just getting him one pony. All his friends would have to wait and take turns. By the way, I'm thinking of buying the farm where they're boarded. You and Jenny could move up there and live there full-time."

"I'm not much for commuting dad."

"Johnny, I told you. You don't have to work anymore. I've set up a trust so you can have the life I always wanted for you. You and Jenny can travel, send Johnny Jr. to the best schools and just enjoy life."

"That's the life you thought mom and I wanted but it never was like that. All we wanted was a regular life with three meals a day, church on Sundays, a week at a rented cottage in the summer and maybe a nice house with a picket fence.

"So can you come by?" he asks me.

"We've got the big IPO coming up so I don't have a lot of time. Maybe a week Sunday. I'll take everyone out to dinner. There's a great chef and sommelier at the Obisidian Club."

I don't know why I keep putting Johnny off. We've been seeing a lot more of each other over the past five years but I've always managed to have our time together at parties, large family functions, dinners out, but never one-to-one.

The fact is, I'm still afraid to be a dad. Still afraid that I'll be a disappointment to him. Afraid he'll see through me and see the loser that I am. Still afraid I'll have nothing to say, too much to say, or the wrong thing to say that will put him off. Our relationship is so good right now, I don't want to blow it.

'Beep. Beep. Beep.'

"Oh Johnny, that's Dragul calling. I need to take it."

"No problem pop. Hey, there's something on the news about Dragul. You'd better talk to him. Bye."

"Bye, son."

"Hi Dragul."

"Al. I'm at 52 Division."

"What? What for?"

"There was another woman and man attacked last night. Both of their throats were ripped out. Both have been completely drained of blood. The police came by my apartment a half hour ago and brought me in."

"What does that have to do with you? Come on. They can't be serious. We've been through all of that. This is just vindictiveness because we kicked their ass the last time."

"Just get here as quickly as you can."

I jump into my BMW and tear the 16 blocks over to the police station. The road is nearly blocked by media vehicles, fans, gawkers and, of course, the religious groups.

I push my way through the crowds ignoring the reporters' questions.

Sergeant brushcut greets me.

"Good to see you Mr. Hamburger."

"Hi Sergeant. Good to see you've been on the fast track these past five years," I say glancing at the same three squashed 'V's on his sleeve before giving a light tug on the lapels of my $3,000 Petrocelli suit. "Would you be so kind to direct me to see my client?"

'Chevron sleeve' unhappily leads me through a set of glass doors toward what appears to be a much nicer interview room than the one attached to the cellblock.

"We've just brought him in for questioning. Det. Ferino is in there with him now. He hasn't been charged."

"Det. Ferino. This is inappropriate. My client has asked for his counsel, meaning me, so you have no right to question him without me being present."

"I haven't asked your client any questions. Nothing says I can't sit here with him and wait until you arrive."

"So what's your point?"

"I wanted to tell you before this whole thing gets out of hand that I don't believe Mr. Mangorian had anything to do with these murders. You remember I was the lead investigator for the Stalker investigation, the investigation around actions, I won't call them crimes, that your Mr. Mangorian was involved in."

"Yes, we all know that very well."

"I know your client's MO and, while to the average cop this looks like the same thing, it doesn't ring true to me. So I'm askin', who out there wants to get your guy? Who out there has the ability to do all of this?"

"I really couldn't say. There are a lot of sick people out there. You should see some of our fan letters. But we've never come across another real Sanguinus. I don't know who would have the capability to set something like this up."

"Like I said, I'll try to keep things from becoming weird until we get in the DNA evidence that clears your client."

"Well, thanks for that, I think. Now can you let us out of here?"

"I can't yet. They'd be all over me upstairs but maybe in a couple of hours."

"Okay, can I be alone with my client," I say motioning the detective away. Ferino complies, shutting the door behind him.

Mangorian looks at me with his piercing yellow eyes but this time I see frustration, not menace in them.

"Al, this is a nightmare."

"I know. I know. This is just ridiculous. Despite what Ferino says I'm getting you out of here in 10 minutes."

I know just who to call.

"Hello, George Mission please. I don't care if he's in a meeting. Tell him it's Al Hamblyn on the phone and he needs to take the call right now."

A minute later a voice comes on the line.

"Hello Al? Is that you Al?"

"Yes, George. You asked if I would consider hiring your firm. The answer is yes but how much of our business you get depends largely on what happens in the next 10 minutes."

Seven minutes later Dragul and I exit 52 Division and land smack into a flotilla of media.

"This is nonsense, but we're going to hold off making an official statement until tomorrow. That way, you won't have to bleep out most of my words," I shout to the reporters.

I spot the stretch limo that V-G has positioned in front and we climb in with George Mission.

When we arrive at V-G's glass and marble Bay Street offices, a team of young, well-dressed and, best of all, aggressive-looking lawyers along with my assistant Regina Naylor await us in the main conference room.

"Okay," says Mission. "What's the story and is this going anywhere?"

"Hard to say," says the well-coiffed, mid-30ish fellow at the centre of the table.

He's just the kind of guy who would have been one of Gracey's prime lieutenants in law school. Obviously, the legal team leader. Obviously, smart and political as well. Brooks brothers suit and tie, Allen Edmonds wing tips, Tag Heuer watch – solidly professional and elegant but not so much to make clients think they're being fleeced.

"This is Gregory Mazpera. He's our head of criminal law. You may have heard about his work – the successful defence of 75-year-old Brian Droshko in the euthanasia death of his wife Helen, and of Pamela Jerome after she killed her husband who had abused her for more than 20 years. The rest of our A-Team is Terri Leung, Jessica Hunt and Harry Paskowski. And you want the very capable Regina Naylor working on the case as well, I presume.

"Yes, to Regina but hey guys, we're way ahead of ourselves. No charge has been laid and I am absolutely certain no charge will ever be laid. Why the hell would Dragul do anything like this? We have a multi-billion dollar IPO ready to launch and, frankly, have you seen Dragul's Facebook site? There are literally hundreds of girls each volunteering to donate blood and at least a half dozen nut bars willing to do it the old way – fang to jugular. Dragul, do you have any idea what they are talking about?"

"Police came to my door this morning and, as you know, I'm not a morning person. They started yelling and demanding things, so I ordered them out. One of the officers said if I didn't voluntarily go for questioning, I'd be charged with obstructing justice. So I let them bring me in.

"I was asked where I went last night after the show and whether I had an alibi. That's when I went silent and called for you, Al. You know me. I'm a creature of the night. I like to wander on my own. So no, I don't have an alibi."

"So that's it?" I say. "Dragul doesn't have an alibi and some girl gets killed so they presume it's him?"

"Uhh, not quite. There was a witness," says Mazpera.

"An eyewitness that puts Dragul on the scene?"

"Not exactly. It was Ben Saxon. He was on neighbourhood patrol and saw someone who was very tall and thin climbing over the back fence of the Rosedale house where the murder occurred. He grabbed his phone and shot a video.

Apparently, it is very dark and blurry, but for a fraction of a second when the perp crossed in front of a lit window, you can see a hand with extremely long fingers and inch long fingernails. He tried chasing the perp but he was too fast and vanished into the night. Saxon's now telling anyone who will listen that it was Mangorian."

"So that's it?" I ask. "Tall, thin, long fingernails – You might as well put out an APB for supermodels. This is more than ridiculous. Do they have any real evidence?"

Mazpera raises a hand and says, "The victims, Shirley Ames, a resident of Rosedale and Mahir Batros, a pizza delivery guy, had their throats ripped out by what looks like fangs. The police are comparing the bite marks, fingerprints and the DNA with records they have from Mr. Mangorian's previous case.

"Mr. Mangorian, is there any light you can shed on this case, anything you know at all?"

"Wait a minute," I say while jumping to my feet.

But Mangorian stretches out his long, bony hand and motions me to take my seat again.

"You are a great friend and my defender Al, but an emotional response will not help this time. We need the facts. Let the police put together their forensic case. It won't hold water because there's nothing to hold. I was never around the locations of either victim."

"Okay, George, Gregory and the rest of you, you're on the case. Leave no stone unturned. Job one is to keep this from ever going to trial. Put on the heat and use every legal, police, political, business and media contact to make sure every shred of evidence that turns up is put through the wringer 19 times. I want no surprises. Regina, your full-time job until this is resolved is to make the media walk a straight line. They will be on steroids out-speculating each other so we have to do whatever we can to control the message. In the end, Dragul will be exonerated, but in the process our $6 billion deal may fall to pieces. Hire that PR firm Muldoon & MacDonald to help you put pressure on everyone in our company, all of our associates, the Crown Attorney's office and the police chief. For our staff and associates, the message is, speak or leak and you're fired. To the others, it's, defame Dragul Mangorian and when he's acquitted, we have an unlimited war chest ready to sue your ass off, destroy your credibility and your career or both. Put it in writing so everyone knows where we stand. A decision to make statements that will later prove false could cost us our $6 billion IPO. If that happens, we intend to get back every penny from whoever takes a cheap shot. We've all got our assignments, so let's go."

Mazpera raises a hand. "Two of us don't have assignments."

"Wha . . . who?" I ask.

"You and Dragul. We have to keep the two of you under wraps and under observation so you have an alibi if there's another attack. I think you two should take a couple of suites at the TT and bring along some staffers as additional witnesses."

CHAPTER TWENTY-SIX

OH BROTHER WHERE ART THOU

Dragul has amazing patience. I guess for someone who passed more than a year in prison like it was a coffee break, this is no big deal. I, on the other hand, have always been a little claustrophobic. So after three days of staying put in the Toronto Triomphe and getting room service for everything, I begin to climb the walls. I flip on the TV and see two guys in a cage bashing each other's brains out. One of them is Bryce Hanuman, our mixed martial arts friend from Late Bite's second unfortunate episode.

That gives me an idea. I rummage through some of the paraphernalia Late Bite collected and I find a volume entitled, 100 Magic Tricks to Amaze Your Friends, written by Late Bite's first guest, magician Jack Ace.

I recruit two of Late Bite's security crew to be my audience. They aren't needed at the show because filming has been temporarily suspended. The network has been airing reruns but our audience share has dropped by almost half.

We've been rotating the security guys in and out to bolster the number of witnesses and to keep their paycheques coming. I know what it feels like supporting a family without an income.

Trick number 4 is a coin vanish. Not too successful. The quarter hits my toe with a thud. Trick number 7 is the opposite. I make a bouquet of flowers appear out of thin air, well almost. There's a bit of hesitation and tugging when the bouquet opens prematurely and snags in my sleeve.

Mangorian, usually not one to get involved in stuff like this, rescues my audience by running through tricks number one through seven as flawlessly as if he were Jack Ace. I bow deeply and thank Dragul for his assistance.

The media, even the tabloid press, have been playing things pretty straight thanks to Muldoon and MacDonald. Their job may have been helped by the fact that the case is sensational enough, two murders with the world's only known vampire as the main suspect. No need to hype that.

More bad news arrived yesterday when Regina reported that the consortium of investment houses backing the IPO have suspended the deal pending the outcome of the investigation.

"Man, could the news get any worse?" I moan.

"It just got worse," says Mazpera.

The V-G lawyer's entrance to our hotel suite couldn't have been more dramatic.

"Worse? What do you mean worse?"

"Police are getting ready to lay charges against Dragul."

"That's nuts," I say. "Where's the evidence?"

"The fingerprints lifted at the scene have no whorls but they do have characteristic sweat beads so they know it's not somebody trying to fake them."

"Hey, there's got to be a way they can fake fingerprints that have no prints. Get Replica Roy. I'm sure he can do it. We'll show them."

"That's not all."

"What?"

"They have DNA. Saliva found on the victims' necks match Dragul's DNA."

We're all stunned into silence.

Dragul retreats into his bedroom and won't speak to any of us.

"Dragul, can you talk to me? Can you say something?" I ask, as I knock twice. There's no answer and the door stays shut.

"Do you think Sanguinus all have the same DNA? Like all of them lack fingerprints," asks Regina.

"There's not another living species where individual members share the exact same DNA profile whether you're talking about eggplants or elephants," says Mazpera. "I checked it out. If they have Dragul's DNA on the victims either he did it or someone had his saliva and planted it on the victims."

"Then that has to be it," I say. "I know him. He couldn't possibly have done it."

"But who could have done that? Who has that much access to us?" says Regina. "It's not like Dragul is out on the fast food circuit leaving his DNA and cheeseburger residue on napkins. We know what he eats or rather drinks and where and when he drinks it."

"Even if someone did get some samples of his saliva, that wouldn't cut it," Mazpera says. "They literally found cups of it all over the victims. No way someone could plant it by collecting a bit here and a bit there."

I grab what's left of my hair and use it for grips to whip my head back and forth in the hope it will dislodge some kind of brilliant idea.

"What time and place – exactly – were these murders committed. There's got to be an answer. Maybe one of us was with Dragul during that time."

Mazpera reaches into his pocket and pulls out a notebook.

"Shirley Ames was murdered in her backyard at 333 Crescent Villa Road in Rosedale. The coroner sets her time of death at 10:30 p.m. and about an hour later, Mahir Batros, the pizza delivery guy, had his throat ripped apart on Gladstone Road in the 100 block. The two locations are about two miles apart and, at that time of night, might take 7 minutes to drive."

"That means whoever killed Ames could easily have had time to kill Batros," says Regina.

"Okay, so we're dealing with the time period between 10:30 p.m. to 11:30 p.m. on Friday, June 8, 2018. I want to know if anyone on our business team, anyone with the show, anyone selling Girl Guide Cookies door-to-door had contact at all with Dragul in that time period."

Mazpera and Regina grab their cell phones and madly start dialing.

Before I can make a call, my cell rings.

"Mr. Hamblyn. It's Det. Ferino. I have a warrant for the arrest of your client. I don't want to make a big show of it, put handcuffs on him and drag him to the station. Will you promise to bring him in tomorrow?"

I promise that I will personally bring Dragul to the station as long as there is no publicity around us coming in. He agrees.

I go back to Dragul's door and knock lightly.

"Go away," he says. "Just go away."

§§§

"What's up?" Regina asks Denny MacDonald the next morning as she stirs sweetener into the smooth dark brew at her favourite King East breakfast haunt, Le Petit Dejeuner.

"If you really believe Mangorian is innocent, I have an idea how to get more eyes on for you."

"What do you mean, eyes on?"

"Witnesses or potential witnesses both human and electronic."

"How do you do that? We really need something. Al's taking Dragul in today. They've issued a warrant for his arrest. Dragul's not talking at all. Won't tell us where he was, what he was doing. You have to know him to know how he can do that. He's unbelievably stubborn when he wants to be. So we're faced with literally having to canvass everyone in the city to find out if anyone saw anything."

"That's why it's called the mass media," says MacDonald. "I set up a series of radio interviews and Hamblyn asks on air for the public, business owners, cell phone shooters, you name it to go through their videos, selfies, and any other photo taken between 10:30 and 11:30 that night on the off chance we can get a shot of Mangorian somewhere other than snacking on a Rosedale cougar and a pizza guy."

"How soon can you do this?"

"How soon can you get Hamblyn?"

§§§

Regina rouses me at 4 a.m. to start the rounds from 5:30 a.m. to 10:30 a.m. to all the radio stations in Toronto, including three stations broadcasting in Italian, Arabic, and Mandarin.

Each message ends with the plea, "If anyone has any footage or photos from that night that you suspect may have captured Mr. Mangorian's image, we need to see it. Call, email, or Tweet us. Reward."

As expected the response is immediate. Hundreds of calls, Tweets and emails swamp Dragul Enterprise's phone lines and email accounts. As expected, the vast majority provides images of everything from a scarecrow with carrots for fangs to Count Chocula. Still, there are a few that bear closer examination but the images are fuzzy and dark. Regina sends them to labs that specialize in improving the image quality, but they all say it's going to take time. Regina looks at the clock, 8 p.m. She hasn't eaten a thing since a slice of toast 12 hours earlier and decides to take a break from the DE's Queen Street office.

As she opens the door, she's greeted by a half dozen teens, four with ballcap peaks at 3, 7, 9 and 11 o'clock and two with GoPros mounted on their helmets.

"You work for the vampire dude?" says the skater who appears to be their leader.

"Yes Mr. Mangorian owns the company that I work for."

"We need to see the dude cuz we got the B.E.v. He sees this, he'll do diamondz," the leader says making a series of gesticulations with his hands that make as much sense as his words.

"Pardon me?"

"Totally off the hook you know."

'Huh?"

"Really sick, . . . like rad, totally ill. Your V-guy, radioman says wants our B.E.v. . . B.E.v.," he says, pointing to the GoPro, then to the sky and alternately flapping his elbows like wings and pointing his two index fingers like beams shooting from his eyes at Regina.

"You mean you have a video with Mr. Mangorian in it?"

"The Betty's got it," says skater two.

"Hamster, she is a Betty," adds skater three.

"Yeah, so Josh's doin' his mad shit, double X Tricktionary," says skater two. "Josh hollers, 'Dudes, B.E.v. me.' I get up a pole and turn on the red eye cuz it's dark. I get it all, airfeet, ollies the 12 set. Hamster that was sick."

"You have a video with Mr. Mangorian in it?"

"Yeah, so V guy gets hardcore B.G.P.s," says skater number three.

"You have a video with Mr. Mangorian in it?"

"That's what I said," says number three and then plays a few seconds of the video.

Regina grabs a fistful of bills from her purse and pushes the cash to them in trade for the memory card.

"There's a lot more where that came from if it's really what we need."

"Right rad, dudette."

Regina bursts into the TT suite and jams the SD chip into a laptop. Hamblyn and two staffers gather around.

"It's pretty clear and they used infra-red mode to shoot in the dark. I guess they didn't know he was there until after they looked at the video. There's . . , oh look was that Dragul, there in the corner?" says Regina.

"Yeah, I think so. Does it go back to him?" I ask.

"In a second. There. That's definitely him, definitely."

"What time is that? The time and date code says 9:50 p.m. Friday, June 8, 2018."

"What's he doing?" I ask.

"Just watching I think," says Regina.

"How long does this go on?"

"I don't know. This is the first time I'm seeing this part."

Just then Mazpera bursts in.

"Does the video show . . . "

"We're just watching it now. So far so good," I say.

"Unbelievable," says Mazpera. "And perfect. They shot from above, a perfect bird's eye view."

Regina smacks herself on the forehead. "I finally got it."

"Got what," I say.

"They got V guy on a B.E.v. – bird's eye view," she says.

"I don't get it," I say.

"Don't worry about it. You're too old."

In the foreground, we see six teens slide down a steel bannister, perform flips down a concrete staircase, and do an assortment of spins and jumps. They also have their fair share of falls, slips and crashes.

"Ouch, that's gotta hurt," says Regina.

The entire time until just after midnight Dragul is seen watching the teens, pacing or sitting down. At no time between the start of the video at 9:50 p.m. and the end at 12:37 a.m. is Dragul out of the frame for more than a few seconds.

"Now this is going to rock their socks," says Mazpera.

Mazpera, Regina, and I go directly to Det. Ferino and present the new evidence. Mazpera places a few calls to people in high positions and we have a quick meeting with Crown Attorney Alicia Patullo and Judge Batten and Dragul is released into my custody.

"Did you see their faces when we showed them the video and the skater boys' statements? I thought Patullo and her boss were going to faint," Regina says.

Then turning to Dragul, she adds, "The videotape clearly shows you definitely have an alibi. They have nothing on you."

"The Police and the entire DNA sequencing industry have a big problem," says Mazpera. "This is going to open one gigantic can of worms if DNA evidence is proved to be unreliable,"

"How is this possible," I ask. "Every blade of grass can be distinguished from the next blade by its DNA."

"There is an exception," Dragul says.

We all whirl around to see him standing behind us.

"There is no mistake. The DNA on the victims matches my DNA but I did not touch them."

We all stare at him, mystified.

"The killer is my brother, my identical twin brother, Vlad."

CHAPTER TWENTY-SEVEN

THE DRINK OF DEATH

"Your identical twin?" I say in astonishment. "I thought you said you were the last of your kind. You didn't mention anything about a brother."

"I thought he was dead. I thought I killed him.

"My brother Vlad and I were the rarest of the rare among my people – twins and identical twins at that. With the birth rate so low, all newborns are celebrated but as identical twins, we were revered. Vlad and I were treated as royalty among our kind.

"When modern times decimated our people, Vlad became increasingly enraged. He took to your cities to satisfy his need for revenge and thirst for blood. For many decades, he fed, killing the homeless and others who wouldn't be missed in order to keep out of the watchful eye of our Council."

"But why would he kill when you, and obviously your Council, prefer to take what you need but leave your victims alive?" I say.

"Partly for revenge but, in truth, it is because of the Drink of Death."

"The Drink of Death?"

"Our mythology holds that the Sanguinus who consumes the Drink of Death, takes the final drop of his victim's blood, becomes all-powerful. But it's more than just a myth. When we take all of a victim's blood, we seem to gain our victim's life force. In medical terms, the last blood a Sanguinus drains from his victim comes from reserves held in the spleen that are rich in cells that form the front line in the human immune system. When these cells are absorbed by a Sanguinus, they act like a steroid, increasing muscle mass, speed, strength and recuperating powers.

"Like a steroid, the Drink of Death can also lead to fits of rage. Vlad became increasingly angered that his killing sprees, sometimes numbering as many as three or four a week, hardly caused a ripple.

"Then Fort Worth happened."

Dragul explains that, over the centuries, the largest Sanguinus colony in the Americas and the capital of the Sanguinus world nation was in North West Texas. It took more than 1,000 years to create a vast underground city of tunnels close to an area that would become the City of Fort Worth. The area sits in a basin over a geological formation called the Barnett Shale. When the Sanguinus established its colony, they found it easy to dig through the shale and the occasional pockets of oil they discovered provided them with light and power.

"The oil rich shale had been exploited for decades by your fellow Sapiens. In traditional oil and gas extraction, wells are drilled straight down, hit or miss. But you Sapiens are a greedy species. The power of oil to run your machines was not enough. You needed more machines, more oil, so you invented hydraulic fracturing. This technique uses pressurized water like an explosive to create long spider cracks in the shale. Success is if one or more of the cracks hits a big gas deposit.

"The technique became popular in Texas in the late 1980s and by the mid 1990s, you applied it on the Barnett Shale. One of the projects struck the mother lode by creating cracks that struck a massive sweet gas deposit. Success for the oil company, but disaster for us. Another fissure cracked the walls of our Fort Worth colony filling our atmosphere with poisonous methane. More than 6,000 of us died that day.

"Vlad went mad. He slipped aboard a freight train headed for the Southern U.S. and eventually ended up in Texas to look for survivors. He met with the remaining members of our Council who gathered to see if any part of the colony still existed. After a week, our acting Council Chief concluded that everyone had perished including the majority of our Council and our Chief. The acting chief ordered everyone including Vlad to return home.

"Vlad had other ideas. His first victim was George Voortman, a 36-year-old who had the misfortune to drive a vehicle that bore the logo of West Texas Oil Exploration. He forced Voortman to drive him to a diner that was popular with oil and gas crews, before shredding his throat.

"Bill Jenkins, a 30-year-old rig crew member, and Ted Schiller, a 42-year-old safety specialist, were motioning to the new waitress, 18-year-old Patsy Jones, for another coffee refill when they heard the café door crash open followed by a hoarse, angry voice shouting but a single word: 'Revenge!' When Vlad was done 32 people lay dead or dying in their own blood.

"Council suspected Vlad would not leave peaceably and had him followed. The coverup by the Council after millennia of practice was perfect. The massacre was blamed on the first victim George Voortman. Texans are fond of their guns and Voortman was no exception. A Stevens 512 Goldwing, 12-gauge shotgun was secured over the rear window of his pickup. That and two shotguns gathered from other vehicles in the lot were put to use effectively camouflaging Vlad's feeding frenzy. Voortman was left sitting in a corner of the diner, two spent shotguns beside him, and a shotgun in hand and most of his head and neck missing.

Investigators would puzzle over why a happily married man who was generally well liked would go on a murderous rampage. There was the dispute over being passed over for promotion a month earlier but, otherwise, Voortman's killing spree came as 'a complete shock,' friends and family would tell the media.

"With so few of us left, Vlad's act could have led to our discovery and our extinction. Our Council was outraged and ordered Vlad's execution. As his brother, as is our tradition, it was up to me to carry out the sentence. Vlad came willingly.

'In honour of our people's memory, we should fight to the death,' he says to me.

"We went to our ancestral lair in the Warsaw Caves hundreds of feet beneath the surface, no weapons, hand-to-hand, fang-to-fang combat. However, I had no intention of losing and allowing Vlad to continue his killing rampage. When we reached the lowest level, I told him I had changed my mind about fighting and just wanted him to flee. I walked out of the chamber first and, as I did so, I pulled a cord that dropped a large steel door behind me, effectively sealing Vlad in the chamber.

"This door won't hold me for long Dragul."

"I know," I said to myself as I climbed six levels as fast as I could to the upper chamber. I moved a flat rock lying against one wall to reveal a cell phone wired to a laser detonator. I pressed '999' and then 'SEND', which initiated a high-power laser pulse that travelled at the speed of light along a buried optical fiber. I heard five muffled 'Whoomps' in a row as the passages to five levels collapsed under the impact of stolen mining explosives."

"You buried him hundreds of feet underground? How could he live through that? "Even if he did, how could he escape?" My mind is reeling that after five years as close as I've been to Dragul, this is the first I'd ever heard of his brother or any part of the story.

"That's a question we'll have to ask him," Dragul says with eyes seeing things not of this room but events unfolding elsewhere in the past, present and future.

As a group, we agree to continue cooperating with police turning over all photos and videotapes but we don't tell them about Dragul's twin.

§§§

"Geez, that Ben Saxon is a pain in the arse. Did you see the interview he gave Photo Flash, the tabloid that's been after Dragul from day one?" says Regina.

"Do I look like someone who gives a crap?" I say.

"Well, you might want to look at this one. Saxon says he has a system that can predict where Dragul will strike next and he can use it to positively show that Dragul is guilty of the murders."

"Dragul has an alibi."

"He didn't know that at the time this article was published. Saxon says he can catch Dragul in the act. If that's the case, he may be able to catch the real killer."

"He couldn't catch a cold."

"Maybe, but Saxon's been close to the scene of one of the murders and was the one who reported it to police. He's got to be onto something. At first, the cops thought he may have done the killing but he always had company on patrol. So, perhaps, he's got a way to track the real killer."

I throw up my hands in capitulation. "Okay, I guess it couldn't hurt. Let's talk to him."

§§§

"Thank you for seeing me, Mr. Saxon."

Saxon is a stick of a man, who appears so wasted I'm amazed he can walk. He glances about my Queen Street office suspiciously.

"Is he . . . Is the Vampire here?"

"No."

"Good, good. Look, Mr. Hamblyn, I know you think I'm a nut or obsessed or something. I guess I am obsessed, but I have good reason."

He reaches into his pocket to retrieve a photo of a pretty girl with carmel-colored hair standing next to a much younger and more robust Saxon. The girl is perhaps 14 years of age and she and her dad are wearing Toronto Maple Leaf jerseys and standing in front of the Air Canada Centre.

"The photo was taken about 10 years ago, a week after her mother died. We went to a Leaf game to get our minds off my wife's death. After that, Rachael became the sole focus of my life. We were best buddies. Best Buddies to the end, we'd say. I never thought her end would come before mine. She was just 18. She was just so full of life."

"Mr. Saxon, police have not closed their investigation. Your daughter is missing but there's a chance she's still alive."

"She's dead. I feel it. I felt it that first day."

"Mr. Saxon, thank you for coming today. I wanted to meet with you to discuss this on-going campaign you have been waging against Mr. Mangorian. The courts found Mr. Mangorian not guilty of doing any harm to people. You have to stop. Mr. Mangorian had nothing to do with your daughter's disappearance."

"Of course you say that ______"

"Sure, we don't like it. It's not good for us, our business but it's not good for you either. You've got to get a life for yourself. Look at yourself. You're a mess. Surely your daughter wouldn't want that for you."

"Look Mr. Hamblyn. I know Rachael is dead. There's nothing I can do about it. I also know police are not going to arrest the vampire for her death. I am long past any thoughts of revenge. I am doing it for the vampire's future victims. I am doing it for all the mothers and fathers who love their children and will lose them to that monster."

"Now Mr. Saxon I don't ____"

"Listen," he says with a sudden intensity, "I'm also doing this for you. I saw how you defended him both in court and in the media. You bleed for him and all this time he is just using you. He is using you and, in the end, he will be your death."

He begins his story about how Rachael was lured to her death. She responded to a pamphlet asking for volunteers to help people in Third World countries. She was to meet other young people to write letters to the Canadian government, asking it to increase foreign aid.

"When she didn't come home by 10 p.m., I went to the place the meeting was held. The security guard said there was no meeting and he didn't see any teenage girls.

"It was all a lie. You are being lured down the same path as Rachael. Like Rachael, because you are good inside, you don't suspect that anyone else could be so cruel, so calculating, so evil. You believe you are doing good, that you are contributing, but you are just falling for his lie. Dragul Mangorian is the Devil and he will say and do anything to have you walk a path to your own destruction."

It continued downhill from there, I explain to Regina the next day.

"What about how he tracks the killer? Did you find out how he does it?"

"Crap, it slipped my mind. He got me so pissed off telling me that Dragul is going to drink my blood and kill me."

CHAPTER TWENTY-EIGHT

A DEADLY DISCOVERY

Twelve hundred miles above the Earth, a radio signal streaks toward two dozen orbiting satellites. The date is May 2, 2000. Within minutes, the satellites absorb the new instructions and begin broadcasting their location more frequently and more precisely, resulting in a 10-fold increase in the accuracy of GPS receivers around the world.

The next day in Beavercreek, Oregon, computer consultant Dave Ulmer thinks of a unique way to test the new accuracy of GPSs by taking "a stash," a container filled with bric-a-brac of little value into the woods and noting its coordinates on the Internet. He then challenges others to use a GPS to find it. The rules were basic: "Take some stuff. Leave some stuff."

Two people picked up on the Internet posting and, within three days, separately, they each found Ulmer's stash, took a trinket, left something else, and then shared their experiences online. In that moment, the sport of geocaching was born.

Eighteen years later, Ayden Dayto and Sophie Simpson examine their handheld GPS that tells them they are closing in on their third geocache of the weekend. The problem is its location in a lush area known as Crothers Woods. The 128-acre park located in Toronto's Don River Valley is blessed with woodland, meadows, wetlands, and a network of deep gullies.

The gullies, or more specifically a steep embankment, provide a worthy challenge to Ayden and Sophie. They had been at the top of the slope and, following a circuitous route along the ridge, now stand at the bottom. The geocache, however, is somewhere in the middle. What ups the ante is the three days of rain earlier in the week that transforms the slope into a natural but muddy slip and slide.

"Hey Sophie, we can get up here," says Ayden who is slathered with mud from a previous failed ascent. He examines the possibilities and decides on a broken trail cut over the years by the pounding descent of downhill mountain bikers that snakes upward and to the left.

Sophie follows but immediately finds herself spun around when her attempt to leapfrog a large rock ends in a short, soggy tumble into a greasy pool of clay and water. Wiping the mud away from her eyes, she starts up again but no longer has Ayden in sight.

When she reaches a fork in the trail, she goes right. A further 30 feet up and to the right, the trail comes to a dead end. The pitch is too great to climb without a tree or substantive shrubbery to hold onto. She's about to turn back when she spots Ayden's mud-covered hand hanging down from a ledge.

'I guess the romance is gone. No attempt at sweet talk or calling out to offer a hand up, just a disembodied, dirt-encrusted arm hanging down. Try to scare me, eh?' she says to herself. 'I'll show him,' and gives the arm a tug.

The instant she pulls on the hand, she knows something is wrong and reflexively releases it, as a shudder courses up her spine. But inertia has already taken hold. The cold, all-too-stiff hand keeps coming, followed by an arm and then a head and then an entire body that crashes on top of a shocked and screaming Sophie.

A team of police forensic investigators spends the rest of the day and all night combing the trail and surrounding area for evidence and more bodies. By the time their work is done, they find a total of six bodies in various stages of decomposition. The bodies had been buried in a shallow depression halfway up the hillside until the rain washed away the cover. The corpse that landed on Sophie is among the freshest, 26-year-old real estate agent Piyush Ganeshes who was dead perhaps five days. The earliest death, supermarket checkout girl Annie Yi, was pegged at a month earlier.

The rest are so caked with mud that their identities and the cause of death are not immediately apparent.

Within 24 hours, the story of the sorry end of the rest unfolds. All of the victims have tell-tale fang marks in their necks with death greeting them after a sudden and complete loss of blood.

The third victim identified is 16-year-old Virginia Salé, a student at Jarwin Collegiate. Her friends and family handed out fifty thousand flyers and stapled even more to every utility pole in Toronto's east-end.

All the newspapers and TV news programs covered the search for the first few days and then her story gradually faded from the foreground.

Victim number four is Tariq Hajjar, 29, a used car salesman, and victim five, Jacob Thandiwe, 26, a graduate student in philosophy at the University of Toronto. Neither had any family in the city and their disappearances went largely unnoticed.

The final victim to be identified is a woman in her 60s with an unruly mop of fuzzy grey hair. The overall description matches that of a woman reported missing three weeks earlier by a certain Rosalie Hamblyn.

§§§

I hold Rosalie closely, her sobs convulsing her body as we walk from Sally's grave.

"Al, you are certain that Dragul had nothing to do with this?"

"How can you even say that? I have enough trouble from the police and from guys like Saxon without you thinking that as well."

"I just need you to look me in the eyes and tell me that Dragul is not involved."

I look deeply into those tear-filled eyes and say, "Dragul had nothing to do with this" and then I open up on our drive home and tell her the full story about Dragul's brother.

"You've got to tell the police," she says.

"Dragul wants to take care of this himself. He says it's the only way. If police are involved, Vlad will just go into hiding, move to another city or country. Besides, the police are using most of their resources to pin the murders on Dragul."

Across town, Ben Saxon scans a large map of the city pinned to his livingroom wall. He takes six red sticky dots and carefully places them next to six of the more than three dozen green dots already on the map. There are only two other red/green pairs, one at 333 Crescent Villa Road in Rosedale and the other on Gladstone Road close to number 110.

As co-chair of Toronto's Neighbourhood Watch, Saxon was front and centre during the search and pointed out to anyone who would listen the similarities between Salé's disappearance and that of his own daughter years earlier. While Saxon's involvement in the search was widely reported, most of his comments were not. Even the tabloid press wasn't about to chance libeling Mangorian once he had the financial capability to hire the country's top law firms and was a major supporter of all of Toronto's key politicians.

The discovery of the six bodies changes all that. Fang marks, blood drained from the victims, it's all too familiar.

CHAPTER TWENTY-NINE

ENTER ALEXEI

"Hello, Alexei?"

"Hello, Rosalee? Is it reeelly you? It has been a long, long time. I see you have done very well for yourself."

"Alexei. This is business, your kind of business. When can we meet?"

§§§

As expected, the discovery of the six bodies places Dragul and our team under a microscope again. All six murders occurred before we put Dragul in lockdown and pulling another skater boys rabbit out of a hat doesn't seem likely, especially for all six. For now, Det. Ferino and the other police haven't laid additional charges, content that he's been released into my custody and we have effectively placed Dragul in our own form of house arrest.

Back at our suite in the TT, Regina, Mazpera, Dragul and I start putting together a game plan.

"We've got to tell police about your brother, Dragul," says Regina.

"No, that's something I must resolve myself. If we get the police involved, Vlad will go deep into hiding. They will never find him. Then they will believe we just invented him," Dragul says.

"But they found you. They managed to capture you. Why would Vlad be any different?" says Mazpera.

"We are different, Vlad and I. He has been a killer and has trained as a killer for 200 years . . . And he has the Drink of Death in him. The police will be unable to find him, and that's their good fortune."

"So how do you resolve it?" I ask.

"In his own time, he will allow me to find him. It cannot be hurried."

"So until then we just wait?"

"There is nothing more to do. Any overt actions we take will result in serious consequences for all of you. Do nothing or you put yourselves and those you love in peril."

"If we can't tell police about Vlad, they will come for you. What are we going to do?" I ask.

"When we find Vlad, we kill him."

"You mean that you're going to hunt down Vlad yourself?"

"Not exactly. You and I are going to hunt down Vlad."

"Whaaat? Why would you want me to help you? In schoolyard fights I was the punchline, literally. I took two karate lessons, bruised a knuckle and then pulled a groin. That was the end of my aspirations as the next Bruce Lee. Besides, we have plenty of money. Let's hire an army of ex-Navy SEALs."

"If we sent in a team of mercenaries, Vlad would disappear. But if I go alone, or nearly alone with only you accompanying me, he will show himself."

"I still don't understand why you need me."

"I don't need you to fight. I need you as bait. It would be unfair to place any other vulnerable person in that role. Besides, we always have each other's back. You are truly my brother, not Vlad. This is a battle for our existence. Either we live or he lives. There are no in-betweens. If Vlad kills me, he will surely come after you next and then Rosalie and Johnny."

"He doesn't even know me. Why would he be after me or my family?"

"It is not as if our connection is a dark secret," Dragul says. "We are seen together many times each week in newspapers and on television. And have you forgotten my daily appearances on Late Bite with your name as executive producer at the top of the credits. Vlad is Sanguinus and when a Sanguinus is in a vendetta, either the Sanguinus dies or everyone connected to his target dies."

I think for a second and realize what he says is true.

"If I'm going with you, I need a bigger role than simply the potential meal. I'll buy a gun and take some quick lessons."

"There would be no point. Vlad will never reveal himself unless it is in a place that he has the advantage. It will be dark, with even darker corners. He sees better in total blackness than you see in the day. He is many times quicker than the swiftest Sapiens. He will be on you before you draw your pistol."

"Then what do you suggest?"

"To begin with – armour to protect your neck – but disguised so it's not immediately apparent. Then something not too obvious that you can use as a weapon."

"That's a job for Replica Roy," I say.

I make a quick call, describe what I need.

"Give me two days," says Roy.

§§§

A sleek Jaguar XKR-S GT Coupe turns into a back alley off Bathurst Street and into a spot marked "reserved for customers." An elegantly dressed, middle-aged, but still beautiful woman enters the rear doorway of 'The Komrade.' She walks through a tiny, steaming kitchen to the main seating area.

"You look goood Rosaleee," says the burly figure who greets her with a bear hug and kisses on both cheeks.

"And the Jag. It must be worth for-tuune, and fast, 510 horsepower, I believe?"

"You still have eyes everywhere, don't you Alexei?"

"It helps one leeve longer when you are in my beezness."

Novorossiysk, a Russian port city on the eastern coast of the Black Sea was the childhood home of Alexei Shaposhnikov. Like many Russian families the Shaposhnikovs lived in a single room within a state-owned apartment shared with other families. One of those families, the Kovachenkos, had a beautiful daughter named Rosalie. As children in the 1960s, Alexei and Rosalie were best friends and playmates. They experimented and had a brief relationship during their teen years but found they were better suited as best friends.

"It's like kissing my sister," he confessed to her one day and she agreed she viewed him as a big brother.

During those formative years Novorossiysk received a tremendous honour. In 1973, it was awarded the title Hero City for its fierce resistance during WW II against the German offensive. From August 1942 until it was captured by the Germans in mid-September 1942, Novorossiysk's troops and its citizens fought bravely to retain possession of the eastern part of the bay, denying the Germans use of the port to supply their war machine.

The honour inspired many of the city's young men to enlist in the military, including Alexei. Standing 5-foot, 7, Alexei was not tall by Soviet military standards, but he was powerfully built. He had worked in Novorossiysk's docks since he was 12, first as an errand boy and by the time he was 14, as a labourer doing a man's work moving cargo.

Rosalie knew Alexei had always been athletic but discovered his incredible physical strength and dexterity during a country outing just before he joined the military.

"What are you doing? Alexei, come down here," a frightened Rosalie said as Alexei climbed up the side of an old wooden chapel that had been abandoned for decades. Once he ascended the three storeys to the peak of the roof, he wasn't satisfied and started to scale the steeple jamming his fingers and toes into existing holes or making new ones to act as holds. His plan was to climb another storey higher to straddle the spire for a 360-degree view of the sea and the countryside.

The spire lay before him but when he grasped it to pull his body upward, the large metal lance snapped off its rusted mount pulling the 17-year-old earthward.

Alexei twisted in the air for the least damaging position to take the impact when he saw little Rosalie in the direct path of both his body and the huge metal spear he was riding.

Alexei wrestled with the spire, bringing its base next to his feet and then kicked outward with all the power his weightless body could summon. The much heavier spire moved just a foot or two to the right and Alexei's body rotated a much greater distance to the left. The spire landed nose first, jamming itself two-feet deep into the moist soil, just missing Rosalie. Alexei stretched out one leg at an off-balance tilt, the way the cargomen do when they fall from the nets. Like a well oiled machine, Alexei's leg touched the ground then crumpled naturally as knee, hip, arms, back and neck follow suit distributing the force across his entire body.

Alexei jumped up immediately. Nothing broken but he knew he would be sore in the morning. Rosalie stood, mouth agape, not knowing whether to scold him for his stupidity or praise him for his amazing physical feat.

"The army is the right place for you," she said. "You are stupid and nothing can kill you."

That same toughness served him well in the military. He easily defeated much larger opponents in hand-to-hand combat training, sometimes fighting three attackers at once. He took to weapons naturally, and had dead-eye accuracy as a sniper.

When he won the maroon beret, a highly coveted prize among soldiers with the highest achievements in weaponry, physical endurance and fighting skills, he came to the attention of Anatoli Pleshkunov, the Special Forces Brigade Commander, of the 431st Independent Naval Reconnaissance Spetsnaz, the Russian equivalent of the U.S. Navy SEALs.

Alexei took to the special forces training like he was born to it, excelling in all things that require toughness and extreme endurance. Under Pleshkunov's tutelage, Alexei takes a rocket ride through the ranks rising to major before his 30th birthday.

What the official record doesn't show is his growing proficiency as an elite operative specializing in stealth, espionage, sabotage and assassination.

With glasnost, the new openness policies of Mikhail Gorbachev, comes the beginnings of decay for the elite Spetsnaz forces. In 2010, following further military reforms the Russian leadership disbands the Spetsnaz units and distributes their warriors among different divisions of the military.

It is time for Alexei to find a life outside of the armed forces.

Thanks to his contacts with former KGB operatives, he has documentation created that makes him a welcome emigrant to Canada in 2011. To the tax man and other prying eyes, Alexei is a shipping clerk, a logistics expert. In reality, he is a broker for specialized weaponry from the former Soviet Union to buyers around the world. Few of the weapons, except those he keeps for himself and his team when some persuasion is needed, find their way into Canada and that's the way Alexei likes it.

Alexei's favourite weapons remain those he trained with as a Spetsnaz operative, the kind of low-tech, stripped-down firearms that do the job reliably but are suitable for covert operations – like the AKS-74U compact assault rifle, VSS Vintorez sniper rifle and the PP-19 Bizon submachine gun. At closer range, he has the NRS-2, a survival knife with a wicked blade and an additional surprise, a side barrel that delivers a single deadly shot in complete silence.

"So, what is this beezness you want me to do?" he asks Rosalie.

"I need you to find a monster, and kill him," she says, as she drops a large folder before him containing information about the strengths, weaknesses and habits of the Sanguinus.

Alexei takes a few minutes to leaf through the package.

"Will you take the job?"

"We are Spetsnaz. Any mission, any time, any place. I need good budget for surveillance equeepment. I need at least seex good men and a few eggstra things," he says with a twinkle in his eye.

"Money is not a problem. You tell me how much, and I'll have the cash today."

"And monster? How I go about findeeng him? Your police, despite their resources, have met no success."

"My husband told me there's a man, Ben Saxon, who may have a system or strategy to track the Vampire. We don't have any idea what it is."

"So, why does not your husband find how this Saxon does it, or why has this pairson not gone to poleece?"

"It's a very long story. Al and Saxon don't get along, and the police have written him off as a crackpot."

"Ah yes, Ben Saxon. I hev read about him in newspapers. And you think this guy is not so crazy, after all?"

§§§

Replica Roy stands arms akimbo before an assortment of human-looking body parts.

"So here it is, a lexan collar covered with foam latex to look like your real neck, albeit after a Timmy's donuts binge. That thing that looks like a torso is a thin lexan chest plate, front and back. Light enough to be comfortable but tough enough to stop a 22 at close range. Taking a bullet would hurt like hell but I'm guessing you'll take bruises over blood and guts any time.

"Lastly, your idea about a stake with a shotgun shell tip poses too much risk. Despite the lexan chest protector, something with enough stopping power for the guy you're going after might permanently blind you, take off a chunk of your face, or kill you.

"I made some adjustments to a survival weapon called a 'wasp knife' because of its unique stinger. The knife has a CO2 cartridge in its handle and an internal tube that follows the blade to its tip. The idea is to stab your adversary and when it's buried, a button on the handle discharges a blast of freezing compressed gas that expands to the size of a basketball. All the internal organs are frozen, or at least the parts that aren't blown to bits. It was designed to take out a grizzy bear with a single thrust."

"But I may not have a chance to stab him," I say.

"No worries. You don't hold the knife. I removed most of the handle and part of the blade and then recessed them into the chest and back plates, two on the front and two in back. If there's more than 10 pounds of pressure on your neck armour or chest plate, the front knives spring out and release their gas. If he comes at you from the back, you hit triggers positioned on either wrist and he'll be impaled and blown to bits as fast as you can say pop goes the weasel. Just make sure the blade goes in deep, the deeper the better for maximum effect."

"Ingenious," I say.

"You're welcome," says Roy, lifting his ball cap and with it what looks like the top half of his head exposing his brain.

I groan.

"Been waitin' to do that all week."

"Roy, shouldn't we have some armour and weapons for Dragul?"

"I told Roy not to bother. Armour would slow me down and Vlad wouldn't show if he felt I had weapons," says Dragul, adding: "Shouldn't we test Al's weapons first?"

"So glad you asked," says Roy.

"Comfy?" asks Roy after squeezing me like a sausage into my warrior suit and then arming the knives.

Considering I'm wearing body armour around my neck and chest and I'm about to face a giant vampire mano-a-mano, I guess comfy is a relative term.

"Let's give it a whirl," Roy says and in a surprising single movement spins and lobs a watermelon basketball-style at my chest.

I feel the impact and a click as twin knives project outward. 'WHOOOMP!"

Frozen bits of pink and green fly in all directions.

"That worked. Now let's try it with the wrist controls."

Roy backs me into another watermelon positioned between my shoulder blades.

"Hit it," he says and I comply by pressing the button on my wrist.

'WHOOOMP!'

"Watch out world. It is I, Al Hamblyn, menace to melons everywhere. I raise my hand to give Dragul a high five but he sighs and says.

"You realize we will be fighting for our lives."

CHAPTER THIRTY

THE WRATH OF ROSALIE

After the way Al ushered him out so unceremoniously, Saxon is surprisingly willing to meet the following day with Rosalie and 'a friend' at the Parkdale Community Law Clinic offices.

"We need your help to get the real murderer," she says.

"Mangorian is your murderer," says Saxon, matter-of-factly.

"He is not the murderer. We have him on videotape showing he was nowhere near . . ."

"That's just for two murders. Another eight people are dead that we know of, and how many others there are is unknown. Many others vanished without a trace . . . including my daughter," he says, his eyes filled with emotion.

"Regardless, whether it's Mangorian or another vampire, I want him found and destroyed," says Rosalie.

"Does you husband know about this?"

"No, and he's not to know. I need your word on that."

"Well, it's not exactly like we're Facebook friends. I'm not about to contact him under any circumstances. But considering your husband's connection, I'm surprised you want to do this."

Rosalie is about to dismiss the question but decides to answer.

"Mr. Saxon, you are a driven man. You are driven because of your daughter's disappearance and likely death at the hands of a vampire. I have a loss too. While I appear a civilized woman, you should know I was born and raised in a place where we know how to settle a score. It is in our nature."

"And your friend?"

"He's a friend and he thinks like me. That's all you need to know about it. Now tell us, how are you able to track the vampire? We need to know how you can forecast where the murders occur. You reported Shirley Ames' murder to police and were able to accurately predict that people, from two specific neighbourhoods who disappeared, had actually been murder victims even before their bodies were discovered. What is it? Have you figured out the killer's pattern? Do you use high-tech surveillance? ESP? What?"

"Paint."

"Paint?" says Rosalie, glancing quizzically to Saxon and then to Alexei.

"Yes, paint. That and my network through Neighbourhood Watch."

"I need a bit more of an explanation," says Rosalie.

Saxon reaches into his briefcase and pulls out a map of Toronto, unfolds it and lays it on Sally's desk.

"When police first asked for our help to trap Mangorian, they told everyone to park cars on top of all the manhole covers so he couldn't escape from the storm sewers. It occurred to me that Mangorian might be using the sewers again, this time not to escape but as a direct route to his victims. He certainly would be familiar with all the routes after living in the sewers for 10 years," Saxon explains.

"So, if there's a second vampire, he might be living in the sewers, too, and be using them to move around. But I still don't see how that helps us," Rosalie says.

"I puzzled over that for awhile, too, until I came up with the solution. I sent a text to all my block captains asking them to add a little something to every manhole cover and sewer grate in their neighborhood. That something was a thin line of paint on the edge of the manhole cover extending onto the lip that holds it in place. For the sewer grates, we put a fine line of paint on the edge of the curb. If someone comes out of the sewer, they have to lift the manhole cover and when they replace it, the paint becomes misaligned. When the grates are lifted, they bang against the curb and chip the paint. A simple walk around the block every day, something all Neighbourhood Watch captains do, anyway, can spot any misaligned or chipped markings. When that happens, the captain sends me a text reporting date and location.

"Every time I get a report like that, I put a green dot on the map. I thought that if I had good records of where the manhole covers were displaced, I might be able to uncover a pattern for the killings, or be able to match missing persons with those who were the most likely murder victims.

"Two days before Shirley Ames' murder, I got a text from the captain for Crescent Villa Road. I went to see and sure enough the cover alignment was definitely off. I called a friend in the city's engineering department to be sure it wasn't public works and he reported no crews had been in the area.

"We canvassed the neighborhood for missing persons but there were none. I was a bit confused and figured that perhaps my idea was flawed. Still, I had a feeling that there was a connection, so we started running Watch patrols for the next few days right around the six or eight homes near the manhole.

"I was with two other Watchers when we heard a scream and glass breaking and saw someone actually jumping over a seven-foot fence. I took out my cell phone to video the scene and, hopefully, the perp. I got some of it, but it was dark. It wasn't very useful to police. At first, the cops thought I might have done it to frame Mangorian but the other two Watchers vouched for me."

The morning after Ames' body was discovered, I checked the manhole cover and again it had been disturbed. I compared that with my missing person files and it dawned on me that the murders and the disappearances all happened a day or two after we recorded the paint misalignments. In other words, the vampire was running dress rehearsals, or scouting for victims a day or two before he, literally, went in for the kill.

"We initially missed it, but a sewer cover behind your friend Sally's home had been disturbed. We didn't get to it until sometime after her body was discovered."

Rosalie holds up a hand to stop Saxon from continuing and then takes a deep breath while his words sink in.

"We need you to plot out information for us so we can set a trap. How long will it take to get us information we can use?" asks Rosalie.

"About 10 seconds," Saxon replies.

"Ten seconds?"

Saxon picks up his cell phone and reads a text from one of his block captains.

"34 Shanly Place. Sewer grate disturbance, 8:45 this morning."

§§§

"Hi Rosalie? Things are just crazy at the office what with the police snooping around and me trying to save the IPO. You're not going to see much of me over the next few days. I'll be staying with Dragul at the TT suite. I just wanted you to know," I say, with my pulse pounding in my ears for making up such a blatant lie.

"That's okay Al. I'm at the Law Clinic. I'm trying to make sense of Sally's case notes and interview candidates for . . you know."

"Yes. That's really great. You are a good soul. Sally would want that done," I say.

There's a long pause before Rosalie responds.

"Yes, all my thoughts are of doing right by Sally," Rosalie says carefully choosing her words before adding, "Al, I truly love you with all my heart. You know that."

"Yes I do, but . . .?"

"Oh, I'm just getting sentimental, you know with Sally gone, we have to remember to cherish what we have and the time we have together," Rosalie says.

"And I do, I truly do," I say and I mean it.

Rosalie turns off her phone and smiles a crooked smile while her mind tumbles back to her first encounter with Hamblyn.

§§§

The ad in the laundromat led Rosalie to a squalid storefront on Ossington Avenue near College long before hipsters rediscovered the area. When Hamblyn welcomed her into his office, dusting off a proffered chair with his sleeve, it did little to allay her initial trepidations. He was not handsome, not that looks are any determinant of legal ability, she thought. Still, his cheap suit and shoes screamed out that if she was to find justice, this was not a good starting point.

The lawyer sounded like he knew his stuff and seemed nice enough. That, she concluded, was his problem. Back when they were handing out the DNA that would become Al Hamblyn, they failed to include a gene for ruthlessness. That's the gene Rosalie decided was necessary to be financially successful as a lawyer.

Partly because his price was right, but mostly because she felt sorry for him, Rosalie agreed to let Hamblyn arrange a meeting with 'that jerk', Bill Ritchie, and his high-priced lawyer, Trevor Hogan.

When Rosalie and Hamblyn walked into the glass and marble edifice that housed the financially successful and genetically ruthless law firm of Smithers Hogan and Boothby, she felt hopelessly outgunned. When the two huddled on one side of a 40-foot cherrywood table, with Ritchie and Hogan leisurely sprawling out as if they were at a posh resort, Rosalie felt the needle on her intimidation meter enter the red zone.

That's when something miraculous happened.

Like a butterfly emerging from its chrysalis, Hamblyn bloomed before her. He took a thick stack of paper from his briefcase, neatly spread them like a deck of cards and in syncopathic rhythm jabbed at one document after another while citing precedent after precedent, for liability, culpability, vulnerability, sexual assault, designation as a sexual predator, assault causing bodily harm, permanent disability, and on and on.

"Even if most of the charges don't stick, and some definitely will, your client won't be showing his face at another strip club let alone the country club for another 20 years."

Before Hamblyn had finished, by the sheet-white expression on Ritchie's face, Rosalie knew they had won. The only question was how much.

She looked once more at Hamblyn with new eyes.

"This is a man who is humble, takes nothing for himself but gives everything to others. This is a man to be cherished."

§§§

The city of Novorossiysk is built over large deposits of marl, a high-quality limestone essential in the manufacture of natural cement, a material useful to form and repair architectural sculptures and designs.

It was in one of Novorossiysk's many cement factories that Oskar Kovachenko, a hard-drinking but handsome labourer who kept the marl furnaces stoked, met beautiful shipping clerk Ludmila Cherkov. After a one-year courtship, the two married and moved into a single room in a state-supplied apartment they shared with two other families.

Rosalie arrived 10 months later. The year was 1968.

The cramped conditions with families living on top of families provided one advantage. When parents went off to work there was always someone's babushka available to watch the children, providing about as much care for the individual as a shepherd attending a flock of sheep.

The children mostly found themselves on their own and so it was that Rosalie was swept into Alexei's world, always looking for adventure and learning about the world. It was Alexei's interest in things international that got Rosalie interested in learning English, at first through books, and later listening to English lyrics in rock and roll songs and, when she could get them, watching movies in English.

When Mikhail Gorbachev instituted glasnost, a policy greater freedoms, like many of the country's youth, Rosalie and Alexei felt they could escape their parents' daily struggle for existence and find joys beyond that of a vodka bottle.

By 1988, the promise of glasnost faded. Jobs were in short supply and non-existent for women. Alexei was in the military. With no job, no allies and parents too impoverished to help, prospects for Rosalie were grim.

In desperation, Rosalie signed on with an agency promising her a rich Canadian husband. All she had to do was present herself, have pictures taken and the agency would do the rest. Once she arrived in Canada, she was told, she could meet eligible Canadian bachelors and, if the chemistry worked, she would find herself a husband. If no satisfactory match was made, they'd find her a well-paid job. Photos and letters from other girls who were living a wonderful life in Canada were plastered across the agency's walls. Rosalie took the bait.

The agency was, in reality, a front for Russian organized crime. The girls were to be sold into prostitution on their arrival in Canada.

By the merest of coincidences, one of Alexei's Spetsnaz colleagues passed photos of young, scantily clad women around the barracks. Alexei's eyes fixed on one photo of a beautiful red-haired girl. It was Rosalie.

"Where did you get these photos," Alexei growled, smashing his comrade against a barracks wall.

The rattled soldier explained his brother took photos for the Russian mob and as a bonus kept copies for himself.

Alexei understood immediately and, through connections forged in missions with the KGB, passed on a message that no one was to touch Rosalie. The message sent a chill through Boris Morozov. He had no wish to cross the KGB. Still, he needed his investment back and placed her with a strip club where he kept most of her earnings. When Rosalie was injured and couldn't perform, he had no more use for her and wrote her off.

"Be gone. I don't ever want to see you again."

Her unceremonious exit meant she had no money for food, only a few pieces of clothing she could wear on the street, and no place to live. One of the girls told her she should sue but how could she? Escaping the cold in a 24-hour laundromat, Rosalie spied a handwritten ad from Hamblyn Legal Services – You Don't Pay Unless You Win.

Over the next several weeks, Hamblyn became much more than her lawyer. He lent her money he couldn't afford to give, and which she couldn't repay, and he found her a warm place to stay with his friend Sally Wiseman.

"Hell, Sally never stays there anyway," he said, fumbling about nervously as he usually did when Rosalie was in his presence.

As the days passed, Rosalie's attachment to Hamblyn became absolute. "This is a good man. This is a man I could love."

CHAPTER THIRTY-ONE

THE TRAP

The occupants of all 10 Shanly Place homes have been persuaded to vacate their houses for the week. The inducement? Tickets to the exotic resort of their choosing, $10,000 in spending money, and six tough, heavily-armed men telling them the neighbourhood will be a very dangerous place over the next few days.

"We expect vampire is targeting one of those three houses at end. One in middle, Number 34, is probably the one because single woman lives there," Alexei tells Rosalie.

On each approach to Shanly Place and, from two angles via the rear yard that backs onto a ravine, Alexei's men lay in wait.

The three homes at the end provide a criss-cross view of each other, ideal for surveillance and to create a crossfire, cutting off escape. Alexei has assembled an elite team of former Spetsnaz operatives, all experts in a range of weapons and all stone-cold killers. They also have specialized expertise, he explains to Rosalie.

"Anatoly is electronics man. He set up command vehicle, night vision cameras, and early-warning sensors. Bogdan and Roman are snipers. Bogdan has recorded kill 2,016 metres, third longest kill shot for Russian Special Forces. Roman has three kills at over 1,000 metres.

"Close range we hev Alexander and Sergei, deadly in hand-to-hand combat and knife fighting. Viktor handles explosives. And then there's me."

Alexei grabs his walkie-talkie to provide last minute instructions and do a final sound check.

"Eef you get chance, shoot to keel. Make certain he is dead before you approach him. He wheel not show any mercies to you," Alexei tells his men. "This man is beast. He is most dangerous adversary you hev ever faced. I know you will take nussing for granted."

Rosalie takes Alexei to the side and reinforces his concerns. "I know you have gone over the information that I gave to you but, I say again, this is no man you face. The vampire sees in the dark better than you see by day. He is much faster and stronger than any man . . . And he knows things. He will not be unaware of your presence," Rosalie says. "Can your men really stop him?"

"Spetsnaz warriors hev animal instinct, too," Alexei says. "Our symbol is wolf because we love adversity. We endure torture, pain, days without sleep, extreme heat and cold, long marches without food or proper clothing. Eef my men cannot stop him, no one can. Spetsnaz are best because we do not have sophisticated weapons like Navy SEALs or Delta Force. We do same job they do with skill but also through cunning, will power and ferocity."

"Trap is set," says Alexei at the controls in the Command Vehicle on the next block. "Now we wait for mouse."

As confident as she is of Alexei's prowess, Rosalie can't help but give a shiver. Who is in the trap, she thinks. Who is the mouse?

The shadows on Shanly Place grow longer until they envelope the block in darkness. The bustle of cars slows and stops entirely after 8. A dog walker strolls leisurely along the street twice, at 9:42 and 9:51. A jogger goes down Shanly at 10:16 and the follows a trail into a ravine that backs onto the cul-de-sac. After that, neither electronic sensors, night-vision cameras, sound detection devices, nor seven pairs of unblinking Spetsnaz-trained eyes sound an alarm this night.

The pink glow of dawn cracks along the eastern horizon waking Rosalie from her slumber in one of the Command Vehicle's captain's chair.

"I didn't mean to nod off," she says apologetically.

"You don't hev to be here. You go home little sister," Alexei says tenderly.

"This is my place. I am like you. I am Novorossiysk. We do not forget. We do not forgive."

Rosalie's cell rings.

"Anything?" the voice at the end of the line says. It's Saxon following up on the night's events.

"No, he didn't show," says Rosalie, partly disappointed but also greatly relieved.

"He will show tonight. I'm certain."

With more time to prepare, Anatoly expands the monitoring zone by placing sensors at every sewer opening within a two-block area. Viktor plants a series of flash bombs, lots of light but almost no sound to exploit the vampire's susceptibility to bright light without disrupting the neighbourhood. The other ex-Spetsnaz spend time cleaning their firearms, checking their ammunition clips and meditating until dusk settles.

Again the evening passes with nothing out of the ordinary. The surrounding streets go quiet by 11 and when the synchronized watches of Alexei's team read 1 a.m., none of the alarms have been triggered.

"He always strikes before midnight," says Rosalie glancing at her watch. At least from all of the accounts we know of, that's true."

"We will maintain our watch until sunrise as planned, no deviation. A trained killer will change his pattern. Spetsnaz are trained to expect the unexpected."

The unexpected happens at 2:15 a.m.

The furthest sensor to the north of Shanly signals activity at the sewer opening and two sniper scopes swivel toward it. Less than a second later, the sensor the furthest to the south comes to life just beating the beeps from a detection module in a ravine immediately to the east.

Three of Viktor's silent flash bombs ignite like ground level lightning but there's no vampire to blind.

"Bogdan, target is north. Roman, target is south. Alexander check what happening east. Viktor see what making flash bombs go off. Everybody else, maintain position," Alexei snaps into his walkie-talkie.

Anatoly sweeps the area with his fixed infrared cameras but comes up with nothing. He directs a drone equipped with a night-shot camera to the north and another to the south. Bogdan peers down his night-vision scope to the sewer access to the north. No target. Roman scans the streetscape to the south. Less than 800 metres to the barking sensor. "An easy shot, if he's there," Roman thinks.

Viktor examines the exploded flash bombs and can't believe what he finds. "They are wired all wrong. That's eempossible. I set them up myself."

A perfectionist, Viktor has to learn more. He cracks open his toolkit and begins taking the mechanisms apart, a distraction that in the next five seconds proves fatal.

"Viktor, you have secured flash bombs? Viktor?" Alexei asks into the walkie-talkie. Radio silence provides him with his answer.

The patio doors of 34 Shanly slide open silently as Alexander slips out under cover of darkness armed with a PP-19 Bizon submachine gun that's equipped with a silencer and a bayonet. Hundreds of hours of training missions, live fire, multiple opponents with real knives, who cut for real, washed all fear from Alexander years ago. An expert in stealth, Alexander has used his ability to move silently to surprise and kill more enemies than he can remember. And if it's the enemy who is in hiding, waiting to spring a trap, Alexander had the well-honed skills to deal with the best fighters attacking him from any direction.

He moves silently into the backyard of 34 Shanly with his senses tuned high. There are no trees or buildings closer to him than 25 yards, too far for an adversary to launch an effective attack from above. His night and heat seeking goggles scan the grounds a full 360 degrees around him. No one is there.

A creaking sound on a rooftop about 40 yards away launches him into fight mode. He ducks to make himself a hard target while, simultaneously, directing his assault rifle toward the rooftop to return fire. No shots ring out.

From Alexei's briefing, Alexander is confident the vampire will not use firearms, but that's on a conscious level. Subconsciously, his training denies him the luxury of assumptions. Whenever, wherever, how ever, the attack comes, he is ready. It is all automatic reaction and animal reflex, the result of years of constant life-threatening drills under live fire and multiple opponent attacks. These skills were proven time and again during Russia's wars with Georgia and the Chechen Republic.

Alexander knows what to expect and he stands ready for any attack whether it comes from the north, south, east or west.

What he does not expect, nor his Spetsnaz training prepare him for, is an attacker who drops straight down from the sky.

Vlad caused the creaking sound by leaping from a rooftop an astonishing 120 feet into the darkened skies. Gravity fulfills the rest of the mission, redirecting him Earthward while amplifying the vampire's 350 pounds through a bone-crushing free fall onto the blind side of Alexander's head.

"Alexander? Alexander?" No response.

Anatoly witnesses Alexander's end when the drone's wide-angle lens captures a figure streaking from the sky, striking feet first and driving Alexander's head into the ground at 60 miles an hour. In the next second, the drone went dead.

Alexei needed no elaboration. His powerful fighter and long-time friend was gone but Spetsnaz training focused him on the task at hand.

"Bogdan, Roman."

The snipers need no instructions. They train their scopes at the rear of 34 Shanly, but a dark figure moves close to the building, thwarting a clean shot.

Anatoly directs the second drone to the obscured area, and a crisp image of the vampire, at the rear of the house, appears on his screen.

"Position C," says Anatoly, alerting Sergei to the entry point via patio doors into the home's livingroom. Sergei, already in position with a silencer-equipped PP-19 Bizon submachine gun, sends a 20-shot burst that rips through the patio doors and anything behind them.

He readies his weapon to unleash a second burst once Anatoly's drone pinpoints the location of, what he hopes is, a wounded target. That's the plan, but it doesn't work out that way. A side window, casement and all, crashes into Sergei, sending him reeling. In practised fashion, he rolls to safety delivering a lethal spray of silenced bullets at the living bulldozer.

'Ta ta ta ta ta ta ta ta ta ta ta.'

The action tears off the ceiling fixture and smashes a lamp. A grey gloom envelopes the room.

Sergei searches the shadows for his quarry directing yet another silenced spray into the darkest recesses. 'Ta ta ta ta ta ta ta ta ta ta ta.'

He realizes he has just a one-second burst remaining if he continues to use the submachine gun in automatic mode. By switching to semi-automatic he may have a dozen shots left but reasons it will take far more than one or two bullets to take down this creature.

The decision is made for him, as chairs, a bookshelf, and an end table hurtle toward him. He fires quick taps through the barrage.

'ta ta ta . . . 'ta ta ta' . . . ' ta ta ta' . . . 'ta ta click click'

At the sound of the click, Vlad rises from the ruined furnishings and strides confidently toward the Russian. Sergei smiles grimly, grasping two short knives from sheaths in his jacket. The vampire is a monster. His head nearly touches the ceiling and his face is death. Monstrous fangs protrude from his lips and vicious, inch long claws extend from his fingers and bare toes.

Sergei throws one knife at the monster's head and the other at his heart. Vlad makes a sweep with his arm, deflects one blade and catches the other and pockets it.

But Sergei isn't done yet. From a sheath at the side of his boot he withdraws the same foot-long fighting knife he used to dispatch three Chechens six years earlier.

Vlad lashes out, claws raking at Sergei's face, but the Russian's knife parries the thrust. The vampire then slashes with his left, ripping through Sergei's jacket, drawing blood before the Spetsnaz warrior's steel glints again slicing the back of the vampire's hand.

The adversaries step back and then charge like warring bulls. The vampire stops a knife thrust by grasping Sergei's right wrist and the Russian's grip on the monster's other hand prevents claws from raking his face.

For a twinkle in time, the two lean face to face.

In a move impossible for a human, Vlad twists one leg and flips it straight in the air, momentarily, sandwiching it between the foes. A deep, evil laugh escapes from the vampire as the death-dealing leg descends with razor-sharp talons slicing the Russian open like a ripe cantaloupe.

The drone hovers by the shattered window and relays Sergei's last moments to Anatoly. Neither Bogdan nor Roman have a direct line of sight on their target but the drone's precise, real-time imaging allows Anatoly to effectively direct their silent fire through the house's clapboard siding.

'Ta ta ta ta."

'Ta ta ta ta ta."

The team selected the VSS Vintorez as their sniper rifle of choice because of its compact size, accuracy, silencer and night-vision options. All of the weapon's attributes now come into play.

"Bogdan, Roman. Target ees crouching four feet north of missing window," Anatoly shouts as each sniper discharges a second burst through the walls, Bogdan, north to south and Roman, south to north.

'Ta ta ta ta ta."

'Ta ta ta ta ta ta."

One bullet catches Vlad in the shoulder and spins him around.

The vampire growls in pain and hurls an end table at the drone that was escorting death his way.

"Target hit but not down," says Anatoly before his screen goes blank.

"Drone ees down. Target last known position three feet north, one foot lower than last burst."

Vlad uses the Russians' momentary blind spot to move through the shadows to crash through the back door of the house where Bogdan is positioned on the roof. In four leaps he is on the second floor. Bogdan scrambles madly on the rooftop, tries to sight his target, fails and then fires blindly through the roof.

'Ta ta ta' 'Ta ta ta'

In the master bedroom Vlad spies a massive four poster bed and snaps off one of the pillars like a popsicle stick with one sharp end. He waits until the firing stops and then hurls his full weight and strength behind the splintered pillar, transforming it into a projectile that cleaves through the bullet pattern in the sheet rock ceiling, through the attic, the chip board roofline, and skewers Bogdan like a piece of meat on a barbeque.

Roman instantly responds firing just below the roofline where his comrade is already dead.

'Ta ta ta ta ta ta'

"Ta ta ta click'

The 20-round magazine is exhausted.

Roman sees the vampire's yellow eyes burning at him and then watches as Vlad makes an impossible leap from the window 50 feet to the roof of the house next door. Roman is bathed in an icy sweat as he removes the exhausted magazine and reaches into his backpack for a reload. The vampire reaches the peak of the roof next door and is poised to leap at the Russian. But the Spetsnaz sniper is quicker. With the new magazine snapped in place, he raises his rifle to fire but . . . too late. Roman slumps over, his lifeless eyes awash with blood spurting from Sergei's finely crafted throwing knife lodged in his temple.

"Roman? Bogdan?" Alexei expected no answer and received none.

All of his elite fighters, save Anatoly and himself, dead.

"Drive away. Get out of here," he says to Rosalie, signaling Anatoly to follow him around the block to stand dead centre in Shanly Place.

The young and the old warrior stand back to back in the street, each holding an assault rifle, knives, and a proficiency in hand-to-hand combat few men on Earth can match.

"Come get us vampire," Alexei shouts defiantly.

§§§

The two hear a crunch from one of the rooftops.

Anatoly screams: "He's coming at us from the air."

The two scan the sky and, with their night-vision goggles, they make out something hurtling down toward them at an incredible speed. Twin streams of fiery death cut through the blackness until both magazines are exhausted. The ghastly task has been effective, slicing through the target so effectively that body parts rain all around them. One piece lands with a soggy thud and rolls to Anatoly's feet. It's an arm still wrapped in a bloody sleeve bearing the Spetsnaz logo of a wolf.

At once, Vlad is upon them, striking Anatoly so hard that the impact is transferred from back to back to Alexei who is sent spinning 30 feet. The vampire grabs the stunned Anatoly, rips into his throat and drinks deeply before casting the dead man aside.

Then he turns toward Alexei who has fury on his face and a fighting knife in his hand.

Vlad stretches to his full height, extends his fangs and the claws on his hands and feet to complete his monstrous pose.

Any other man would be stricken with fear. But Alexei is not any other man. He always believed it would end like this and he relishes the thought. Alexei's greatest fear, when Russia dismantled the elite Spetsnaz units, was not death but dying weak, old, and forgotten in a public home for the elderly.

This is as it should be, death in glorious battle. Such thoughts always occupied his mind when he engaged in mortal combat, a warrior's mindset so there is no particle of reservation, no holding back in the bloody business at hand.

The vampire's much longer reach and razor sharp claws are a significant advantage, and an advantage that means Alexei cannot initiate the attack. He will wait for the monster to make a move, find an opening, and not stop until only one of them still stands.

Systema, the martial art created for the Spetsnaz, drills patience into its fighters. A weaker opponent can prevail over a much more powerful adversary if he bides his time, and pits only strengths against his enemy's weaknesses. As an expert in systema, Alexei is a master of patience, and a master of the many martial arts incorporated into the Russian fighting system.

Alexei sees a glint in the Sanguinus' yellow eyes and he knows an attack is imminent. The vampire lunges forward like a beast swiping wildly with those razor claws. Alexei calmly steps back at 45 degrees, out of range and at an angle forcing Vlad to reposition before he can attack again. Alexei knows the attack had been merely a feint to hide his adversary's real plan and to probe for weaknesses.

The monster moves in once more with both arms churning like death-dealing windmills. Again, Alexei steps back, not taking the bait because he knows two-arm attacks are no real threat. To get the reach and power necessary for a disabling blow, even a vampire, needs to stand at an angle. Otherwise, strikes carry the force of the arms only, lacking the killing power when the body's full potential is put into play.

As if reading Alexei's mind, the vampire steps back and then immediately lunges forward at an angle with razor tipped claws stabbing toward Alexei's neck. This time Alexei stands his ground stabbing at Vlad's deadly digits hoping to lop off one or more of the claw-bearing fingers to even the match. The knife cuts into the webbing between thumb and index, forcing Vlad to jump back. In relative terms, the wound is no more than a bee-sting.

The vampire now adopts the stance of a boxer, still at an angle where both claws are held tighter to his body but where both lethal hands can employ full strength when they engage. As the vampire steps forward, Alexei bends his own left knee so his head and torso lean backward 60 degrees, an action that appears to be a retreat – shifting the head out of harm's way – thereby inviting the attacker to move in more aggressively. When the vampire starts to step forward on his left leg, rather than stepping back with his right, Alexei sweeps it forward in perfect counter-balance with his head, dynamically intercepting the vampire's foot with his heavy army boot and lifting it high in the air.

The surprise judo move – de ashi harai – topples the 350-pound vampire backward. With a human adversary, Alexei would pounce on him and stab him in the heart but even supine this creature has too many weapons. Instead, Alexei's knife seeks a home in the vampire's leg. A strike to a major artery or key tendon will impair movement and make Vlad easier to kill.

Spetsnaz fighting strategy holds that the strongest legs win. A full half of all Spetsnaz physical training is directed to increasing the strength and stamina of its soldiers' legs because 50 per cent of the body's muscle power is in the legs.

There's an old boxing saying that goes, 'kill the body and the head will die.' In real life-and death-combat, Alexei knows if you kill the legs, your enemy dies. Once the enemy is too weak to march or is hobbled, he is easily dispatched.

Alexei's six and-a-half-inch blade finds the calf but tears only meat as the vampire howls and flips backward acrobatically. Regaining his balance, Vlad rocks for a second and then launches forward like a fullback heading for the goal line but with teeth and talons flashing.

Alexei dodges a vicious raking movement from the right and uses a beat lunge against the vampire's left clawed hand and, surprisingly, it works. The fencing maneuver creates a small space parallel to Vlad's arm for the knife to bite flesh. Then the vampire does the super human. He presses in hard against the cut of the knife, so it slices deeper into the rib cage, but misses vital organs. The passed arm now encircles Alexei's, locking it down.

Without his knife and the ability to retreat, Alexei's empty left hand is all that stands between Vlad's razor claws and those awful fangs.

Fangs or claws? Alexei can only block one while he tries to adjust his grip on the knife. Fangs mean instant death. The choice is clear. Alexei sacrifices his body. Claws thrust finger deep into the Russian's stomach inspiring a Niagara of blood and guts as they withdraw. Claws rip into the chest launching a sputtering crimson tide before plunging once more into Alexei's stomach. For a second, time is motionless as Alexei watches the fluid of life spurting from his chest while beads of the vampire's saliva drip on his neck from its hovering fangs.

"Phuut."

Vlad reels in pain from the small-caliber bullet that tears deep into his chest, a special surprise from the hidden side barrel in Alexei's NRS-2 knife. For a moment, the vampire teeters and then drops in one direction, and Alexei, a smile of satisfaction on his face, falls in the other.

\CHAPTER THIRTY-TWO

BATTLELINES

"Hello. Mr. Hamblyn?" says a voice that's vaguely familiar to me.

"What? Who? What time is it?"

"It's Ben Saxon. We've got to meet."

"How the hell did you get my cell number? What are you doing calling at . . . at . . . For Christ's sake. It's almost 2:30 in the morning."

"Shut up and listen."

I drive to Shanly Place, my foot full out on the accelerator, giving no heed to stop signs, traffic signals or other vehicles. I see Saxon and pull into what looks like a war zone. Two tough-looking guys lie dead, really dead, their throats and chests ripped apart, and a third man, or at least parts of him are scattered about. Some of the houses are visibly damaged by gunfire and impacts of some kind and I see a fourth figure on a rooftop who – Is it possible? – seems to be impaled by a giant spear.

"You said Rosalie was here. Where is she?" I say frantically.

"I don't know. I don't know," says Saxon looking even more frightened and paranoid than usual. "She was supposed to be in the mobile command centre," he says pointing to a van that looks like someone hacked it apart with a giant can opener. One side is almost entirely missing and, visibly, there's no one inside.

"Who are these men? What do they have to do with Rosalie?"

"I don't know that either. I think they were Russian mercenaries. I overheard Rosalie speaking to them in Russian. I think she hired them to track down and kill the vampire."

"Nonsense. Mangorian is back at the hotel. I just left him," I say beginning to suspect the whole thing is part of a ruse by Saxon to entrap Mangorian and me.

"Not Mangorian, the other vampire, Vlad."

My jaw drops open and for a minute, I can't breathe.

"How . . . how do you know about Vlad? "

"Rosalie told me about him. Wanted me to help find him. Something about avenging Sally."

My mind reels. My blood runs cold.

Far down the street, we see the reflected red, blue and white ribbons of police cars approaching.

"I can't afford to be held by police. I've got to get out of here," I say as I jump into my car and burn rubber heading away from the coloured lights.

A minute later, the police cars, including an unmarked police cruiser, pull onto Shanly Place and Det. Ferino climbs out in the midst of the horrifying carnage. He checks his watch. It's 2:47 a.m.

Ferino spies Ben Saxon and heads directly to him.

"What is this? What the hell happened here?"

"I'm not sure. They set up a trap for the vampire . . . It didn't work. He killed them all," Saxon says his voice and his legs failing him.

"Mangorian did this?"

"No, not him . . . his brother."

"What? What are you saying? Mangorian has a brother?"

"Yes, and he's bigger and meaner. You . . . you might be able to see some of it on video. The truck . . . it has cameras. I don't know what happened to Mrs. Hamblyn. I don't see her anywhere."

"Mrs. Hamblyn? What does she have to do with this," he says grabbing Saxon by the lapels and giving him a shake. "Snap out of it man. Where did they go?"

With that Saxon faints.

"Help. I need some help here," Ferino calls to his officers. "And ambulances or the coroner's meat van. I don't know. We just need help and lots of it."

The forensic team and the coroner's office arrive and take control of the scene.

Inside of the destroyed van, Det. Ferino watches the playback of several of the recordings.

"Unbelievable," says one of the uniformed cops. "But why was there so little noise?"

"They were really professionals. They used silencers. And it's a good thing they did. If neighbours started showing up, we'd have a lot more bodies on our hands," says Ferino.

"Man that guy really put up a fight," says one of the cops. "I'm glad we got here after everything was over or there'd be a lot of dead cops, too."

"Whether this was Mangorian's doing or not, he's involved. Hamblyn's involved. Hamblyn's wife is involved. You three are with me," he says pointing at the nervous cops next to him.

"Let's pick 'em up."

§§§

When I arrive at the TT. Dragul and Regina are waiting for me.

"Vlad has Rosalie. We have to go after him," I say while I madly scramble into my bedroom and haul out the special package Replica Roy prepared. I'm scarcely able to breathe. It takes another five minutes before I've calmed down enough to get the rest of the story out.

"Maybe she got away," Regina says helpfully.

"No, Vlad has her," Dragul says grimly. "He knows what she means to Al and, therefore, how much she means to me. He intends to use her as bait to bring me, bring us to him."

"If that's the case, let's go right now. I'm ready," I say. For the first time in my life, a dark hatred burns in my core that gives me strength that I never possessed, never knew I possessed. I am ready to fight, ready to kill, ready to die.

I open the large case that Replica Roy has packed, check the contents, and then say to Dragul: "I'll bring Rosalie back, and I will kill your brother."

"Blind hatred will get you killed. It will get all of us killed, especially Rosalie. We have our plan and we need to execute it perfectly, you and I, if we hope to survive."

Regina looks at Dragul strangely and says, "You are his twin. You are a Sanguinus. Why are you so afraid of him?"

"The Drink of Death has transformed Vlad. His strength and speed are unimaginable, far surpassing mine. And worst of all, the Drink, affects his brain. There will be no reasoning with him. He is a pure killing machine."

My cell rings.

"Al, it's Greg Mazpera. Police have a warrant to arrest Dragul and you. Det. Ferino is on his way now."

§§§

The mental fog slowly lifts rousing Rosalie from the deepest sleep she's ever had. As sense begins to percolate in her brain, the thought comes to her,

"Where am I, not in my bed, not at home?" Her eyes flutter open, at least she thinks they're open. It's so dark that an awful fear comes to mind. "Have I gone blind?"

A fine crack in the ceiling perhaps a hundred feet away spits out a tiny trickle of light giving her peace of mind that her vision is intact.

She tries to move but can't. Is she still dreaming that dream of helplessness when feet refuse to respond to orders from the brain? As a young girl she had a recurring nightmare of faceless hordes pursuing her with escape undermined by her own body, feet that fumbled, hands that couldn't hold.

As the next level of consciousness falls into place, she understands why her body isn't responding. She's bound, hand and foot.

Then memories of the night begin to return to her. Alexie's warriors, tough, unbeatable men who survived wars, insurgency, extreme deprivation, 100-mile marches, and life and death hand-to-hand combat with as many as three enemies at time, all dead. My dear Alexei. My invincible superman. My big brother. Dead. Against Vlad, they never stood a chance.

But why is she not dead? Where is she now? The ground she's lying on is cold and damp. The air is foul and musty. She hears the faint music of moving water and the tiny scratchings of something small scurrying by.

"It's a rat. I'm in a sewer."

Memories of the night so vividly recorded in Rosalie's mind return as she hits the replay button for that awful mental video.

Alexei's face, no longer reflecting the crazy, risk-taking boy she knew those many years ago, is a portrait of pure seething rage, a grim gladiator called to the arena for his greatest and final battle.

"Drive away. Get out of here," he barks, giving Rosalie the lingering look of undying brotherly love. That look said, "I love you. I will die for you."

Rosalie starts to do as directed, starts the van but her tear-filled eyes make it impossible to see, impossible to drive. A monitor at the rear of the van relays sounds of Alexei shouting, "Hurry, hurry."

Rosalie clambers to the rear and has a front row seat via one of Anatoly's night vision cameras for the real-time, real-life drama that begins to unfold.

"He's coming at us from the air," she hears Anatoly say.

A moment later two automatic weapons erupt, sending silent tongues of white-hot fire skyward followed by a rain of body parts.

Rosalie's heart leaps.

"Can it be? Is the battle won?"

Before the moment of exultation is embraced, a dark figure appears from the side and crashes into Anatoly knocking him and Alexei off their feet. The vampire is on Anatoly so fast that Rosalie is not certain what she is seeing until the Russian's body falls lifeless.

Rosalie has seen Dragul many times but this figure, rendered by night-vision in greens and blacks, is truly a monster, a hideous contortion of his brother and in enormous proportions.

Alexei is on his feet again, armed only with a knife. The vampire attacks and, at first, Rosalie fears it is over. But her hero easily avoids the rush and seems, incredibly, to be the one in control. Again the monster moves in whirling arms with every finger dagger-tipped death. Rosalie holds her breath and bites down hard on her lower lip.

Once more, Alexei handles the attack unfazed, amazingly forcing the creature back.

In a move so quick it takes her breath away, the vampire comes at Alexei with those razor claws seeking his jugular.

The veteran of so many Spetsnaz conflicts coolly holds his position and like a champion fencer makes a precision thrust through the melee of claws and fangs to strike something that makes the vampire fly back.

The monster takes a more cautious approach to prevent Alexei's talented knife doing more damage. This time it is Alexei who seems to retreat. The vampire immediately moves in but . . but . . Now the creature is flying in the air and crashing on his back.

Rosalie stares in amazement. What happened? How is this possible? For the first time, she begins to feel that there's a chance for victory as Alexei moves in on his fallen foe.

Alexei's knife darts in once, twice, and on the third lunge he strikes something that causes the vampire to scream and retreat with a backward somersault. Just as Rosalie begins to breathe again, the monster rushes with enormous speed and power, attacking with his every weapon. Alexei weaves, bobs and uses the knife to stop lethal claws from tearing at his neck when, incredibly, Alexei's knife finds an opening and jams into the monster's chest.

Rosalie holds her breath, waiting for the vampire to fall. Instead, the two figures appear locked together. It's too close, too close, she screams in her head. Then her worst fears are realized when Vlad's terrible talons thrust once, twice, three times into Alexei's helpless form. Images flash into Rosalie's mind of that cocky boy of her childhood transforming into a powerful fighter and now held helpless by a monster whose fangs descend on Alexei's still pulsating jugular.

There's an odd muffled "phuut" so quiet Rosalie isn't certain she actually heard it. But at that moment, Vlad stiffens, releases his hold on Alexie, and the adversaries fall like the two halves of a split log.

Rosalie watches the screen with mixed emotions. Her grief at the loss of her 'big brother' is deep, but knowing the monster is dead, and that Alexei died the way he wanted, consoles her.

Peace is short-lived. She watches aghast as the vampire struggles to rise, grabs Alexei's still warm body, and drinks straight from his heart.

In a madness born of the unrelenting fighting spirit of the men, women and children who defended Novorossiysk with their lives, Rosalie starts up the van and heads around the corner for Shanly Place.

Vlad is still there. He has drained Alexei and now sucks whatever blood remains in Anatoly's heart to renew his strength and heal his wounds. Rosalie drives straight at the vampire, her foot crushing the accelerator for all she's worth.

Whether it's the blood lust, his weakened state, or pure arrogance, Vlad continues to feed as Rosalie bears down on him. At the very last instant, he becomes aware of the truck barreling at him and jumps sideways, taking a glancing blow.

The vampire is stunned so Rosalie pulls the van around to drive at him again. This time Vlad is prepared and easily dodges the cumbersome vehicle.

Rosalie tries for a third run, but Vlad has attached himself to the side of the truck, iron talons on his hands and feet ripping into the van's fibreglass body. With a mighty pull, Vlad tears off the side of the van, slides inside and sits next to Rosalie.

Rosalie grabs one of the Spetsnaz throwing knives and holds it between her and Vlad.

Vlad emits a deep, evil laugh that causes Rosalie to shudder.

"I fear no man but, like all my kind, we fear your women. It is the women, women like you who have been the undoing of my race. Despite our strength and all of our abilities, we are as nothing compared to the power of your womb."

Vlad snatches the knife from Rosalie's hand.

"And now I need some of that power before we reach our final chapter." With that, he takes Rosalie and drinks deeply from her neck.

CHAPTER THIRTY-THREE

THE SHOWDOWN

My cell phone rings at 4:03 a.m.

"Al. It's Rosalie."

"Rosalie. Thank God. Where are you?" I say with relief flowing through every part of my being.

"Vlad has me. He wants to meet with Dragul."

I tighten up again and can scarcely breathe.

"Are you . . . are you all right?"

"He took some blood from me but not enough to hurt me."

That information doesn't make me happy but I've seen how others have gone through it with no long-term effects.

"Where are you?"

"We are in Dragul's old lair in the sewers," she says hesitantly. "I don't want you to come, just Dragul."

"What does Vlad want with you? Will he let you go?"

"I'm not sure. Certainly he won't release me until after he sees Dragul. I think he means to kill him," she says, adding, "Al I want you to promise me that you're not going to come."

"I can't promise that."

"You can't help. All you can do is get killed."

"I need to see you, make sure you're safe."

"You'll see me after Dragul comes. Don't complicate things. I need you to promise me you won't come. Please promise me."

"I promise," I say, but it's a big, bold lie.

A light drizzle makes the walk down the slope of the Don Valley treacherous. If not for the steadying hand of Dragul I might have plunged hundreds of feet into the darkness after more than a couple missteps. There's a sidewalk at the bottom. We follow it to a large sewer outlet where the one-ton safety grate has been pushed aside.

All I see in the tunnel is a deep, unyielding darkness. Dragul has no problem seeing in the dark but I need the help of a small flashlight to guide my feet safely along.

After a few miles at a run, the tunnel makes a left turn. We make the turn and before us is a large, dark shape. I flash the light toward the shape but the darkness swallows it before it reaches its target.

I look and the figure steps from the shadows. He has Dragul's face and height but his body is much more massive. His shoulders are twice as wide and his biceps and thighs are huge like steroids on steroids.

"How . . . what. He's a giant," I gasp.

"The Drink of Death," Dragul says.

"Hello Dragul. So glad you accepted my invitation."

"It's been a long time, Vlad."

"Yes, a long time. You've been constantly in my thoughts every moment. For 20 years I fantasized about ripping out your throat and crushing your skull. I dreamed of your lifeblood turning the ground red. All this for you my brother."

"We do not have to do this. The Council is no more."

"I know. Just another reason why we will do this."

"If you live as I do, no one will hunt you. I have more blood than I could ever drink."

"You are a fool Dragul. You deny your nature. This petty life you live filled with trinkets and silly people like this fat morsel you brought for me, that is not a life, certainly not a life for Sanguinus like you and I."

"So now let me sample the little present you brought for me."

"Not a present. You have the Drink in you so I have brought an ally."

"The Sapiens have turned your head to mush. You call this pudgy thing an ally?"

"More so than you think. He and I are the brothers that I'd hoped we could be."

"Brothers? Brothers? You dare use that word when you entombed me hundreds of feet underground to survive on fare that in even the meanest environments would have repulsed our ancestors."

"I did it to save your life. I knew that, if you had the will, eventually you would escape."

"Escape? I would hardly say 20 years of digging with a pan, a spoon and my bare hands scratching at an air vent to make it big enough for me to fit through was a master escape plan. This time you come to a place of my choosing. No cowardly tricks like before."

"Council ordered your execution. If I didn't kill you, they would. This was the only way to save you."

"Save me? Our underground stores lasted a few months and after that I was forced to live as our ancestors in the worst of circumstances, dining on devil worms & snails. I dug so long and hard, I tore the flesh off my fingers."

The fearsome creature makes me quake with fear but I have to ensure Rosalie is all right.

"My wife, Rosalie, where is she?"

"Oh yes. A very brave one. Her strength is now my strength. I'm afraid her soldiers injured me so much that I wouldn't be able to present myself to Dragul the way I wanted. So she provided me with the Drink I needed to be at my very best."

"But I spoke to her."

"A necessity to bring you to me. She served her purpose in that capacity and then I needed her to serve me in another capacity."

"She's . . . she's dead," I say.

"Very much so, over there," the monster says pointing to a dark shape in the corner.

I run over and my flashlight passes over the beautiful, pale face of my Rosalie. So still, so peaceful, so beautiful. I feel for a pulse. There is none. Her body is as cold as the ice now coursing through my veins.

I fall to my knees and weep as I've never wept in my life, great sobbing convulsions rocking through my body.

"I will kill you," I say. I see a broken chunk of concrete the size of my fist and I throw it at the vampire with all my might. Vlad sees it coming, doesn't move and lets it strike him on the chin. The concrete cracks in two upon impact. The monster is unaffected.

"No," says Vlad. "I will kill you and my brother."

Vlad kicks off his boots and stretches ugly green-tinged toenails that extend like daggers. He reaches to the ceiling, nearly touching it as his fingernails lengthen and transform into razor sharp claws. And then opening his mouth as if in a silent howl, I see the fangs grow longer and extend outward at a 45-degree angle.

To my amazement, Dragul goes through the same transformation into something I'm not sure I entirely know.

Time slows as the two circle, taking deep cavernous breaths that sound like that of immense beasts and then exhale their horrid fetid breath like weapons at one another.

Two sets of demon eyes flash. It is like watching tractor-trailers bent on a head-on crash.

The two Sanguinus come together, so fast, and with such power, it takes my breath away.

Vlad's size gives him the advantage as he ploughs Dragul across the chamber into a solid concrete wall.

Pinning his smaller adversary to the wall with his left hand, Vlad slashes mightily with his right, talons leaving gaping crimson tracks across Dragul's forehead and cheek. I look for an opportunity to jump in but there is none. I think to myself, 'Why don't I have a gun like I originally wanted.'

Blood is streaming freely from my friend's face but the claws miss his eye, leaving it blood stained but functional.

Dragul smashes Vlad's left elbow so it folds, bringing his larger adversary closer to him in a desperate attempt to keep the slashing right claws from gaining the momentum needed for a second deadly swing.

The brothers seem about to hug in a death embrace when Dragul grasps the back of Vlad's head and brings it down to his chest while thrusting his right knee straight up directly into big brother's face, once, twice, three times before Vlad throws his body backward in a wild bid to escape. Thank you Bryce Hanuman.

Vlad's face is now awash with blood, and the tip of one fang snapped clean off.

The two move back to the centre of the chamber still sizing up each other as they circle. Vlad charges, thrusting Dragul backward so hard he leaves the ground, and comes to a hard splashdown in a stinking puddle.

Panther-like, Vlad leaps at Dragul, claws and remaining fang fully extended, but the smaller fighter rolls and twists out of harm's way. He is almost to his feet when Vlad throws his full weight against him knocking him to the ground once more and this time with the larger adversary landing on top, pounding and stabbing. Dragul uses the curve of his right foot to hook Vlad's left knee and aided by claws deeply anchored in flesh, sweeps his opponent so he is now in the top position where he has greater striking power. Score two points for Hanuman.

Still, Vlad's greater strength is starting to take a toll on Dragul. Vlad manages to squirm free and faces Dragul for what I fear is the final clash.

Again, Vlad drives Dragul into the sewer's concrete wall. The two thrust and parry with gleaming fangs and razor tipped toes and fingers.

Dragul tries the Muay Thai clinch again but Vlad isn't one to fall for the same trick twice.

Slowly Dragul seems to wear down under the relentless onslaught of his gigantic foe. Looking more like hamburger than man, he lunges violently to the right to dislodge himself from Vlad's grip. Vlad strikes with talons and fangs toward the movement when Dragul suddenly spins clockwise to catch Vlad from behind and brings his full force behind his brother, smashing him against the wall, raining talons, fangs, elbows and knees into Vlad's back and neck.

The giant screams in rage as Dragul presses him against the wall with all his strength. Vlad is too strong and puts both feet on the wall and pushes off with a mighty heave. The two fly 30 feet across the chamber and crash into an unforgiving wall with Dragul taking all of the impact.

Dragul is unconscious or dead. I can't tell.

Vlad, slashed and bleeding everywhere, staggers toward me.

"Now for the Drink of Death," he says glowering at me.

He brings his fangs close to my neck and I panic. I grab at him to bring him in close so the wasp knife can deliver its deadly sting.

Vlad puzzles at this. Victims push away. They do not pull in. His hands realize they are not grasping flesh but something hard – my neck and chest protector – when suddenly the wasp knives on the chest plate do their trick, projecting outward delivering their icy treat. But the giant isn't coming in for the kill as planned. His hesitation leaves a crucial gap between us. One knife scratches him but not deep enough to do any damage beyond a baseball-sized freezer burn on the surface of his chest. He howls in pain and jumps backward and, in the process, rips off my armour sending me spiraling against the wall so hard I border on consciousness.

He glares at me with unbridled hatred in those alligator eyes and readies for a lethal lunge. Out of the corner of my eye, I see something moving quickly. It is Dragul, still alive. He leaps on his brother's back wrapping his legs around his adversary, further securing his position by anchoring 10 toenails around 10 ribs. Dragul's left arm wraps around the giant's neck while, with the right, he alternates mallet fist strikes to Vlad's temples and machete fingernails across his face and eyes.

The giant's visage is a red, pulpy mess, but he manages to unlock Dragul's leg vice leaving chunks of flesh dangling from Dragul's toes.

Then Vlad runs full speed toward the chamber wall, pivoting at only the last instant so Dragul takes the full impact on his shoulder and knee. Like a ball rebounding from the wall, the giant launches himself across the room repeating his pivot and brutal landing over and over again. On the sixth crash, I hear a loud crack and Dragul's right leg flops uselessly to the side.

A seventh smash to the wall easily dislodges Dragul's remaining grips and the giant swings around to employ talons, teeth, and hammer blows.

My friend is dying. Dragul looks more like a pile of offal than a person with each succeeding second. I'm helpless, helpless to defend my friend. Then I see it. Just as Dragul falls to his hands and knees, we make eye contact. A toe on his good leg catches the strap of the remains of my armour and with an extraordinary effort he sends it sliding to within a few feet of me.

I fight the fearful paralysis gripping my body and reach for the back plate. There are still two wasp knives that haven't discharged. I work them free of the armour and grasping one in each hand, I run toward the giant who is hunched over the bloody sprinkler system I know as Dragul.

The giant is completely engaged in the final kill, leaving me a clear shot at his back. I aim for the right side hoping the shank's explosive charge destroys the monster's heart.

I raise my right hand as high as I can reach and, with all my power, I jam the dagger at the monster's back. For an instant, time is frozen, as I puzzle why my thrust doesn't feel quite right. And then I see it. The blade did not penetrate the giant's rib cage.

Vlad whirls his monstrous head to look at me with one fiendish yellow eye. A knife remains in my left hand but my arms and legs do not respond to my brain. I feel death very near.

Vlad's arm snakes over his back, at an impossible angle, to grasp my throat when the blade finally discharges.

Again, freezing death fails to hit its mark leaving only a large icy welt on his back. The frigid blast tumbles me backward out of the Vampire's grasp while the last knife is pitched harmlessly forward.

Vlad reaches for me again, but his powerful arm is held in check. It is Dragul's last gasp. His left arm has a tenuous grip on Vlad, especially now that the monster turns back on him with his remaining fang fully extended. That terrible three-inch canine descends ready to deal death. The notion of killing me next flashes through the giant's mind when he spots something curious, something that should not be there.

By rote, his fang continues on its deadly path toward his brother's throat when an arm held up in a weak attempt to block the attack suddenly, through sleight of hand worthy of Jack Ace, reveals a thin metallic blade.

The point of the wasp knife I had dropped, moves just six inches more in a smooth, ascending arc, passing the unmatched fangs, dissecting the upper palate of the mouth, and comes to rest between the two hemispheres of Vlad's brain. Vlad stares at Dragul, astonished, as his face momentarily billows, as if viewed in a carnival mirror, before a muffled 'whoomp' spurts freezing blood and brain matter like a fountain in all directions.

The nearly headless vampire sinks onto its haunches, black blood gurgling from what's left of his head and neck, impelled by a heart that has yet to know any different.

Dragul isn't looking any better. His breath is choppy and blood runs freely from his face and from countless wounds on his ragged chest.

"I'm dying but I'm content."

"You can't die. You are the last one."

"You didn't mind helping to kill the second last one," he says, his laugh cut short by a fit of coughing, accompanied by spurts of blood.

"Dragul. You must gain your strength. Drink my blood."

"I can't. It won't help. I need so much blood, it will be your death."

"We don't know that."

"I do and so do you. Only the Drink of Death will save me."

"Look Dragul. I was a dead man walking before I met you. My life was worthless. I was worthless. No one cared about me. I was a laughing stock. Now people I love respect me. I can now leave enough money for generations of Johnny's family to live comfortably. I'm respected in the community and in my profession. What more can any man ask from life.

"And then there's Rosalie. My beautiful, loving, precious Rosalie. As beautiful and as incredible as she was, she loved me. She loved me. She saw things in me to love that no one else ever did. And because of you Dragul, I had five more wonderful years with my Rosalie. Rosalie, the love of my life is gone. What good is it for me to keep on living without her? I want to be with her. I need to be with her. Drink my blood my friend. I will die a happy man. I owe my wonderful life to you. Now I return it to you."

"You are certain?"

"I have no regrets. You have been my greatest friend. I love you better than a brother. You gave me life. Let me do the same for you. Please do it. Drink my blood," I say. "It's now or never."

"My friend. My great friend. I will remember you always," says Dragul.

Dragul reaches to me, tenderly smooths back my hair and gently places his mouth on my neck. I feel no sensation of pain, just a slow fogginess descending upon me. I feel happy to be on this journey. I feel I am doing the right thing and I'm going to a better place, to be with Rosalie. Through the fog I see all the people I've known in my life. My mother, Rosalie, Johnny, Regina, Jerry, Gracey, Mrs. Alvarez, and, of course, Dragul. Dragul's face lingers before me through the darkened haze of the sewer.

CHAPTER THIRTY-FOUR

HAMBLYN'S PEACE

Patches of light and colour begin to swirl and I'm back somewhere I recognize.

Dragul is wearing shackles, around his neck and wrists. I see a chrome clock hanging on a bleak, beige wall. I remember that wall. I remember that clock but I'm too tired to do anything but sleep . . . sleep . . . sleep.

Tick!

The door of the interview room clangs open and two cops with their Glock 22s drawn and pointing at Mangorian scream: "Take your hands off him. Put your hands in the air now, right now. Don't move a muscle."

With a clank of the manacles around his wrists, Mangorian raises his hands.

The younger cop, keeping his pistol trained on Mangorian with one hand, grabs the ankle of the fallen man and then drags his body far from Mangorian's reach while the sergeant calls for help.

"Bobby, is he?"

"Definitely dead," says the younger cop. "No pulse, no heartbeat."

"Poor bastard," says the sergeant. "I feel like an asshole calling him 'Hamburger'. Seemed like a nice guy. Not one of those shyster lawyers in their $2,000 suits. Seemed like the guy just needed the work."

"The shit's going to fly over this one," says the constable.

"That's just politics. We were in here the second we saw him grab the guy. There was nothing we could do," the sergeant says.

"Why the hell did he walk around the table?" says the younger cop. He picks up the dead lawyer's notebook and looks at it. The page is blank other than a title, date, and time at the top:

Al Hamblyn

First Interview with Dragul Mangorian

Sept. 15, 2013, 9:00 a.m.

He glances at the chrome clock.

9:26 a.m.

"I guess we'll never know but one thing's certain, this murdering bastard will fry," the sergeant says.

"I will not fry as you call it," Mangorian says with his yellow eyes ablaze. "First of all officers, you know that Canada does not have the death penalty. Secondly, I did not murder Mr. Hamblyn. He was a genuinely unhappy soul and I merely assisted his suicide. In fact, he begged me to drink all of his blood."

"He begged you?" stammers the younger cop.

"Yes, it was a necessary exchange. I gave him what he wanted. I made him happy. He gave me what I needed. He gave me life."

"You made him happy? He's dead," the sergeant says incredulously.

"Gentlemen, you need only to look at his face to confirm the veracity of my words."

Both cops look at the puffy, white face staring up at them.

The look was not of terror, agony or even sadness. The dead lawyer wore a wide smile and his still-open eyes gleamed with contentment.

"Gentlemen, now that Mr. Hamblyn is uh . . . incapable of performing his duties, I would like to avail myself of another lawyer."

EPILOGUE

"Hello, Alexei?"
"Hello, Rosalee? Is it reeelly you? It has been a long, long time."
"Alexei. This is business, your kind of business. When can we meet?"

- END -

ABOUT THE AUTHOR

Hi, my name is John Matsui. I've been a writer my entire adult life, first as a newspaper reporter, editor and columnist and then as a communications consultant. Now I've turned my pen to the world of thriller novels.

In *Late Bite*, my first novel, I take the vampire genre and turn it on its head. *Late Bite* introduces what I hope you will find is a compelling set of characters who struggle under strange circumstances in a world that all too closely resembles our own.

Late Bite is the first volume in the three-part Toronto Chronicles series.

I live in London, Ontario with my beautiful wife Judy.

UPCOMING THRILLERS BY JOHN MATSUI

GRAVITY GAMES

Book 1 of the

Nathan Sherlock Mystery Series

WANTED: DEAD OR DEADER

Book 2 of 3

The Toronto Chronicles

THE SUPER HERO SUICIDES

Book 1 of

The Z Squad Series

34047237R00129

Made in the USA
Charleston, SC
29 September 2014